A SMALL SACRIFICE

A JANE LAWLESS MYSTERY

by ELLEN HART

2009

D1286332

Copyright© 1994 by Ellen Hart

Bella Books, Inc.
P.O. Box 10543
Tallahassee, FL 32302

All rights reserved. No part of this book may be reproduced or transmitted in any form or by any means, electronic or mechanical, including photocopying, without permission in writing from the publisher.

Printed in the United States of America on acid-free paper

First Bella Books Edition, October 2009

Cover Design and photo by: Kathy Kruger, Whistling Mouse Illustration & Design

ISBN-10: 1-59493-165-8
ISBN-13: 978-1-59493-165-9

About the Author

Ellen Hart is the author of twenty-five crime novels in two different series. She is a five-time winner of the Lambda Literary Award for Best Lesbian Mystery, a three-time winner of the Minnesota Book Award for Best Popular Fiction, a two-time winner of the Golden Crown Literary Award, a recipient of the Alice B Medal, and was made an official GLBT Literary Saint at the Saints & Sinners Literary Festival in New Orleans in 2005. *Entertainment Weekly* named her as one of the "101 Movers and Shakers in the Gay Entertainment Industry." For the past twelve years, Ellen has taught "An Introduction to Writing the Modern Mystery" through the The Loft Literary Center, the largest independent writing community in the nation. In the spring of 2008, Ellen, William Kent Krueger and Carl Brookins (who have traveled together for 9 years promoting their individual novels as The Minnesota Crime Wave) began a monthly TV show, *The Minnesota Crime Wave Presents*. Segments are available on YouTube and the MCW website, www.minnesotacrimewave.org. Ellen's newest novels are *No Reservations Required*, A Sophie Greenway Mystery (Ballantine, June 2005) and *The Mirror and the Mask*, the seventeenth Jane Lawless mystery (St. Martin's/Minotaur, November 2009). She lives in Minneapolis with her partner of 31 years.

An author writes, not in a vacuum, but for an audience. Many thanks to Linda Hill, Karin Kallmaker and everyone at Bella Books for bringing this story, long out of print, back into the light of day.

Ellen Hart, 2009

For R.D. Zimmerman and Lars Peterssen.
Here's to the wonderful candlelight dinners we've
had together, to drive-by signings and Lars's
fabulous chocolate pecan cookies.
May we always be friends.

CAST OF CHARACTERS

CORDELIA THORN: Artistic Director for the Allen Grimby Repertory Theatre in St. Paul. Member of the Shevlin Underground.

JANE LAWLESS: Owner of the Lyme House Restaurant in Minneapolis. Old friend of Cordelia Thorn's.

ORSON ALBERN: Owner of the Blackburn Playhouse in Shoreview. Member of the Shevlin Underground.

THEODORE (THEO) DONATI: Member of the Shevlin Underground.

DIANA STANWOOD: Actress. Owner of the Summer Green Playhouse in Summer Green, Wisconsin. Member of the Shevlin Underground.

ANNIE WHITTIG: Professor of Theatre Arts at Northwestern. Married to Curt. Member of Shevlin Underground.

CURT WHITTIG: Stage Manager for a community theatre in Chicago. Married to Annie. Member of Shevlin Underground.

HILDA BARNES: Caretaker/Gardener at the home of Diana Stanwood.

AMITY SCARBOUROUGH: Fourteen-year old daughter of Diana's deceased lover.

CHICKIE JOHNSON: Junior-high-school friend of Amity's.

JOHN HUBBLE: Director of the Summer Green Playhouse.

O, For a Muse of fire, that would ascend
The brightest heaven of invention . . .
            King Henry V
            Shakespeare

Prologue

University of Minnesota
Spring 1972

Orson bent over the morning paper, sipping from a tepid cup of coffee. Halfway down the front page he read the headline, "Body of Minnesota Business Legend Stolen from Eastwood Cemetery." The article went on to say that the granddaughter of Edgar Davis Collingwell, the founder of the Collingwell Baking Company, had posted a ten-thousand-dollar reward for information leading to the arrest of the individual or individuals responsible. The gravesite, near the entrance to the cemetery, had been tampered with two nights ago, sometime after midnight. Since the body had been buried prior to 1930, no cement vault was used. The grave was an easy target. Nothing like this had ever happened at Eastwood before, and officials were baffled as to a motive.

God, thought Orson, as he glanced around the dining room of his cramped campus slum, could he use that kind of money. In the wake of last night's party, stacks of dirty dishes, filled ashtrays

1

and empty bags of chips were scattered around the room. Neither of his two roommates had bothered to clear away any of the mess. Then again, neither had he.

Drumming his fingers impatiently on the table top, his thoughts returned to what the reward money could buy. Ten thousand dollars. Lord. As a third-year theatre major, he was as penniless as the proverbial church mouse. By the time he got his M.F.A., he'd be buried in unpaid loans. He didn't have a rich family picking up the tab, unlike his Gatsbyesque roommate, the golden Curt Whittig. Thankfully, Curt liked the student slums. He even paid most of the rent. And on weekends, he threw parties for the other theatre majors. Curt was majoring in theatre himself, though he was more interested in the high-tech aspects of lighting and stage design. Orson and Theo Donati, the other roommate, had only one agenda in mind. Acting. More specifically, the legitimate stage. Their rivalry had become a source of contention—as well as amusement. But one way or another, however long it took, Orson was going to prove that his was the greater talent. Unfortunately, Theo had the exact same goal. Only time would tell.

Orson looked up as Theo entered the room. He didn't try to hide his surprise as his eyes took in the suit and tie. And briefcase. Something was up. "Should I salute?" he asked, finishing the bitter coffee in one gulp.

"Stuff it," said Theo, stopping in front of a mirror to adjust his tie. His shaggy hair had been clipped short and combed away from his forehead, making him look a bit like Al Pacino. "And quit staring," he ordered, kicking an empty bag of corn chips out of his way. "Christ, this place is a freaking pit. Who the hell are those two people out there in the living room watching cartoons?"

Orson shrugged. "Leftovers from last night's prom. I think they passed out on the living room floor."

Theo grunted, sitting down at the table and pulling the newspaper in front of him.

"Aren't you coming this morning?" asked Orson. He, Curt and Theo, and three others, Cordelia, Annie and Diana were known humorously in the theatre department as the Shevlin Underground because they nearly lived in the cafeteria in the basement of Shevlin Hall. They were also fast friends. Every Monday morning they had a standing date for breakfast. "I'm driving. Cordelia and Annie should be here any minute."

"I've got an appointment," muttered Theo. "I'll have to pass." His eyes fell to the article Orson had been reading. "Jesus. Did you see this? A body was stolen. Gives you the creeps, doesn't it?"

Before Orson could respond, the doorbell rang. "That must be our other half," he said, rising from the table and charging down the long narrow hall to the front door. Instead of being greeted by two young faces, he was met by the sight of mounds of deep purple and white lilacs. One of the mounds had Cordelia's voice.

"Your hovel needs a bit of sprucing up, Orson. Find us some vases. Chop chop."

He put his hand on his hip and grinned. "Sorry. Fresh out of *vases*. But I might find you an ice-cream bucket or two."

"I suppose that will have to do." One of Cordelia's eyes peeked through the purple, narrowing in disgust at the two people sitting on the couch. "You need a bouncer. "

"You applying for the job?" asked Theo, breezing into the room followed closely by Curt. He squinted into the second mound. "Is that Diana behind there or Annie?"

"Annie," came a rather husky voice.

"Hum. Then where's Diana?"

Orson moved over to the closet door and opened it. There, among the sneakers and the tennis rackets, wrapped in a quilt and snoring like a truck driver, was the sixth member of the group, Diana Stanwood.

Curt took the flowers from Annie's arms. "She got pretty ripped last night. Last I looked, all the bedrooms were occupied, so I'd say she found the next best spot."

3

Everyone stood silently, gazing down at her. "I don't think she'll be coming to breakfast," announced Annie. "That's too bad."

"Why?" asked Theo. "She won't die if she doesn't get her soft-boiled *egg*. Neither will I."

Annie tweaked him under the chin. "We're going to study for Hanson's mid-term this morning. Remember? Orson knows the stuff backwards and forwards. He's going to coach us."

Cordelia nudged the sleeping form with her foot. Diana let out an angry snort and turned over. "No sweet rolls for this princess." She unloaded her flowers on Orson and then raised an eyebrow at Theo's strange clothing. "Willy Loman. *Death of a Salesman*," she pronounced.

"I'm not auditioning for a part," said Theo, "if that's what you're suggesting. I have an appointment."

"Where?"

"None of your business." He pulled on his cuffs. "Did anyone ever tell you you're entirely too nosey?"

"Frequently." Cordelia was a large—some might say shiplike—young woman, nearly six feet tall. She had mounds of flowing auburn curls and an expansive manner. In other words, Cordelia was a *presence*. Everyone watched in amused silence as she swept into the room, snapped off the TV set with great distaste and then waved her arms at the couple sitting on the couch. "Shoo." she scowled. "Show's over. Rocky & Bullwinkle have just been canceled."

The couple didn't move.

"Did you hear me?" She tapped her foot, waiting until she was confident of their full attention. "Your life is hanging by a thread unless you depart. Evaporate. Set sail. Sally forth. Take wing."

They blinked.

She lowered her voice to a more ominous tone. "And if you aren't gone by the time I count to five, I'll break your knees. Got it?"

In an instant they had scrambled to their feet and were out the door.

Cordelia brushed her hands together with a satisfied smirk and then returned her gaze to Theo. "You don't think I'm going to accept that brush off as some kind of answer to why you're dressed so strangely. I've never seen you in a suit. I didn't even know you *owned* one."

Theo gave her a secretive grin but said nothing more.

Nuts, thought Orson as he sprinted back down the hall to the kitchen. If Cordelia couldn't get Theo's destination out of him, no one could. He found several plastic buckets under the sink and began stuffing the lilacs into them. "Curt, bring the rest of those flowers back here. And everybody—that is, everyone who's headed over to Shevlin—my VW is leaving in five . . . no, make it ten minutes. You can buy your tickets after you're seated." He began filling one of the buckets with water. What the hell was Theo up to?

Orson was the first one out to the car. Cramming six people into a Beetle was a trick, but one they'd mastered over the years. Today, without Theo and Diana, there would be only four. Piece of cake. Unfortunately, the doors no longer locked. Not that it mattered. The car was so rusted and dented it was invisible.

"What's that plastic sack in the back seat?" asked Cordelia, twirling her finger languidly. "We better put it in the trunk. That is, if you have *room*." On the last word, she bugged out her eyes. It was common knowledge Orson was a pack rat. He collected everything that wasn't nailed down.

"Looks like a garbage sack," said Curt. He brushed a blond lock of hair away from his eyes.

Annie gazed at him with barely concealed lust. It was also common knowledge Annie had a thing for Curt.

Cordelia had a sneaking suspicion Curt and Theo were sleeping together. If it was true, she felt sorry for Annie. Theo and Cordelia had made no secret of their sexuality. They referred to themselves lovingly as The Inverts. Orson and Annie were clearly hetero. But Curt and Diana—who knew? After all, it was 1972. Other than your priest, your pastor or your parents, who cared?

Orson grabbed the sack and started for the trunk.

"Yesterday's lunch?" asked Cordelia smiling snidely.

Annie moved closer to Curt, slipping her arm through his.

"Actually, I don't know what it is," replied Orson. "I suppose I should take a look." He opened it, peering at the contents for several seconds before looking up.

"What is it?" asked Curt, seeing Orson's face pucker with disgust.

"This must be some kind of joke."

Cordelia inched closer and glanced into the sack. "Yuck." she exclaimed, patting herself on the chest.

Orson reached inside and drew out a skull.

"Been doing some late night work over at the biology lab?" asked Curt.

Ignoring the question, Orson knelt down and dumped the contents onto the sidewalk. Bones, bits of wood and shreds of cloth all tumbled out together.

Cordelia watched a look of recognition dawn on Orson's face. "What's going on?" she asked. "You act like you know what it is."

He closed his eyes for a moment. "I'm probably way off base, but did you read that article in the morning paper? The one about that body stolen from Eastwood cemetery?" He didn't look up. His gaze was transfixed by the sight of the bones.

"No," said Cordelia. "I don't read right-wing rags."

He wiped a hand across his mouth. "One of you needs to go call the police."

"Why?" asked Curt.

"You're probably going to think I'm crazy, but this may be . . . the body."

Annie pulled Curt closer. "How awful."

"What's it doing in your car?" asked Cordelia, raising a skeptical eyebrow.

Orson shook his head. "Beats me." He stood slowly, his mind working something through. Finally, after looking each person square in the eye, he said "I want you all to understand one thing. This is *my* car. And I'm the one who opened the sack and made the connection. If I'm right, you all have to admit this to the police."

"So," said Annie. "What's the big deal?"

"The big deal," repeated Orson, a slow smile pulling at the corners of his mouth, "is . . .right now, you may just be speaking to a very rich man."

Cordelia bounced joyfully around the kitchen as she put the finishing touches on the meal she was preparing for tonight's celebration. The new Stones album was playing loudly in the dining room. The smell of lasagna filled the apartment, spilling out the back door into the alley and no doubt making the rest of the student tenants drool. Cheap red wine was chilling in the refrigerator—she knew that was tacky, but everybody liked it better cold. The salad was made. And the garlic bread—*lots* of garlic bread—was just about to go into the oven. All of this in honor of the evening's special guest. Orson.

After a morning of questioning, tests and more questioning, it appeared that he would be receiving some kind of reward for finding the remains of the filched dead body. Cordelia was thrilled. However that sack got into his back seat, the family of Edgar Davis Collingwell was relieved to have it back. She couldn't wait for Orson to arrive and elaborate on his day. He was driving over with Curt and Theo. Annie was still at the costume shop, but would make it for dinner. And Diana was asleep in her bedroom. Her hangover was huge.

The East Bank slum Cordelia shared with Annie and Diana was almost a mirror image of the guys' apartment. She figured it was a popular floor plan during the west-ward expansion. On one end was a tiny living room. No fireplace. Decoratively cracked plaster and unwaxed hardwood floors—scuffed by students and marred by heavy furniture since the dawn of time—completed the ambiance. A long hallway led to the dining room and kitchen. Both of these rooms had wonderful views of brick walls, initially terribly arty, but ultimately confining and depressing. Off the hallway were three bedrooms. The only real difference between the two apartments was the decorating—or lack thereof. Cordelia was heavily into her purple phase. The wall color and *objets d'art* scattered here and there confirmed her influence. Annie liked posters of handsome blond men. A Robert Redford shrine had been set up in her bedroom. Cordelia, whose room contained only one star photo—Bette Davis—told Annie she was fixated on *blond*, but Annie just shrugged it off. Diana liked clothes. Her room was a jungle of outrageous costumes hung on hangers dangling from strings she'd affixed to the walls in a crisscross pattern. As far as anyone could tell, Diana fixated on only one person. Herself. No photo of any kind had found its way to her walls.

"Smells good in here," said a voice from the doorway.

Cordelia turned to find Diana limping into the room, her long brown hair a tangle, her clothing crumpled. She must have just gotten up. Ultimately, Cordelia had confidence that Mick Jagger *could* wake the dead. "You feeling better?"

"Yeah. We got any tomato juice?"

"Sorry."

She ran a hand through her matted brown tresses and shambled over to the counter, picking a cucumber slice out of the salad and crunching it. "What's the occasion?"

Cordelia dropped her minimal effort at concern and brightened. "It's Orson. He found some human bones in a plastic bag in the back seat of his car."

"Doesn't surprise me. You never know what you're going to sit on in that heap of his." She pretended a shiver. "Still, I suppose

8

any old reason for a party."

"Just listen, will you? See, there was a grave robbery at Eastwood cemetery two nights ago. Someone stole the remains of some wealthy cookie maker."

Diana did a double take. "Is this a joke?"

"No joke. You know the one—Collingwell Mills? They make Chocolate Bombs, Minty Marvels."

Diana held up her hand. "I would never have made it through high school without them."

"Exactly. Anyway, somebody dumped the remains in Orson's car. He found them this morning when we were on our way over to Shevlin. And the best part is, there's a reward."

"How much?"

"I'm not sure. I think it depends on whether the information leads the police to the grave robbers."

Diana selected another cucumber slice and nibbled the edge. "And I missed all this?"

"You were snoring so belligerently in the closet, we didn't want to wake you."

"Really. How flattering." She moved to the screen door and stared out at the trash cans in the alley. "Lucky bastard."

"Yeah. I hope so. That's why we're throwing the party tonight. The guys should be here any minute." Cordelia watched Diana's back. Something was wrong. She hated playing Mom, but since she looked like an earth mother—or Mama Cass, take your pick—she was often cast unwillingly in the role. "What's up, dearheart? You seem kind of depressed." Then it dawned on her. Sure. Diana was up for the lead in an experimental play over at Scott Hall. She must have blown it. "Is it that Carver piece? Didn't you get the part?"

Diana turned around, a smug look on her face. "Oh ye of little faith." She fluttered her eyes.

"Don't toy with me."

She sauntered back to the counter and leaned against it, dramatically closing her eyes. "I was so emotionally and technically brilliant during the audition, how could they even *think* of giving the part to Rowena Todd? My timing was impeccable. My movements . . . delectable." She opened one eye. "Of course I got it."

Cordelia threw her arms around her and together they giggled, dancing around the kitchen floor. "Then we'll have even more to celebrate tonight. But one word of caution. I hope your acting loses a bit of its . . . broadness before opening night. I doubt they want Theda Bara playing a drug addict."

She laughed at the allusion. "Spoken like a true director. You know, buddy of mine, one day, you're going to be the best. The top of the heap. And I'm going to be there, cheering."

Cordelia blushed.

"It'll happen," continued Diana. "For all of us." She seemed to have regained her zip. "So, where's the wine?"

Cordelia shook her head. She wished Diana could party occasionally without all the booze. "Why don't we wait till the boys get here?"

"You have no sense of timing," said Diana, her head already inside the refrigerator. "Here it is." She withdrew the jug and held it up, a mischievous grin on her face.

The doorbell sounded.

"I'll get it," said Cordelia, stuffing the garlic bread into the oven. She raced down the hall to the front door. Orson was the first to enter, followed by Theo, no longer in his suit and tie. Curt and Annie brought up the rear.

"We found Annie lurching over the Tenth Avenue Bridge," said Orson, handing Cordelia a bunch of daisies. "We decided to offer her a ride. Otherwise, there wouldn't be any food left when she got home." He put his arm around her and gave her a squeeze.

"Good point," said Theo, flopping on the couch and lifting his feet up on the coffee table. He spread his arms wide over the back and gave everyone his most beatific grin.

Too beatific, thought Cordelia. She was determined to get

his little secret out of him before the night was over. Why had he cut his hair? He looked so . . . establishment. She shivered inwardly as she thought of the draft lottery. It might not be long before he was forced to cut it anyway.

Diana appeared in the doorway with the jug of wine and six plastic wine glasses. Plastic was a student necessity when dealing with the various cattle that mooed in and out of their apartment on a daily basis. Glass wouldn't last a day. "So," she said, handing the jug to Annie and passing out the glasses. "Do we really have something to celebrate?"

Cordelia smiled exuberantly. Except for one other person, a high-school buddy by the name of Jane Lawless, the people she loved most in the world were all in this room.

"Come on," said Curt, grabbing Orson by the shoulders and shaking him. "Out with it."

Orson couldn't contain his emotion any longer. He burst out laughing as he sat down on the couch next to Theo. "You're talking to a new man. Money, although not everything, does give one a certain . . . renewed outlook. Yes. I'm going to get the reward."

Everyone cheered. Cordelia bent down and gave him a kiss on his cheek, mussing up his shaggy black hair. Diana began dancing around the room, pouring a glass of wine here and there.

"The granddaughter of Edgar Collingwell was so beside herself with joy to have the old guy's bones back, she called her bank right away. It seems, even though they can't positively ID the remains just yet, they found a ring in the sack. It belonged to him. They're doing lots of tests on the contents—even the sack itself. And my car was gone over with a fine-tooth comb. They especially liked the assortment of lamp shades in the trunk."

"God, I remember the day we found those," said Theo, stretching his arms high over his head. "We were in Dinkytown eating a leisurely breakfast when you saw that guy's U-Haul pull to a stop right outside the restaurant. You would have thought it was a Brinks truck passing out cash the way you bolted out of there."

"Say," said Curt, scratching his chin, "come to think of it, I lent you twenty bucks that day. You never paid me back. "

"He's good for it now," winked Cordelia.

"And besides," offered Annie, "you never know when you're going to need a battered lamp shade." She leaned back in her chair as Diana filled her wine glass. Evening sunlight streamed in through the front window, striking her red hair and turning it into a soft flame.

Curt glanced at it briefly before returning his gaze to Theo. Annie might look lustfully at Curt, thought Cordelia with a kind of detached amusement, but at least for now, Curt reserved his lustful eyes for another. Cordelia had already formed some rather cynical opinions on the course of true love.

"Anyway," said Orson, nudging Theo in the ribs, "I should get the money sometime next week. But there is one other issue."

"What's that?" asked Diana, filling his glass and then stepping back. She set the jug on top of the TV set.

"Oh, it's nothing much. Just . . . well, I think I've found the girl I'm going to marry."

"Woman," roared Cordelia, ignoring his cow-eyed expression. Would these boys never learn.

"Right. Woman."

"Not the granddaughter of old Collingwell," said Curt. "She must be well into her forties."

Orson sipped his wine. "Nope. The *great*-granddaughter."

"How do you know she'll marry you?" asked Theo. He smirked at Curt.

"I don't. But I'll bet I'm right."

"How much will you bet?" asked Theo, still smirking.

"I don't know. I hadn't thought about it."

"Fifty thousand dollars?"

"Come on," said Annie. "Where would you get that kind of money?"

Theo shrugged. "I'm not always going to be a student."

"Actors don't make shit," offered Curt pleasantly.

Again, Theo shrugged. "Maybe. Or maybe they just don't take the right parts."

"There you go again," snapped Diana, her wine glass already empty. "You may have a talent for acting, Theo, but you have no sense when it comes to money. Now me—"

Everyone hooted and jeered.

"Queen of the bounced check, " shouted Annie.

"You mean queen of the borrowed buck," laughed Cordelia, turning at the sound of a knock. "Who the hell is that?" she muttered as she crossed to the door and opened it. She could smell the garlic bread. It was time to take it out of the oven. "Yes?" she said, peering impatiently at two men in business suits.

The taller of the two said, "We're looking for Theodore Donati. Is he here?"

She cocked her head. "Who wants to know?"

The man took out his wallet and showed her his ID.

"Christ. FBI? What do you want with him?"

"Is he here?" The man didn't look particularly friendly.

Theo stood and walked toward them. "I'm Theo Donati."

"We'd like to talk to you," said the taller man.

"What about?"

He hesitated, then said, "Impersonating an IRS agent."

The room became silent.

"Who the hell told you that?" demanded Theo, his back stiffening.

"This is ridiculous," said Curt, moving up behind him. Diana and Annie followed. "I know this guy. He'd never do something like that."

Cordelia was aghast, yet as she watched them talk, she couldn't help but wonder. Of all her friends, Theo had the greatest tendency to do dumb things—to live on the edge. Could it be? Slowly, Orson stood. Even though he said nothing, Cordelia could see the frightening intensity in his stare.

"Do you deny it?" asked the agent.

"Of course he denies it," shouted Diana. "This is harassment. It must be that anti-war march you were in last month."

"Don't say anything," said Curt, putting a hand on Theo's shoulder. "You need a lawyer."

The FBI agent motioned to the man standing behind him. In an instant, Theo's hands were cuffed and he was being led out to a waiting car.

Curt followed, his voice trembling as he tried to talk them out of it. Everyone else seemed paralyzed.

The scene progressed as if in slow motion. Diana poured herself more wine. She stood in the corner, dazed, massaging her right temple. Annie watched Curt out the window, wringing her hands together as she saw him try to get into the back seat of the car with Theo. Orson just stood in the center of the room. His eyes were wide open, but he seemed someplace else.

And lastly . . . Cordelia. She felt the daisies slip from her hand, falling to the floor with a small thud. The garlic bread was burning. It was as if she had just witnessed an explosion. Her ears tingled. Her body was numb. And worse. An inner sense told her that the ramifications of Theo's actions would touch all their lives. The world, as she'd known it, might never be the same again.

1

Late Summer 1994

"What are you staring at?" asked Jane. She and Cordelia were sitting in Jane's living room, drinking a relaxing cup of after dinner coffee and discussing the events of the day.

Cordelia blinked. "Was I staring?"

"Unless you're having problems with catatonia, yes. You were. Is something wrong with my hair?" Jane touched the back of her French braid. Normally, she thought her hair was one of her best features. Deep chestnut brown. Graying at the temples. Maybe it was her new glasses. Not that she thought moving from silver wire rims to gold was a big deal. She did find that she was wearing them more lately.

"No. It's just . . . I was wondering. I suppose we look a lot different than we did back in college."

So that was it, thought Jane. "You're thinking about your friends from—"

"The Shevlin Underground."

"Right." Jane smiled. "Are you worried about your meeting tonight with Orson?" Jane knew Cordelia had received a rather cryptic phone call from him two days ago asking that she come to his house at eight on Friday evening. Tonight. From the way Cordelia kept drumming her fingers on the rocking chair and staring at the clock, she was as nervous as a cat. Or a poodle. Jane had known more nervous poodles in her day. All of Cordelia's cats appeared to be lumps of perfect serenity. It was a poor metaphor. Then again, nervous as a poodle somehow didn't cut it.

"Not worried, exactly," said Cordelia. "More apprehensive. Orson refused to be specific about why he wanted to see me, but from the tone of his voice, I'd say it's serious. I can't for the life of me figure out what's going on. He just got back from Summer Green."

"What's Summer Green?"

"It's a small town in Wisconsin. He grew up there. I thought I told you all this."

Jane sipped her coffee. "Must have been your *other* best friend."

Cordelia mimicked a smile. "Well, you remember Diana Stanwood?"

"Sure. Of all the people in your group, she's become the most famous. "

"You wound me when you say things like that, Janey. My star is rising."

Jane cleared her throat. "I used to catch her occasionally on that soap opera. What's the name? *The Sordid and The Shallow?*"

"For your information, she's also done a lot of work in the legitimate theatre. Mostly New York. Before she left last year, she had the lead in a new production of *A Doll's House.*" Cordelia shook her head sadly and looked away. "But something happened. I don't know. Orson said she wasn't getting along with the director. Diana told me she left the production because of exhaustion. I'm not sure who to believe."

"So, you're wondering if this meeting tonight has something

to do with his trip to Summer Green?"

Cordelia set her empty cup on the coffee table and began to rock. "Diana's living there now. A little over a year ago, Orson told her about this old country church on the edge of town. A fire destroyed the rear of it. The congregation decided not to rebuild. Instead, they erected a new church on the other end of town. Near The Mall." She rolled her eyes. "They've been trying to sell the partially burned one, but with no luck. That is, until Diana came along. Orson convinced her it would make a perfect space for a playhouse. He knew Diana was having trouble figuring out what to do with her life. As much as possible, we all still try to take care of each other. Keep in touch. Since she's had good financial management all these years, she's not hurting for money. And I guess it turns out he was right. When she saw it, she got really excited. She spent all last winter having it rebuilt. Most of the summer was spent finding a permanent company. On Labor Day, The Summer Green Playhouse will officially open."

"I assume you're invited."

"But of course." Cordelia waved the question away. "Since the town is midway between Appleton and Green Bay, it will draw from both cities. A perfect spot. Last time I called, she'd decided to do a fall, spring and summer season. No winter."

"Good thinking."

"Summer Green is a beautiful little town. Orson and I drove there once about ten years ago. He doesn't go back very often. All of his family is gone, but he still knows a lot of people. He went to school with just about everyone."

"I suppose being president of Collingwell Mills doesn't give him much free time."

"Between that, his family and running the Blackburn Playhouse in Shoreview, he doesn't have a minute."

One of Jane's dogs hopped up on the couch and nestled his head in her lap. She stroked his soft fur as she asked, "Have you seen Curt and Annie recently? I remember they stayed at your house several years ago. You brought them over to my restaurant for dinner."

Cordelia shook her head. "With Annie's teaching schedule at Northwestern, she doesn't get much time off. Curt is another story. After graduation, he just never seemed to settle down. It's hard to believe he and Annie have been married for thirteen years. She's been his rock. Other women might have given him the heave ho, but not her. He's tried his hand at so many projects, but nothing ever sticks. I guess he's stage manager at a community theatre in Chicago right now. Every time I see him, he seems so . . . listless. I don't think he's really been himself since—" Her voice trailed off.

"Since what?"

"Well, he never really got over what happened to Theo."

Jane remembered the time well. She and Cordelia had both attended the University of Minnesota, but Jane had never been part of Cordelia's inner circle of theatre friends. Even so, she'd known Theo slightly, and admired his talent. The night he was arrested, Cordelia had come over to the sorority where Jane was living. She was beside herself with worry. She couldn't fathom what had happened to make him do something so bizarre. She didn't necessarily believe the FBI, but she couldn't ignore Theo's reaction. He'd left her apartment with little protest. Almost like a lamb to the slaughter. After his conviction for impersonating an IRS agent—made worse by the accusation that he'd stolen over fifteen thousand dollars from the office safe—he'd simply disappeared inside himself. Cordelia said everyone in the group had visited him in prison at one point or another, but he wouldn't open up. To this day, his reasons for committing such an act remained a mystery.

Even though Jane had known Cordelia's friends only peripherally, she remembered that back in the early seventies, Orson, Theo and Diana had cut highly romantic figures. All penniless aspiring actors. On stage, their styles were very different. Orson's skills were more cerebral. He came across as quick, intelligent, wry. Comedy came naturally. His voice was powerful, deep and resonant. He could play the part of a much older man because of his size and bearing.

Theo, on the other hand, was all passion. The audience felt his intelligence as well, but only as it was filtered through his emotions. Consequently, he seemed more vulnerable. Less sure of himself. People identified with Theo. The viewer experienced the play through him. Jane often heard Cordelia refer to him as the heart and soul of their group. And even though the Shevlin Underground wasn't a formal title, it had been a tight circle. Others in the theatre department envied the six of them, not just for their talent, but for their friendship and loyalty.

And Diana? On stage she was like a slow explosion. Sometimes Jane didn't even notice her presence at first. But by the end of the performance, she had taken the audience captive. Her range was much broader than either Theo or Orson's. Unfortunately, Jane had always been a bit put off by Diana. When she wasn't in front of an audience, she seemed . . . deflated. Oh, she could be charming, but she could also be nasty. Cordelia had never minded *nasty*. She found it amusing. Jane, on the other hand, didn't find the quality—or Diana Stanwood—particularly appealing. Fourteen years ago, right after Theo had been let out of prison, Diana had visited Jane's restaurant in south Minneapolis for Sunday brunch. The usual celebrity commotion had ensued, with people forming a line to get an autograph. Jane found it tedious. Diana had drunk too many Bloody Marys and talked too loudly. Mostly about herself. Cordelia finally had to help her out.

Jane noticed Cordelia looking at the clock again. "Is it about time to leave?"

"It appears so."

"Maybe Orson wants you to direct something at his playhouse."

"We've discussed my schedule at the Allen Grimby. I'm directing four plays this season. I don't even have time to brush my teeth."

Jane gave her a sympathetic nod. "I suppose that means our

ten-mile run is off for tomorrow morning."

Cordelia gave an indignant snort. "I'll have you know that Mugs, I mean, Mary Katherine—I have to remember to use her real name. When I do, she blushes. And *I* just *melt*. Janey, it's better than chocolate truffles from the St. Paul Hotel. Anyway, Mary Katherine's put me on an exercise regimen. I go to the gym now every . . . well, every *other* day."

Jane grinned. She liked Cordelia's newest love. "Good for you."

"Not that I want to be thin. Heaven forbid. I do *not* want to take up *less* space in the world. I should like to take up more. My cosmic context is large—always will be. But I want to be healthy." She sighed. "So I beat the crap out of myself on those torture machines several times a week."

Jane laughed. The clock on the mantle struck the half hour.

"I'd better hit the bricks," said Cordelia, rising from the rocking chair and striding into the front hall, "and get this meeting over with."

Jane helped her on with her coat. "Good luck."

"Thanks. By the way, dinner was wonderful. As usual. I will say, the risotto could have used a bit more Parmesan."

"I'll make a note of it."

"And a little less spinach."

"Spinach is good for you. Ask Mugs."

"And the salmon. Where did you buy it?"

"Good night, Cordelia."

"Don't get huffy."

"Give my regards to Orson."

20

2

Cordelia expected Orson's wife, Ingrid, to greet her at the front door when she arrived, but instead, Orson himself appeared—dressed all in black—and led her into his study. Other than a quick hi, he said nothing. The entire house was silent, unusual for this time of night. Normally, his teenage kids were pole-vaulting through the kitchen on their way to the evening's entertainment—partial destruction of the family room. Ingrid must have taken them out tonight. That knowledge made Cordelia even more ill-at-ease.

Stepping hesitantly into the room, she came to a sudden stop. There, seated on the couch, a golden lock of hair falling casually over one eye, was Curt. He smiled up at her, his expression pleasant but subdued. As he stood to give her a hug, she blurted, "What are you doing here?"

"I asked him to come," said Orson, sitting down behind his desk.

"Why?" She looked from face to face. "Did Annie come too?"

Curt shook his head. "She wanted to, but her class load wouldn't allow it." He gave Cordelia the hug and then stepped back. "But she'll be in Summer Green next weekend for the intervention."

"Excuse me? The what?" Cordelia put a hand on her hip. What the hell was he talking about?

"Just sit down, will you?" said Orson. "I'll explain everything."

Out of the corner of her eye, Cordelia caught sight of another figure emerging from a rear door. She turned, expecting to see one of the kids after all, but instead, found herself staring into the eyes of a man she hadn't seen in over fourteen years. Not since her last visit to the prison. "Theo."

He grinned, and then looked a bit annoyed. "You recognized me."

She was so stunned, she forgot to close her mouth. He looked much the same as he had in college, though older with a few more wrinkles. His hair remained dark and longish, no traces of gray anywhere, but now professionally styled, not combed by the wind as it had been so many years ago. And he had grown a beard. Jeans, boots and some gold jewelry finished the picture. He'd put on weight, and it looked good. He still could have doubled for Al Pacino. "Did you think I *wouldn't* recognize you?"

He shrugged, touching the beard. "It's new. I'm not used to it yet."

They held each other's eyes for a second longer and then both burst out laughing, throwing their arms around each other and holding on for dear life.

"How come you've never made it up here before?" she demanded, a pout forming. From the look Theo gave Orson, she knew the truth instantly. He had been here. He simply hadn't contacted her. She took a second to let that sink in.

"This place has some bad memories," he smiled. "You understand."

She didn't. She also didn't understand why his whole life had been so damn secretive, but for now, she decided to let it drop. She didn't know what was going on, so it was best to tread lightly.

After getting out of prison, Theo had lived for a short time—just a couple of months—in Chicago. Cordelia had made plans to visit him there, but before it could happen, he'd disappeared. No one knew where. About a year later he resurfaced in Florida. He'd been living in Miami ever since, refusing to let anyone come see him. No one even knew his address, or what he did for a living. Once, two years ago, he'd stayed with Diana in New York. But he'd never returned to Chicago to see Curt and Annie. Annie had made that clear on more than one occasion. Cordelia knew there was still a certain friction between Annie and Theo. Annie had won her man, but Curt and Theo *had* been lovers in college. From comments Annie had made over the years, it still rankled.

Orson visited Diana frequently in New York. Cordelia had also stayed several times at Diana's apartment near Central Park, but never for more than a couple of nights. And never when anyone else was there. So, however you looked at it, this was the first time in many years that so many members of the old group had been in the same room together at the same time. She knew it wasn't an accident. She returned her scrutinizing gaze to Orson.

"Just sit down," he said impatiently. "Dr. Bernson should be here any minute."

Cordelia's frustration was rising. "And who, pray tell, is Dr. Bernson?"

Orson's expression grew pained. "All right. I've already explained some of this to Theo and Curt. It's not a pleasant subject. That's why I thought I'd wait and let the doctor handle it. But since you're obviously about to explode, I'll fill you in on everything I know."

Cordelia plunked herself down in front of the desk. She tried not to glare, but her face wouldn't cooperate.

"On my last trip to Summer Green," Orson began, making

an arch of his fingers, "I became increasingly frightened by the extent of Diana's drinking. I know it's been bad for years, but this felt different. Maybe it was because we were spending so much concentrated time together, I don't know, but when I mentioned it to her, she wouldn't even discuss it. She said it was none of my business. One afternoon I was talking to a friend of hers and I discovered that Diana's new doctor in Appleton said if she didn't quit drinking and fast, her liver wouldn't last a year."

Cordelia was stunned. "Did the doctor tell that to Diana?"

"Of course he did. But apparently Diana has chosen to ignore the warning. She's so wrapped up in this new playhouse, she told me she doesn't have time to deal with anything else."

"But if she doesn't ... I mean, she might—" Cordelia couldn't finish the sentence. It was too awful to even contemplate.

"Exactly," said Curt from his position on the couch.

"Have you ever heard of something called an intervention?" asked Orson.

"Vaguely," answered Cordelia.

"It's when friends and family—in this case, the five of us—get together and, with the help of a therapist, try to hold up a kind of life mirror to the person who's drinking too much. Our experiences with their drinking become that mirror."

The doorbell sounded.

"At last," said Orson, breathing a sigh of relief. "That should be Dr. Bernson. She can explain this a lot better than I can." He rose and headed quickly out of the room.

While he was gone, Cordelia looked at Curt and then Theo. So that's why they were here. "You mean, Orson wants us all to go to Summer Green and tackle Diana? Tie her up and force her to listen to reason?"

"That's not what it's like," said Theo. "Besides, if we took that approach, it would never work."

Cordelia knew one thing. Someone was going to have to explain this to her more fully. But she did agree. If what Orson said was true, Diana needed help.

Orson returned to the room a few seconds later, followed closely by a small dark-haired woman in a navy blue linen suit and heels. She carried several packets of paper in her arms and smiled at everyone before taking a seat next to Curt. After introductions were made, she set the papers down and leaned forward, ready to take charge of the meeting. Orson resumed his chair behind his desk, and Theo sat down next to Cordelia. "Is this everybody who's coming tonight?" she asked, directing the question to Orson.

"Yes. There will be one more person at the intervention. Annie Whittig."

"My wife," said Curt, not looking at Theo.

"Fine. Well, remind me to give you an extra packet of information to take home for her. I'd like you all to fill out these forms before next weekend." She passed them around.

Cordelia studied the first page. It asked her to list the ways in which she had seen alcohol negatively affect Diana's life. And, interestingly, the next page asked her to list the ways in which Diana's addiction had affected *her* life negatively. She could think of dozens of answers to both.

"I'd like to begin tonight by talking about the disease of alcoholism in general terms," continued the doctor, folding her hands together loosely. "Alcoholism is, by definition, a disease of denial. The last person to know how sick he or she is, is the person with the disease. Normal perception becomes altered. The individual is not only out of focus while drinking, but also when sober. It's my personal opinion that people drink over feelings. Though many other tangential issues may be involved, the core issue is self-esteem. This often sounds strange when you realize how many interventions are done on doctors, lawyers, professionals of all kinds. We resist the notion that someone so obviously successful could also feel rotten about themselves. But self-image problems aren't confined to any single stratum of society." She paused to allow the meaning of her words to sink in. After a moment she added, "To most people, alcohol is a beverage. To the alcoholic, it's medication."

"What happens during the intervention?" asked Theo.

"Well, first of all, before the intervention ever takes place, I see to it that all the pre-admission work is done. In this case, we're going to ask Diana to fly with me that same day to a clinic in Minnesota."

"Is that the way it's usually done?" asked Cordelia, surprised it would happen so fast.

"It is. We need to create a sense of urgency in your friend. Since her doctor has said the liver is severely damaged, it's even more urgent. Her life is literally hanging in the balance. Near the end of the intervention, I'm going to ask each of you to explain how your relationship with her will change if she doesn't get on that plane. She has to know you all mean business."

Curt nodded. "But how do we get started? How do you explain *your* presence?"

"Well, when I arrive at the house, I'll tell Diana that I'm a family therapist who has been asked to be part of a meeting called by all of you because you're worried about her. The element of surprise is crucial. I can't stress that strongly enough. Then we begin immediately. I believe Orson said he would go first. You'll all use the sheets you've filled out. There's no shaming. No attacking. But we do use tough love. In specific terms, you all tell her how you've seen her abuse of alcohol affect her life. Each of you gets a turn. Then we move on to how her drinking has negatively affected *your* life."

"And these . . . interventions? Are you usually successful?" asked Curt.

"In nine out of ten cases, we are. For me that means we'll be able to move your friend from her head to her heart."

"What about her chances in treatment?" asked Theo.

"That's harder to predict. But at least she has a chance if she can break through the denial. Otherwise, I'm told her doctor has given her a year to live."

Everyone's eyes fell to the carpet.

Finally, Orson said, "How long does it take?"

"A normal intervention takes a couple of hours. Sometimes it can go longer. I did one last week that lasted over five. It all depends on Diana."

"Why us?" asked Cordelia.

Dr. Bernson's smile was gentle. "Because you love her. I understand most of her family is gone. Orson tells me you've all known each other since college. That's good. It gives you a vantage point from which to view her life. I'm most interested in the quality of your individual relationships. Blood ties, in and of themselves, mean nothing."

"I'm just curious," said Cordelia. "I know this isn't common knowledge, but did Orson happen to mention to you that Diana is . . . a lesbian?" Cordelia knew Diana wasn't out to most people. She'd been married briefly many years ago and had used that as a cover. But since the early eighties, she'd been living with her personal secretary, Jill Scarbourough. Still, it wasn't an obvious living arrangement. Until Jill's death, two years ago, they'd kept separate bedrooms.

"He did. As a matter of fact, I work primarily through a gay and lesbian institute in St. Paul. The fundamental issues are the same—medicating the pain, self-esteem problems—but the reasons for those issues are often different. It's hard to be a member of an oppressed and stigmatized group and not show the effects. Society dumps a lot of shame on anyone who deviates from the norm. Hiding and denial are often used as defense mechanisms against a hostile atmosphere, but hiding and denial intensify an alcoholic's problems. There are many dynamics associated with gay and lesbian alcoholism that are unique. We'll work with her on all of that."

"So," said Cordelia, leaning back in her chair. "When is this all going to happen? Did I hear Curt say something about next weekend?"

Orson nodded. "I hope you're free. Annie was having some difficulty getting five days off—"

"Five days." Cordelia swallowed hard.

"Right. Diana is expecting all of us to be in Summer Green for the opening performance at her new playhouse on Saturday night. But we're supposed to arrive on Friday. She's planned a party. And then on Monday, she's throwing a Labor Day picnic. I told her I'd arrange everything. She's like a little kid, she's so excited. And besides, I think it would be a good opportunity for all of us to spend some time together again. We'll need that before . . . well, before Dr. Bernson arrives on Tuesday."

"It's the first day I have free," said the doctor.

"But I'm in rehearsals right now for two different plays," protested Cordelia. "I don't suppose it could wait until—" She knew it was pointless to ask. Of course it couldn't wait.

"It's a small sacrifice," said Theo, his face betraying the intensity of his feelings, "when you compare it with what we might lose."

Cordelia nodded, lowering her eyes. Of course he was right.

"Besides," added Orson, "it might be fun."

"Sure. A relaxing, stress-free vacation," agreed Cordelia.

Orson narrowed one eye. "Look, we haven't been together in years. I, for one, think that should change."

"Right-on," said Curt, knowing he'd just said something not only dated, but obtuse. "And far-out," he declared. His grin told everyone he didn't care.

Cordelia wondered if she recalled the past a little more clearly than everyone else. She not only remembered the caring, she also remembered the rivalry and the volatility. "Well, I agree we should do it. No question about that. But all I can say is, I hope we keep from killing each other." She arched an eyebrow at Theo. Like her, he wasn't smiling.

3

"So," said Jane, watching Cordelia shamble into the downstairs pub of the Lyme House, the restaurant Jane had owned for many years, "Are you all packed and ready to head for Wisconsin?" She motioned to Johnny, one of the early afternoon bartenders, for another cappucino. Cordelia looked like she could use some caffeine.

Easing herself onto a bar seat, Cordelia heaved a deep sigh. "I guess I'm ready. I've cleared everything with the powers that be at the Allen Grimby. Jeff Kelling is going to take over my directorial duties until I get back. He's competent, but uninspired."

"Then they'll miss you all the more. And besides, you won't be gone that long." Cordelia fluffed her auburn curls. "It may turn out to be the longest five days of my life."

Jane knew Cordelia felt strongly about the intervention. It had to be done. She also knew Cordelia wasn't looking forward to this *reunion*, as Diana was now calling it. Diana had phoned her two nights ago and talked for several hours about her hopes and plans for the visit. She'd even gone so far as to suggest that everyone in the old group consider leaving their current jobs and homes to relocate in Summer Green. The playhouse would finally have a permanent staff. It would be like old times. Together, they'd make it the biggest and best regional theatre in the nation.

So much for Diana's grip on reality.

"Well," said Jane, pushing a bowl of fresh popcorn toward Cordelia as the cappucino arrived, "At least you know you're doing the right thing."

"That's what I've been telling myself all week. The needle seems to be stuck."

"Come on. It won't be that bad."

"Easy for you to say." She took a sip of the frothy drink, appearing to relax just a bit. "You'll be here, in the bosom of your family. Promoting your new cookbook. Being interviewed by the press and adored by the culinary public. Eating your beef Wellingtons and salivating over your plum puddings."

Jane held up her hand, knowing when Cordelia was on a roll, she could go on like this forever. "Plum pudding doesn't appear on the menu until November."

Cordelia tapped her fingers impatiently on the counter. "Raspberry trifle then. Pretty soon you're going to be right up there with Julia Child and the Frugal Gourmet."

Jane smiled at the exaggeration, but didn't correct her.

"And don't forget your promise," continued Cordelia without so much as a pause. "My cats need to be fed and cuddled once a day. I would have asked Mugs, but she's going to be in Cleveland."

"Cleveland?"

"It's one of her home security conventions. I know it's her job, but she's almost incommunicado when she's there. It drives me crazy."

"Don't worry. Your cats will be fine."

"Lucifer likes to hide next to the spaghetti noodles in the

pantry. If you can't find him, that's where he'll be."

"I know."

"And Melville—"

"—likes to pretend he's a book. He sleeps on top of an old copy of *Moby Dick*. I know, Cordelia. I've been taking care of your cats for years. I'm aware of all their idiosyncrasies."

Cordelia raised an eyebrow, tossing several popcorn kernels into her mouth. "All right. But remember, these are my *children*."

"Put your mind at rest. Beryl may even go over and babysit. Bounce them around the bathtub a few times."

"Oh, they'd love that." Cordelia's expression brightened. "Your aunt is a peach, Janey."

"I know. But she may not get to be a peach much longer if the INS has anything to say about it."

"What do you mean?"

"Unless Dad can pull some more strings and get her another extension, by March, she'll be back in England."

"What a dreary thought."

Jane nodded. "But listen, kiddo. You've got enough on your plate right now. We'll worry about that later."

Cordelia squared her shoulders and climbed down off the stool. She finished her cappucino is three quick gulps. "I'll call you sometime during the weekend."

"Fine."

"Wish me luck?"

"All the luck in the world," said Jane, putting her arm around Cordelia's shoulders and walking her out.

After many hours of driving through some of the richest farmland in America, Cordelia saw a sign that said, "Summer Green, 4 miles." She felt her hands tense around the steering wheel. She'd never been afraid of confrontation before—she'd even prided herself on her forthright handling of sensitive issues in both her work and personal life. But somehow, this was different. So much was riding on the outcome of the next few days. She'd dutifully filled out the forms Dr. Bernson had given her. It provided a good perspective from which to view Diana's life as it touched her own. What she'd once seen as merely high spirits mixed with bad judgment, now formed a more ominous picture. Diana had been having problems with alcohol ever since college. Cordelia felt more than a little guilty that she'd turned such a blind eye, allowing her friend to drown quietly.

Then again, the apprehension she was experiencing wasn't limited to Diana and the intervention. All week she'd been wondering what it would be like to spend time again with the Shevlin Underground. Even the name now caused her acute embarrassment. It was so . . . so silly. So dated. So hopelessly *young*. And, if nothing else, no one was young any longer. Even though she was excited to see her friends again, she knew the old tensions were just under the surface. They would all be walking through a mine field until they got to the final day. If they got that far.

Stop it. She ordered herself. Her melodramatic nature was running amok. The visit would go just fine. Oh, there might be the unavoidable glitch or two, but what the hell. They were all human. She had to think positively. For one thing, they loved each other. That was never in question. Each person, in his or her own way, was making a certain sacrifice to be at the reunion. They'd each be on their best behavior because nobody was an idiot. They all knew, like Cordelia, what the potential problems were. Everyone would put Diana first. No, it would be just fine.

Just fine.

As she slowed the car to forty, she began to see more houses and lawns instead of cows and corn fields. Another sign at the edge of town proclaimed, Welcome to Summer Green, Radish Capital of the Upper Midwest. Cordelia laughed out loud at that bit of hype. God, what people couldn't get excited over. At the bottom was the population—3,487. Over three thousand avid radish-lovers. Each, no doubt, with a recipe for creamed radishes on toast or radish preserves handed down directly from Grandma. She'd have to alert Jane. Perhaps a new cookbook should be considered.

Another half mile and she spotted a billboard. This one advertised the new Radish Hill Mall. Cordelia bit her lower lip. It was clear what had just happened. Sure. Rod Serling owned the hardware store. She'd finally entered The Twilight Zone. She'd always had a sneaking suspicion it was somewhere in the Midwest.

Orson had given her a rather crude map before she left. Now, if she could just find Main Street. She looked up at the street signs whizzing past and realized that the highway had ceased to exist and she was already on Main. Up ahead, she could see stores on either side of the street. The town was probably deserted, except for a small child, a dog and an old man. The townspeople had mysteriously vanished. A metallic object had been sighted falling from the sky into a ditch just south of The Mall. Two men, dressed in leopard skins and Robin Hood hats, had walked into town and entered the cafe. Fade to morning.

Cordelia knew she needed to eat something before she actually started to hallucinate. The tuna sandwich, corn chips and Ho Hos she'd packed for the trip had been devoured before she'd left the Twin Cities city limits. She was just like a kid. She could never wait. Passing through the business district—such as it was—she turned left onto Oak Avenue and picked up speed. Once again the houses began to dwindle as the road turned into a highway. By the time she spotted the church, now turned playhouse, she was back to fields and cows.

Diana lived next door to the church in what had once been the parsonage. It was a lovely sight, the evening hues subtle, like a Wyeth watercolor. Driving up to the white wood-framed buildings she couldn't help but notice how the simplicity of their design fit perfectly into the rustic surroundings. Clean, sharp lines. Cordelia pulled her car off the road and sat looking at the restful, yet slightly smarmy scene. Give me downtown St. Paul any day, she mumbled, listening to the disconcerting silence. The fading summer sunlight had imbued the buildings with a kind of angelic glow, casting deep shadows along the east side of the parsonage. The church steeple, which once housed a bell tower, now served as the anchor for a large wooden sign: The Summer Green Playhouse. Diana had mentioned that the fire which destroyed the back of the church had spared the carved wooden pews. She'd left them untouched, knowing they lent a kind of reverent formality to the interior. To her, theatres were intensely spiritual places. People sitting in the dark, listening to other people in the light talk about the experience of being human.

Cordelia crooked her neck and saw that, though most of the tall pointed windows on the side were clear glass, some of the old stained-glass panels still remained. Two of them flanked the arched double doors in the front. She couldn't wait to get inside and see what Diana had dreamt up for the stage. She'd hired an architect from New York City. A personal friend.

As Cordelia sat and contemplated the deepening sunset, its reds and golds settling into the grassy fields, a white Cadillac rolled over the distant rise. It came to a stop in front of the parsonage. The windows were dark, preventing her from seeing inside. Whoever was behind the wheel was probably just satisfying his curiosity because, after a moment, he drove on. Maybe it was a resident of the town, though by now, everyone must have had their fill of this new construction. It was probably the biggest event to hit Summer Green since the radish blight of '05.

She returned her attention to the church and the gloomy graveyard which stretched behind it. Not a particularly welcoming sight for visitors to the new theatre. Nevertheless, unlike Brigadoon, it wasn't going to disappear. Diana had made the best of it by keeping the lawn manicured. Here and there, flowers sprouted in thick clumps. She might even be able to use it to her advantage by offering prospective repertory players their own plot should anything untoward happen during a performance. Cordelia snickered at the thought. After all, perks *were* perks.

Out of the corner of her eye, she caught sight of a figure skulking in the shadows near the back of the parsonage. She squinted to get a better look, thinking it might be one of her group. They were great skulkers, all of them. But this person appeared to be elderly. Gray haired. She also seemed to be peeking in one of the side windows. Jesus, was this the town Peeping Tom? The idea that she was actually witnessing *a peeping* gave Cordelia the willies. She honked her horn, but her reaction had been too slow. The woman had already disappeared around the rear of the house.

Yuck. As she was about to pull back onto the road and head for the parking lot, the same white car she'd seen a minute ago rumbled by once again. Just as before, it stopped in front of the house, but closer to the front windows this time. Was someone casing the joint? The happenings inside the parsonage seemed to be of interest to one and all. As the sky grew darker, the lights inside grew brighter. It was possible now to see into the front room. She checked her watch. Nearly eight. Lights were also glowing inside the playhouse. She decided to take the direct approach. She rolled down the window of her car and leaned her head out calling, "Hi. Great house, huh. My name's Cordelia. What's yours?" The chill night air smacked her square in the face.

No sooner had she called her greeting than the Cadillac revved its motor and sped off. But before it did, she fixed on the license plate. She couldn't get the number, but she caught the state. Illinois. Interesting. An out-of-towner. From the same state as Curt and Annie.

Good riddance she thought to herself as she pulled her car into a parking space right next to Orson's Lincoln. She turned off the motor and got out, her nose twitching as she sniffed the itchy summer air. The scent which assaulted her was very different from what she'd grown accustomed to in south Minneapolis—

car exhaust mixed with just that right hint of ozone. Not that she had anything against city life. God *made* her for concrete and late night bistros. But this smell was decidedly pleasant. Earthy and sweet, with a slight whiff of cow. She could do without the cow—unless it gave chocolate milk.

"Bellboy." she shouted, hearing no response except the buzz of mosquitos. All itching for blood.

"Ahhhhhh," she sighed, heaving her heavy bags out of the trunk and letting them thump to the ground. "Ain't country living grand?"

4

Cordelia approached the screened porch, her ears pricking at the sound of Janis Joplin being played somewhere inside at the correct, ear-splitting decibel level. She smiled as she recalled Annie's record collection. Lots of Janis, Elton and Jethro Tull. Music had been such an important part of their lives. It had been the backdrop, the atmosphere against which they laughed and loved. Climbing the steps, Cordelia rang the bell knowing no one would hear. But, surprise, surprise, as she peeked through the window, she saw Orson dash into the hall and come barrelling toward the door.

"We wondered when you were going to get here," he declared, out of breath.

Cordelia swatted a mosquito away from her face and handed him her bags, realizing with a sense of relief that she didn't have to tip. Then, sweeping into the small foyer, she took a moment to look around. Well, well. Straight out of St. Mary Mead. Diana had done nothing to modernize. Instead, even the furniture furthered the image of small town life—*tasteful* small town life, circa 1920. Except, here and there, her personality did leak out. A dramatic arrangement of red gladiolus in a tall Lalique vase dominated the central hall. Signed photos from famous friends dotted the walls. A huge teddy bear from F.A.O. Schwartz sat in a rocking chair under the stairway, monitoring comings and goings. Cordelia knew the bear was from F.A.O. Schwartz because she'd been looking at one just like it in Minneapolis. She also knew the price.

"Everyone's in the parlor," said Orson, straining under the weight of five days worth of Cordelia's clothing. He had to shout to be heard over the music.

Cordelia nodded, noticing a floor to ceiling poster of Diana which served as the focal point in the dining room. So much for humility, not that Cordelia had ever been much into humility herself. At least Diana didn't have candles burning at the shrine. In the poster she was dressed as her character in "The Bald and the Snooty"—or whatever the name of that soap opera was. Cordelia never watched daytime TV, yet she was painfully aware that Diana had become famous playing the highly seductive mega-bitch, Morgana Richmond. Such stereotypes. It made her feel slightly nauseous. Nevertheless, actors had to be pragmatists. The part had made Diana a rich woman.

"I'll take these up to your room," said Orson, puffing up the stairs.

"Thanks." She followed the music into the first room on her right. The parlor was another period piece, with one sop to the modern. A comfortable leather couch. The rest of the furnishings were antique. The small room had an almost stark quality to it, though the smell of food and the soft glow from a wood fire made the scene inviting. Theo was standing with his back to her, leaning over a table filled with chafing dishes. He seemed to be unable to make up his mind. Curt was stretched out on the couch, paging through a soap opera magazine. He looked bored and tired. The trip from Chicago had no doubt been a long one. And Annie, her red hair done up in frizzy bun, was sitting cross-legged on the floor in front of the stereo, poking intently through Diana's old records and new CDs. Cordelia saw that the speakers were mounted on the wall above the fireplace. Another sop to modernization.

Diana, however, was nowhere in sight.

Attempting to restrain herself from sprinting over to the food table and diving head-first into the bean dip, Cordelia crossed regally to the hearth and rested her arm on the mantel. She waited for Janis to stop yelling and then cleared her throat.

Everyone turned to look.

"Cordelia." shouted Annie, turning down the volume and jumping up. She threw her arms around her. "I didn't hear you come in. "

"I'm a master of stealth," she grinned, hugging her back. Theo also came forward, giving her a welcoming kiss. "We thought you might have had car trouble."

"Nope. I was simply mesmerized by my bucolic surroundings."

Curt snorted. He remained on the couch, but offered a deep, heartfelt, "Moo."

"Hello to you too," replied Cordelia. "Did anyone think to bring the insect repellent?"

"The house is completely stocked," said Orson, returning to the room and dumping himself into a chair. His face had reddened from his brief stint as hotel staff.

Cordelia put a hand on her hip. No one would cast a man who looked like Raymond Burr as a bellboy, she thought to herself. When it came time to leave, she must remember to choose someone else to carry her bags back down. "Where's our host?"

"The company's doing a full dress rehearsal tonight," said Orson. "All very hush hush. Diana didn't want us anywhere near the church. She wants the production tomorrow night to be a complete surprise."

Cordelia nodded, spying a keg of beer sitting on a table in the far corner of the room.

Annie followed her gaze. "Diana said we should all help ourselves. I guess she thought a keg was pretty funny. Sort of for old-times sake."

No one laughed.

Janis droned on about Bobby McGee.

"Christ, put another record on," said Curt. "I'm sick of hearing that woman scream."

Cordelia noticed Annie stiffen. She wondered how things had been between the two of them recently. By the tone of this interaction, not so friendly.

Annie walked back to the turntable and switched everything off. "There. Is that better?"

He glared at her. "I hope we're not going to spend the entire weekend wallowing in nostalgia. My stomach can't take it." He stood, tossing the magazine on the couch, defying anyone to challenge him on the subject.

The first skirmish, thought Cordelia. There would be more.

"This reminds me of the night we realized we all had the flu," Theo piped up, ignoring Curt's angry look. "Remember? We were all in incredibly rotten moods. "

"Wasn't that the same time we all took turns making chicken soup?" asked Annie.

Theo nodded. "Whoever felt the least rotten would go to the store and buy more chicken and vegetables.

"And garlic. Don't forget the garlic," insisted Cordelia.

"God, we were sick for weeks," groaned Curt, thawing just a bit.

"I'm sure we kept re-infecting each other with the food," offered Orson.

Everyone laughed.

"Remember that time we decided to go sledding," said Annie, warming to the conversation. "I borrowed those sleds from my cousin."

"Right," agreed Orson. "Cordelia had just finished that paper, and we wanted to do something to help her celebrate."

Theo draped his arm over Cordelia's shoulder. "All I remember is Diana barrelling down the hill heading for the river."

"She must have closed her eyes," said Annie, shaking her head. "I was so scared. Remember how cold it was that day? If she'd gotten wet—"

"If it hadn't been for that snow fence," scowled Orson, "she would have gone straight into the water."

Curt hooted. "And then you, Theo old boy, wouldn't even use your sled. You said it was too dangerous."

"Oh, that wasn't it. He wanted to try out his newly memorized soliloquy," grinned Cordelia.

"Of course," agreed Orson. "You stood on top of that hill and gave a rare performance."

The room grew still as everyone remembered the magical moment. Theo, surrounded by mounds of freshly fallen snow and a cobalt blue sky, had spoken words from Hamlet.

"Act two," smiled Orson. "Do you remember any of it?"

"Of course." Theo gave a small bow.

"No you don't," said Curt. "That was twenty years ago. You couldn't possibly."

Theo cleared his throat. After a pause he began,

Now I am alone.
0, what a rogue and peasant slave am I.
Is it not monstrous, that this player here,
But in action, in a dream of passion,
Could force his soul so to his own conceit.

The words seemed to stop him.

"Go on," prodded Annie.

Theo looked over at Curt.

"Someone feed him the next line," said Orson.

Again, Theo held up his hand. Very soberly he continued,

Yet I,
A dull and muddy-mettled rascal, peak,

like john-a-dreams, unpregnant of my cause,
And can say . . . nothing.

"What's this?" asked a forceful voice from behind them. Everyone turned to find Diana framed in the doorway. Her hair, her skin, her clothing, everything was the color gray. She was wearing a gauzy, fringed flapper outfit and a thin band around her twenties' haircut. The makeup she wore emphasized the gauntness of her now aging face. She was a mannequin—a ghost with a mischievous smile.

"What happened to the party?" She moved into the room like she owned it. Which she did. "Annie, put on some music. Hamlet is much too dreary for a celebration. I feel like . . . how about some vintage Elton John? What do you say?" Her grin was irresistible.

"Fine," said Annie. She found a new CD and the music once again resumed.

"Much better," said Diana. She grabbed Cordelia's arm and gave it a hearty welcoming squeeze as she waltzed her over to the keg.

Conversations resumed.

"This should stay cold for several hours," said Diana. "Hey, you don't have anything to drink yet. Who the hell is the host around here?" She filled two mugs, and handed one to Cordelia. "Bottom's up," she smiled, finishing hers in one try. "Acting always makes me thirsty."

Cordelia took a small sip. Normally, she liked tap beer, but tonight it tasted bitter.

"You look fabulous," said Diana.

"Thanks. And you look . . . like a corpse."

She gave Cordelia an impish smile.

"How's the play going?"

"Good. Really good. I don't have the best talent to work with yet, but the company as a whole is solid. You'll see tomorrow night." She refilled her mug and eased over to the food table.

The doorbell chimed. Cordelia saw Orson disappear into the foyer. He certainly took his role as butler seriously. A moment later he came back and motioned Theo over to the door. Odd. Was the visitor for Theo? Who would come calling at a parsonage in the middle of nowhere? After a short conversation, they both left the room. Cordelia's curiosity moved instantly into high gear. She was itching to get over to the window to see what was going on, but she couldn't just dump Diana.

"Have a radish," said Diana, picking one up and taking a tiny bite. "They're an obsession around here."

Cordelia attempted an understanding smile, the one she reserved for people on the brink of insanity. "I noticed." She also noticed Diana's figure. She'd lost a great deal of weight since the last time they'd seen each other. Not that Diana had ever had a weight problem. In fact, the radish she was holding was probably tonight's dinner. Cordelia eyed the Swedish meatballs in the tallest chafing dish.

"What's on the agenda for tomorrow?" asked Annie, walking up and slipping her arm through Diana's. Curt had resumed his position on the couch, arms crossed over his chest, eyes closed.

"Well," said Diana, finishing beer number two. "I thought we'd stick around here in the morning. If I recall correctly, we all have different opinions as to what constitutes breakfast time."

"Not a moment before ten," said Cordelia. "I refuse to be up before the birds."

Diana took a deep breath. "Right. And then in the afternoon, everyone can explore the town at their leisure. I've written up some of the sights to see."

"That should take about ten minutes." Cordelia set the beer down.

"Still the big city girl?"

"What do you think?"

"You may not believe this," said Diana, "but I thought of myself that way too. Once. I was wrong. There's something about the American character that makes me believe we're all from a small town. Deep inside, we all grew up in a place like Summer Green."

"Hopeless romanticism," remarked Cordelia, trying not to be disagreeable, even though she disagreed.

"Just listen to us," laughed Annie. "We haven't changed a bit since college."

"Right. I still tie-dye my underwear." Cordelia gave them a pained smile. "Helps me maintain a youthful outlook."

"No. Really. Think about it."

"You mean Diana still *knows* everything," said Cordelia.

"And Cordelia still has to *control* everything," smirked Diana.

"I beg your pardon?" Cordelia's hand rose indignantly to her chest.

"And Annie quietly gets everything she wants. She never lets anything stand in her way." Annie said the words without a trace of humor.

"Well, whatever." Diana gazed into her empty mug of beer. "Just remember, give the town a chance. It might grow on you. And then in the evening, you'll all put on your finest big city duds and take your place in the front pew of the new Summer Green Playhouse. I'm going to knock your socks off." She glanced around. "You know, this celebration calls for something stronger than beer. Wait here." She dashed out of the room.

Cordelia seized her opportunity. "I'll be right back, Annie. I have to . . . freshen up." Didn't people always need to freshen up?

"Ah . . . sure."

"Don't eat all the food before I get back."

"I wouldn't dream of it." She selected a radish.

Christ, what was *wrong* with these women. Bean dip and meatballs and they grab the freaking radish? She didn't have time to dwell on it. Striding into the foyer, she crossed to the front door and peeked out the window. Orson was standing on the porch, deep in the shadows. Theo had moved out to the end of the walk. He was talking to a bald man who was leaning on—oh my god, there it was again. The Cadillac. So they *had*

44

been watching the house. The conversation seemed to be calm enough. No shouting. But it made her uneasy. Why didn't the guy come inside? Why all the secrecy? After a few moments, the man got into the car and Theo headed back up the walk. When he got to the steps, Orson stepped out of the shadows. Cordelia opened the door just a crack to hear their conversation.

"How did he find you?" asked Orson.

"No idea."

"I don't understand. It can't be a coincidence. The odds against it have to be astronomical."

"Apparently not."

"What are you going to do?"

"That depends on you."

Orson didn't move.

"You still my banker?"

"Jesus. When is this ever going to end?"

Theo smiled. "You owe me your life, buddy."

"I know."

"What are you looking at?" asked Diana, poking Cordelia in the ribs. She was holding a bottle of vodka.

Cordelia jumped. She turned around and tried to look innocent. She'd never been very good at that. Not even when she was a baby. "Why . . . nothing." She smiled. "Just . . . appreciating the sunset."

"The sun goes down in the west, Cordelia."

"Oh. Right." Some people were such a store of useless information.

"Is that for me?"

She glanced at the booze. "For all of us." Diana turned and breezed back into the parlor.

Reluctantly, Cordelia followed.

"Can I have everyone's attention?" called Diana, waving her hand like the prom queen she wasn't. She looked around the room. "Where's Orson and Theo?"

"Right here," said Theo. They both moved in behind her.

"Good. I want to propose a toast," said Diana. "Does everyone have something to drink?"

Curt handed Theo, Orson, and Cordelia a mug of beer.

"Great," said Diana. "Before the toast, I want to say one thing. Thanks to brother Orson's big mouth, I'm sure you've all heard the news that I'm at death's door. Well, buckos, we're all dying. Everyone of us. I just may have a better idea of the date. I don't want to make that little tidbit the focus of this gathering, is that clear? Doctors have been wrong before." She held up the bottle. "All right then, to us. To the best bunch of friends anyone's ever had. And to our reunion after far too many years. We all came for our own reasons. Whatever they are, may we each find what we're looking for."

They clinked their mugs together, Diana using the bottle as her glass. She unscrewed the top and took a swig.

Except for Elton John, the room grew quiet. No boisterous *here here's* accompanied the toast. Cordelia could see each person silently retreat into himself or herself. Thoughts grew louder than words.

And, for the second time that night, Cordelia looked up and saw Theo staring at Curt.

5

Around one in the morning, after everyone had gone up to bed, Cordelia crept quietly into the kitchen and picked up the phone. She punched in some numbers and then waited. After a few seconds a woman's voice answered, "Hello?"

"I missed you. I simply *had* to hear your voice."

"Excuse me?" came the confused reply.

"This is not a crank call, dearheart. This is a plaintive cry from a faraway land."

Jane let out a deep growl. "Cordelia."

"C'est moi. Were you asleep?"

"No. I always sound like my head is under a pillow."

Cordelia sat down behind the counter. The room was dark except for a hood light on the stove. She could hear a soft buzzing.

"Couldn't you have missed me a few hours ago?" asked Jane. "Before it became the middle of the night?"

"I wasn't even thinking about you a few hours ago. I was

having too much fun."

"Oh, I get it. And now you're bored."

"Well . . . not exactly." Her eyes searched the darkness for the source of the buzz. "Something isn't right here."

"You mean in Summer Green? I take it you made it without mishap."

"The drive was straight out of a Norman Rockwell painting, Janey. You know Wisconsin. Cheese flowing down the hillsides like lava. Cows, chickens and bratwurst all grazing together in the open fields." She swatted away a mosquito as it dive-bombed her face. Ah ha.

"Then what's the problem? Can't find an espresso bar when you need one?"

"Cute. No, actually something happened tonight. I need to run it past a disinterested party."

"Is that what I am?" She snorted. "You make me feel so special."

"Well, I mean, you know everyone here. You simply don't know them as well as I do. But just listen, okay? You tell me what you think. When I first got here, I noticed this Cadillac casing the parsonage where Diana lives. It stopped in front of the house for a few seconds and then just sped off."

"Curiosity seekers?"

"That's what I thought. But later, the doorbell rings and Orson says it's for Theo. So, Theo goes outside. I happened to glance out the front door a few minutes later and there's the Cadillac again. Only this time, Theo and a bald man are standing next to it, talking."

"Could you hear what they were saying?"

"Nope. Too far away."

"Did they seem angry or upset?"

Cordelia played the scene over again in her mind.

"Not really. But finally the bald guy gets back in the car and drives off. That's when Theo comes back up to the porch and starts talking to Orson."

"Where was Orson when all this was happening?"

"Standing in the shadows on the porch. I'm sure the bald guy never saw him. Anyway, Orson says something to Theo about wondering how the man found him. Then Theo tells Orson he needs money. Calls Orson his banker."

"How did Orson take *that?*"

"Before he could say much, Theo reminded him that he—Orson—owed Theo his life."

Jane whistled. "Do you know what he was referring to?"

"I haven't the vaguest idea." Cordelia could hear the faint buzzing again. The mosquito was back for round two. "I can't help but wonder if it has something to do with the time Theo spent in prison." She flailed at the air in front of her as the speck flitted past. "And something else strikes me as odd."

"What's that?"

"Diana seems to be angry at Theo. She barely spoke to him all evening. I wasn't the only one who noticed it."

"Did someone comment on it?"

"Yeah. Annie. She got me aside before everyone went up to bed and asked if I knew what was going on."

"Sounds like you're having a great time."

"Actually," said Cordelia, smacking the counter but missing the intended victim, "tonight was wonderful. We all sat around the fire and reminisced. I laughed so hard my fingernails hurt."

"Well, I'm sorry I can't help you more," said Jane, trying to stifle a yawn. "You'll work it out."

"Yeah," said Cordelia, slamming her fist down hard on a plate. She could just *feel* the mosquito's smug smile as it whizzed past her face. "I'll keep you posted."

"You do that."

"Nighty night, dearheart." Cordelia set the phone back in its cradle. Climbing down off her stool, she spotted an aerosol can of RAID on the far counter. "Say your prayers," she whispered, her eyes gleaming wickedly.

6

Before going to sleep, Cordelia made the mistake of leaving the window open in her bedroom. She awoke on Saturday morning to the sound of a DC-10 attempting to make a crash landing on her pillow. Knowing she had mere moments to react, she shot out from under her quilt and hit the floor, covering her head with her hands. Seconds ticked by. When nothing happened, she cracked open one eye. Hmm. No dust balls under the bed. How hygienic. Next, she hoisted herself up on a chair. It took a moment before her mind completely focused. When it did, she realized the sound she'd heard wasn't a jet engine, it was a lawn mower. By the roar it made, a damn big one. Anybody could make the same mistake, she thought to herself as she yanked her pink satin pajamas into place. She found her fake zebra-skin robe in a heap on the floor and trudged out the door, heading for the stairs. She might as well see who else was up.

As she passed the parlor on her way to the kitchen, she saw

someone had already cleaned away the mess from last night. Gremlins, no doubt. She knew Diana had passed out on the couch and had to be carried up to bed. A bad beginning to their stay.

"Who are *you?*" asked a young voice.

Cordelia turned to find a girl standing at the bottom of the stairs. She had brown hair, cut very short—almost a crew-cut—and very green eyes. And, she was chewing gum. Loudly. She couldn't be more than fourteen. The army fatigues she wore looked like they came straight off the rack at Bloomingdale's. Combed cotton. Nicely tailored. Cordelia raised a highly approving eyebrow. She wanted to touch the collar, but knew it would be gauche.

"You must be one of Diana's friends," said the girl, realizing she was being scrutinized. She bumped past Cordelia and flopped down on the couch. She had a magazine under one arm and quickly took it out, covering her face.

Cordelia noticed the title. *The New Republic.* A bit different from the other reading material scattered on the end tables. With the exception of *The Independent Film E Video Monthly,* and *Interview,* Diana appeared to read mostly soap opera gossip. But then she knew the *gossipees* personally. Cordelia had great faith that one day, gossip would be recognized as the primal need it so obviously was. For Pete's sake, that's why we *had* celebrities. So we could talk about them.

She cleared her throat. "My name is Cordelia Thorn."

The magazine didn't move.

"What's yours?"

A page turned. "Amity. Amity Scarbourough."

The last name was familiar. Cordelia thought for a moment. Of course. Jill Scarbourough had been Diana's personal secretary and lover for many years. She'd recently died. This must be her daughter. "It's nice to meet you. I knew your mother, though only slightly."

"Me too," came the quick response. Another page was turned.

The kid was fast. Cordelia sat down. She didn't mind talking to a magazine. It gave her an opportunity to stare at the fatigues with total abandon. Perhaps she could have her dressmaker sew one in a larger size. She knew Bloomingdale's failed miserably at large sizes. No doubt, fat women weren't supposed to look like they'd served in the Gulf War.

Amity lowered the magazine to see where Cordelia had gone. She gave a little wave. "I'm right here."

"You're weird."

"Thanks."

"What'd you say your name was?"

"Cordelia."

The magazine lowered even further. "I like that name."

"Me too. What are you doing in Summer Green?"

"Hiding."

"From whom?"

"My grandparents. After Mom died, I went to live with them. We didn't get along."

"Umm. So you came here."

"Yup. Two days ago."

Really. No wonder Diana hadn't mentioned anything about her the other night on the phone. "Have you checked out the town yet?"

"What town?"

Smart kid. They were going to get along. "Have you had any breakfast?"

"Yeah. I had a bagel. It was awful. Totally gummy. I don't know how Diana can eat that crap."

"Thanks for the warning. I think I'm going to head into the kitchen. Being up before dawn has made me ravenous."

"It's after ten, but I know what you mean." The magazine rose. "Later."

"Later," repeated Cordelia.

The kitchen which greeted her weary morning eyes was cleaned and polished. A far cry from last night. It was the one room in the house which didn't look as if it had come straight out of an antique Sears catalogue. The cabinets and counters were all new white laminate. A center island served as both a work space and an eating area. Six stools fit comfortably along one side. She turned to the window as she shuffled to the refrigerator, noticing an elderly gray-haired woman outside on a riding mower. Cordelia narrowed her gaze to get a better look. Damn if she wasn't the same person Cordelia had seen last night looking in the side window.

"Top of the morning," chirped Annie, entering the kitchen with a newspaper tucked under one arm. She was already dressed

Cordelia glared. She'd forgotten Annie was one of those tediously cheerful morning people. "Right," she grunted.

Annie gave her an amused smile. "There's orange juice in the fridge. And fresh blueberry muffins on the counter."

Come to think of it, Cordelia did smell something wonderful. "Who made them?"

"Hilda Barnes. She's outside cutting the grass. She's sort of a jack of all trades. Gardener. Cook. I think the minister who used to live here hired her as a housekeeper. When Diana moved in, Hilda knocked on the front door and offered her services. She lives about a mile up the road. Her husband died many years ago. She just likes to keep busy, I guess. If you'd been up a couple of hours ago, you would have met her. We had a nice talk."

Cordelia raised a skeptical eyebrow. She got out the juice and poured herself a hefty glass. Then she sidled over to the muffins and selected the largest. "Where is everyone?"

"Diana and Theo are still upstairs sleeping. And since it's such a lovely morning, Curt went for a walk after breakfast. "

"You didn't go with him?"

Her mouth tightened. "No. I didn't. And Orson drove into town. He has a lot of friends around here."

"I know," said Cordelia between bites. The muffin was

delicious. Real blueberries. "Local boy makes good."

"That he has."

Cordelia pulled up a stool and sat down across from Annie. She might be perky as hell, but she didn't look happy. "So, what's new with you?"

"Not much. My teaching schedule is pretty full this term."

"You still like it? Teaching, I mean?"

She nodded. "It's the only thing I've ever really wanted to do. I can't act. I'm not good at the tech stuff, like Curt is, and I've no interest in directing. But I love the theatre."

Cordelia finished her muffin and washed it down with the juice. Then, reaching for a mug, she poured herself a cup of coffee. Nice touch, having the coffee maker on the center island. "You want some?" she asked, still holding the pot.

"Why not," said Annie. She grabbed a mug. "You know, fresh squeezed orange juice always reminds me of that winter I came down with pneumonia. Remember?"

"I brought juice to the hospital every day," said Cordelia, smiling at the thought. "Along with an assortment of Robert Redford photos."

"You were all wonderful. Orson and Theo did those silly drawings and then plastered them all over the hospital room. And Diana stayed with me at night. I'll never forget that. She'd leave in the morning and go to class and to work, but every night she'd be back. She must have been exhausted, but she kept it up until I got well. The doctors terrified me. I don't think I ever said that to anyone. But I felt so warm and safe with all of you. So . . . loved. It was the first time I think I realized how special you'd become to me. I've had lots of friends since, but I've never felt that same intensity. Maybe it only happens once in a lifetime."

Cordelia had wondered about that too.

"And Curt." Annie's eyes grew wistful. "He came in the evenings with his guitar and sang to me. That's when I first realized my feelings for him went beyond friendship. He was so gentle. And so beautiful. He read me poetry and silly limericks.

Tried to get me to smile. Seeing you all again has made me miss that time in my life terribly. I wonder if we can ever get it back."

Cordelia squeezed her hand. "We can try, dearheart. We can give it our best shot." She poured Annie's coffee. "I hear Curt is stage-managing for a community theatre in Chicago."

She nodded, taking a sip. "It's not full time, but it's something."

"You aren't hurting for money are you?"

"No. My salary's pretty good now. And Curt's parents give him anything wants. We're fine. But as far as I'm concerned, they've crippled him. He's never been very self-motivated, and since he doesn't need a regular job to survive, he just drifts."

Cordelia already knew about Curt's inability to settle on a career. She'd been surprised that he'd settled on a marriage partner.

"He's a good man, but we've had our problems. Especially lately."

"Want to talk about it?"

Annie shook her head. "I don't know. Maybe. We've started arguing over small things. Nothing that has any importance. But our home has begun to feel like an armed camp. I know he's unhappy, but he never does anything about it. I suggested a marriage counselor, but he drags his feet. Won't make a decision. One minute he thinks it's a good idea, the next he's not so sure. I know he loves me, but—"

Cordelia turned the mug around in her hand. "How do you feel about spending the weekend with Theo?"

She looked away. "Okay, I guess. What can happen? And besides, I couldn't turn my back on Diana, no matter what the cost. Actually, the more I've thought about it, the more I see that this visit might be a good move. Maybe we can finally get our problems out in the open. I've always known Curt's feelings for Theo were never resolved. After Theo was put in prison, Curt just crumbled. That's when we first really talked. He knew I liked him when we were in college, so he purposefully kept our relationship light. But later, he needed a confidant—especially after graduation when we all scattered to the four winds. He followed me to Chicago. And then we got married. Maybe that was a mistake, I don't know anymore. It's what I wanted. I thought it was what he wanted too."

"Does Curt think he's gay?" Cordelia had often wanted to ask the question, but she and Annie had rarely talked this intimately in the years since college.

She shook her head. "Curt considers himself bisexual. We've never had any sexual problems, if that's what you mean. For him, it's more the person than it is the gender."

Cordelia nodded. It was what she had suspected. "Didn't Theo spend some time in Chicago right after he got out of prison?"

"Yes, though we didn't see him very much. And then one day he was just gone."

Cordelia had always wondered why he'd left so abruptly. To be honest, she'd never really understood why he'd gone to Chicago in the first place. Her gut feeling told her it had to do with Curt, though she could be wrong. "Well, I'm sure Theo and Curt will have ample time to talk while we're waiting for the other shoe to drop."

"I know what you mean. That's exactly how it feels. Everyone's so jumpy."

"Maybe I'm a coward, but I'm not looking forward to Tuesday's little meeting."

"I'm not looking forward to any of this."

Cordelia knew the subject had once again returned to Curt and Theo.

"I'll just say one thing," said Annie, pushing her mug away. "If Theo hurts Curt any more than he already has, this time, he'll have me to answer to."

It was obvious Annie's emotions were stretched as taut as a drum. Even though her voice was calm, Cordelia could read the tension in her eyes. And it worried her.

7

Diana stood in the bathroom and splashed water into her face. Mornings were always a shock. An entire bottle of aspirin couldn't help this hangover. Maybe a sledge hammer—right between the eyes. Or an entirely new head. She looked up, catching sight of herself in the mirror. "Oh crap," she scowled, seeing the damage much more clearly than any camera. It had been quite a party last night. Terrific to see her friends again—the four she could still call friends. But it was hell to watch them watching her. She hadn't counted on that. She felt like a zoo animal. Damn that Orson. He had no right. Maybe she did drink too much, but so what? Her life was completely fucked. It was the only thing that helped.

"Makeup," she called, turning around too quickly and losing her balance. "Oops." She caught herself on the edge of the sink. God, she felt awful. She was still dizzy. That was often the worst part. What she really needed was another drink. Walking very carefully back into her bedroom, she opened her lingerie drawer and felt around for the bottle. Her heart sank when she realized it was empty. She should have remembered to grab a fresh one from the liquor cabinet before coming up to bed last night. Not that she actually knew *how* she'd gotten upstairs. She didn't remember a lot of things these days.

In a depressed funk, she slid to the floor in front of her closet and began to cry. What was the use? Everything she touched turned to ashes.

Everything except . . . Jill. Her lover. Her companion. Her lifeline. They'd been happy for so many years, making plans for the future. Not that life together had been perfect, but it was good. But then—.

Diana pulled her legs up close to her body and began to rock. It wasn't fair. The one part of her life that made sense—God should have looked out for Jill. The doctors should have been able to prevent her death. But then, everyone knew you couldn't prevent a New York truck driver's stupidity.

Her head fell back against the wall. And now, what the hell was she supposed to do with a fourteen-year-old? She knew nothing about kids. School would be starting in a matter of days. Army fatigues and ripped tank tops wouldn't go over well in Summer Green. It was too much. She couldn't deal with any more right now. "Jill, what do I do?" she whispered, covering her face with her hands.

Jill's death had been the worst. Nothing could even touch the pain. But, crazy as it sounded, what happened the morning of the funeral was almost as bad. Since that day, nothing had been the same. Looking up, Diana saw the picture she'd attached to the inside of her closet door. It was stapled about three feet off the floor. A photo of her nemesis, minus two small body parts which no one would miss. The button she'd affixed to the chest was nothing short of genius. Cordelia had mailed several of these buttons to her after Diana had made a hefty contribution to the Minnesota Abortion Rights Council. No, it was the perfect touch. Just the right statement. Why didn't anyone ever get the parallel?

She stared at the photo, her eyes starting to burn. "Notice the rat-like expression," she said out loud, as if to a crowd of onlookers. She swept her hand to the picture. "The sly, pinched smile. The oily condescension of someone who always knows best." No doubt about it, this rodent had never been a friend, though the disguise had been masterful. The name Judas came to mind.

Her eyes fell to a kitchen knife just inside the door. A moldy chunk of cheese and a box of crackers rested next to it. Must have been a late night snack. She couldn't remember when. Picking up the knife, she felt its weight, running her hand appreciatively along the razor sharp edge. Suddenly, in one lightning swift movement, Diana slammed the blade into the picture. The knife sank deep into the door.

"Have a nice day," she whispered, easing herself into a standing position. "You never know when it's going to be your last."

8

After lunch, Curt decided to check out the graveyard in back of the parsonage. He'd spent the morning walking south along the highway. He hadn't run into much, except a couple of farms and three friendly horses. Everything was so lush and green, yet the air felt heavy with a kind of end-of-summer sadness. Even though autumn didn't officially arrive for almost a month, it wouldn't be long before the fields were covered in snow. Curt hated winter. Hated the cold and the damp and the bitter winds. Yet the root of his melancholy had nothing to do with the seasons. He simply couldn't stay around the house today, trying to ignore Diana's drinking. She'd started early. If she didn't get a grip, tonight's performance would be a disaster. Orson had taken her aside and tried to talk to her about it. He wished him luck. The others all seemed to have so much to catch up on. Curt just felt tired. All he wanted was silence.

He knew Annie was upset with him. She'd tried to get him to open up last night before turning in, but he couldn't. She wanted to know if it was hard to be around Theo again. What could he say when he didn't know himself. One thing he did know: Theo had taken on the force of a symbol in his life. Curt's reaction to him was completely out of proportion to what had actually happened. He'd become a symbol of a kind of confused longing. But hadn't Curt always sensed an emptiness inside himself—even before he'd met Theo? He crouched next to a grave stone and looked around. Sometimes he felt like an archaeologist attempting to dig up a lost life. His own. Annie could never understand that. She wanted him to live in the present because that's where she was. She didn't understand limbo. She didn't even believe it existed.

He squeezed his eyes shut, trying to focus. His mind was slippery today. He couldn't hold it still. Getting up, he began to run. The cool wind felt good against his face. His senses took over, the exertion making his body feel strong. He stretched his arms high over his head and tried to relax. The graveyard was bigger than he'd first thought. As he came to a massive elm, he put out his hand and leaned against it, catching his breath. The tree was old, its leaves already yellow. Not because of the season. It was dying. Close to its enormous roots was a row of head stones, all from the late 1800's. Curt moved toward them, fascinated by how the years had erased the names and images. He bent down and touched the surface of the first. The date was unreadable. Glancing to his right, he jumped at the sight of a hand lying motionless in the grass. It was holding a can of cola. Curt shot to his feet, nearly losing his balance. "Christ. You nearly scared me to death."

Theo's eyes were open and he was staring up at the cloudless summer sky. "Thought I'd get the lay of the land. See the real *coffin's* eye view." He propped himself up against a gravestone. "You out for a run?"

"Yeah."

"It's too nice to stay inside." Theo paused, chewing on a blade of grass. "So, why don't you pull up a rock and have a seat."

"I don't know. I'm feeling kind of anti-social today."

"Oh, come on." When Curt continued to hesitate, Theo added, "I'd like to talk to you."

It seemed a reasonable enough request. Not that they'd made any attempt to talk so far during the visit. They just threw words at each other. He moved around a carved pillar and sat down, keeping a good distance between them. "All right. What's up?"

Theo scratched his beard. He took a sip of cola.

Curt could tell he was nervous. That was interesting.

"Annie looks great."

"Yeah. I agree."

"You two still pretty happy there in Chicago?" Theo's eyes rose to the sky.

"Get to your point."

"No point. Just curious."

"We have our ups and downs. Just like everyone else. How about you? You like it in Florida?"

"I'm living in Texas right now."

"Really? I didn't know. Why the move?"

"Oh, the climate I suppose. Among other things."

"You always have reasons, Theo. You just don't share them."

Theo's gaze dropped to the horizon. "You sound angry."

"I don't know what I am. Maybe you're right. I mean, Jesus, I don't even understand why you went to prison. You never answered my letters. You won't give anyone your phone number so I can't call. If you really want to talk, maybe that's a good place to start."

He shook his head. "Why get into all that now."

Curt just stared at him. Why did he think this conversation would be any different? "Right. Sorry. I just thought that since we loved each other once, I deserved more than your standard brush off. But I was wrong. Forget it."

Theo looked down. He was quiet for a long time. Finally, he said, "We wouldn't have stayed together. It never would have worked."

"Why?" Curt felt his stomach lurch.

"I wasn't ready to settle down back then. I'm not sure I'll ever be ready."

Curt laughed out loud. "A word of advice, Theo. Get some new lines. You're starting to sound like one of Diana's soap operas."

"You never saw yourself the way I did. You were such a lost kid back then. Your mom and dad were the original ice king and queen. You deserved more from them *and* from me. But I couldn't give you what you wanted. I still can't."

Curt was suddenly furious. "That piece of psychobabble is supposed to explain my life? What happened to *us*?"

Theo's face grew very sad.

"It's not enough. Where have you been, Theo? Why did you leave Chicago so abruptly—you never even said good-bye."

"You didn't need me. You had Annie. Besides, you needed a clear shot. I was only in your way."

"A clear shot at what?"

"Happiness."

Curt snorted. He got up and began to pace. "I know you've always prided yourself on what a great actor you are, but I can tell when you're lying, Theo. And you're lying now. Why?" He stopped, waiting for an answer.

"I'm not lying about us. You wanted a life like Ozzie and Harriet. I couldn't give you that."

"That's a crock of shit."

"Is it? You wanted a stable relationship. Someone to come home to. Someone who would listen to you and love you, eat dinner with you and soothe your world-weary soul. I couldn't be that person."

"Why not?"

"Because it's not what *I* wanted." He took a deep breath, giving himself a moment to regroup. "Curt, listen to me. If what you need to be happy is another man, then go find him. It may

63

take some time, but Annie will understand. Some things work and some things don't. She knows that. She's a realist."

And she hates your guts, thought Curt, though he had the sense not to say it.

"Trust me, there are plenty of guys who want to nest, build a home, live monogamously. I just don't happen to be one of them."

Curt was silent. This conversation felt like shadow boxing. Nothing of substance. Theo kept talking in circles, never really answering a direct question. But he couldn't hide forever. Curt had seen the way he'd looked at him the night they arrived. Theo had thought he was being cool, standing in the shadows while everyone's attention was elsewhere. Curt was talking to Diana, waiting for Annie to come up from the car. He was wearing his mirrored sunglasses so Theo couldn't see his eyes. But Curt could see Theo's. The pain in them was undeniable. And the longing. It was all there. The love. The passion. The sadness. It wasn't as simple as he was suggesting.

"What's wrong?" asked Theo. "What are you thinking?"

Curt shrugged.

"Damn it Curt, what did you expect from this reunion? Did you think we'd get back together?"

He couldn't believe his ears. What arrogance. "No, Theo. I'm not a kid any longer. I refuse to let you make this sound like we're back in college. You're the captain of the football team and I'm some pimply-faced ex-lover who can't let go. Don't flatter yourself. I expect nothing from you."

"Yes you do."

"Go to hell."

Theo reached out his hand, but Curt backed up.

"I don't need you to fulfill my life, Theo. But I do need to understand what happened so my life can go on. Is that so incomprehensible? Do you even understand what I'm saying?"

Theo slammed his fist on the ground. "You're missing my point."

"Am I?"

"What do you want from me, Curt?"

"The truth."

He looked away. After a moment he said very softly, "I don't love you. I did once, but not now."

Curt stood very still. "I don't believe you."

"What?"

"I said, *I don't believe you*." He shoved his hands deep into his pockets and waited.

Theo was stunned. But he recovered quickly. With a slightly crumpled smile he said, "It would be easier if you did."

"Easier for whom? You?" Brushing the grass off his jeans, Curt started back toward the parsonage.

"Wait," said Theo, grabbing his hand as he walked past.

Curt shook it off. "You've said what you wanted to say."

"But you haven't."

"What's the difference? You're not interested."

"Don't be angry with me, Curt. I know I've hurt you. "

As Curt stared down at him, he was overwhelmed by a feeling of disgust. He had to get away. Striding toward the parsonage, he heard Theo call, "Look at your life, man. You may already have what you need. You just can't see it because I'm in the way."

Curt ignored the words, breaking into a dead run.

9

Cordelia stood in front of the full-length mirror in her room, zipping up the formal gown she'd brought for the opening performance of the new Summer Green Playhouse, now just two hours away. She knew she was over-dressing but didn't care. Any old chance to wear something gorgeous was a chance taken. She'd considered bringing along her tux but had been in a flowing mauve and silver beaded silk mood when she'd packed. So, alas, that was to be tonight's costume. Not that she was unhappy with the way she looked. She might be large, but she was still a knockout.

Outside her door she heard the sound of footsteps. Then a hard rap. "It's open," she called as she adjusted her earrings. After a second, another knock.

"Just a minute," she said impatiently, as she scurried around the bed. Flinging open the door, she beheld the same tall gray-haired woman she had seen earlier in the day cutting the grass.

Tonight, she'd shed her overalls for a rather baggy cotton dress. Pink and blue flowers on a cream background. Cordelia approved of the look. Sort of a 1950's grandmother. The woman had very sharp features and an expression like a chicken hawk. Her shoulders were square and quite strong for a woman of her advanced years. "Yes?" said Cordelia, her hands rising to her hips.

"Ms. Stanwood wanted me to tell all her guests that she's over at the playhouse and won't be seeing any of you until after the show. She asked me to prepare a light supper. Just some cold chicken, potato salad, homemade biscuits and a radish tray. It's downstairs in the dining room. I've laid everything on the sideboard so you can help yourself." She said the words as if they were a prepared speech.

Cordelia nodded. "That's kind of you."

"Kindness has nothing to do with it. It's my job."

"I see. Well, thanks anyway."

"Just leave your dishes on the dining room table. I'll get them later."

"Fine." She waited. The woman didn't move. Instead, she seemed to be trying to get a better look inside the room. Blatant nosiness. Cordelia was intrigued. "Is there something else?"

"No. Just looking. It's a free country last I heard."

"Would you like to examine my suitcases? I could show you photos of my cats."

"What are you implying?"

"Why nothing." She glanced down the hall. All the other doors were closed. Everyone else was, no doubt, busily getting ready. Her gaze returned to the woman. "I don't believe we've been formally introduced. My name is Cordelia Thorn."

"I know."

"I don't doubt it."

"Hey."

"And *you* are?" Cordelia's tones had become entirely too rounded.

"Hilda Barnes." She stuck out her hand.

Cordelia shook it limply. "I enjoyed your blueberry muffins this morning."

"Yeah. I'm a good cook. Some people are artists, and some aren't." She eyed Cordelia's dress.

"I beg your pardon?" Her eyebrow arched slowly upward as she straightened her plunging neckline. Was this criticism from the same woman who had planted the entire front yard full of marigolds? Definitely Park Board taste. Cordelia sniffed. "Well, this has been delightful, but I have to finish dressing."

"You known Ms. Stanwood long?"

"Since college."

"All of you people staying here are old college friends?"

"Last I heard."

"Old friends are the best kind."

"I'm glad you think so."

"It's about time someone came to help."

"What do you mean?"

She tipped her head back and mimicked drinking from a glass. Then she winked.

Cordelia got the point. "Who told you we came to help?"

"I got eyes. Ms. Stanwood's all right by me. I know she's a little weird. Got some unusual . . . inclinations, if you know what I mean. But then she's artistic. I understand the artistic nature. I got one myself." She lowered her voice. "Don't let that bearded man ruin things."

"Excuse me?"

"I clean Ms. Stanwood's room. I'm not blind."

"To what?"

A door opened and Orson's head popped out. He whistled when he saw what Cordelia was wearing.

Hilda moved quickly down the hall. "Mr. Albern, Ms. Stanwood wanted me to tell all her guests that she's over at the playhouse and won't be seeing any of you until after the show. She asked me to prepare a light supper. Just some cold chicken, potato salad, homemade biscuits—"

When Hilda got to the part about the radish tray, Cordelia could see Orson flinch, but, stalwart man that he was, his attention remained rapt. Strange woman, thought Cordelia. What the hell had she been talking about?

10

As the final curtain came down on the first performance of *Blithe Spirit*, Cordelia found herself leaping to her feet with the rest of the crowd. The performance had been nothing short of brilliant. Diana's comic timing was impeccable, and the rest of the cast had risen to the occasion. Even Diana's periodic slurred words only added to the hilarity. If the audience had only known the truth, they might not have laughed so easily.

Diana had broken her word to Orson. She hadn't stopped drinking after lunch. But even so, she'd made it through the performance and, to her, that was probably all that mattered. The reviews—from as far away as New York and L.A.—would be fabulous. She would receive national attention because she was a national celebrity. She had a hit on her hands and was riding a career high. Her own playhouse. The star. Even though it was a small production, her name gave it clout. No, this would be a night to celebrate. Cordelia glanced at Orson who had been seated in the pew next to her. As their eyes met, she knew he was thinking the same thing. How dreadful was the party going to be which Diana had planned for later?

Right now, it was time to go backstage and hope the congratulations wouldn't be fueled by too much champagne. Cordelia spotted a *Minneapolis Star Tribune* reporter near the rear exit and gave her a wave. Theo was already making his way to the stage door. And Curt and Annie had resumed their seats, waiting for the crowd to clear. As Cordelia turned to watch the audience make its noisy exit, she gazed up at the stained glass windows above the front entrance, silently saying a prayer. Tuesday was a long way off. A lot of things could happen before the intervention. If they ever needed some cosmic help, it was now.

"Where are we?" asked Cordelia, as Theo pulled his Acura into a dirt parking lot and stopped. Orson was in the back seat, stuffing his pipe with tobacco.

"This is Al's Roadhouse."

"Figures." Cordelia gazed out the window at a reasonably attractive wood-framed building. At least it looked clean. Other cars had already arrived. From what Diana had said, she'd rented the place for the night. Everything was on her. "Probably the hottest spot in the entire county."

"Actually, I think it is," said Orson.

"We're about three miles from the playhouse," Theo added, turning off the motor. "Diana tells me she comes here often."

Orson opened the rear door and got out. He lit the pipe and then stood leaning against the fender, looking up at the stars.

"Let's get inside before the mosquitos smell blood," said Cordelia, poking him in the stomach.

They waited for Theo to lock the doors and then, arm in arm, they climbed the steps to the entrance. They were comrades, bound together by a shared history and now a common goal.

Cordelia felt contented in their presence, momentarily overcome by a feeling of gratitude. The second she stepped inside the roadhouse, her thoughts returned to earth. Cigarette smoke enfolded them in an acrid haze. She spotted Diana sitting at a table in the back talking to Annie and Curt.

"You want a pitcher of beer?" asked Theo.

Cordelia lowered her eyes and gave him her best *you've got to be kidding* stare.

"Right. One pitcher of cherry Coke coming right up."

"I'll help you with the glasses," said Orson, following him to the bar.

Cordelia weaved through the crowd, extending congratulations here and there. As she got to the table, she saw that Diana's eyes weren't particularly focused. Her head was propped on one hand, a cigarette dangling from the other.

"I thought you gave up Virginia Slims," said Cordelia, pulling up a chair and sitting down.

"I've come a long way, baby—but not that far," snorted Diana. "And don't be such a party pooper. Have a drink and relax." She blew smoke out of the corner of her mouth.

With a valiant effort, Cordelia did not roll her eyes.

The champagne at the playhouse had taken its toll. Diana was already pretty high. She was sipping now from a glass in front of her. It looked like pure vodka.

Like everyone else, Cordelia knew tonight was going to be a big blowout, and she wasn't looking forward to it. Still, it was better to keep a close eye on Diana than let her trip over a cow and fall down a ravine. At least until the intervention. After that, the ball was in her court.

"Did you see the article in the Chicago paper about us?" asked Curt. He fidgeted with a napkin.

Cordelia's head popped up. "About *us*?"

"I have a friend who works for the *Sun Times*," explained Diana. "I gave him the information about the opening tonight, and I also told him about my five best friends from college who were coming for the weekend. He thought it made a great story, so he printed it."

"All our names and occupations," muttered Curt, his expression growing sour. "There are a bunch of copies back at the parsonage if you want one for your personal scrapbook." He glanced over at Theo who appeared to be talking intimately with a handsome young man at the far end of the bar. Curt's face sank even deeper into a funk.

"It was the least I could do," said Diana, entirely missing the dejection in his voice. Curt's *occupation* had always been a sore point. "I'm so proud of you all."

"I'm amazed by what your architect friend did with the stage," said Annie, attempting to change the subject. "I like the idea of making it a modified thrust. The audience feels more a part of the action."

"Yeah," agreed Diana, "Donald's a magician." She giggled into her glass. "I sort of *groove* on the idea—how's that for a good seventies word?—that I'm performing in a church. The stage is the altar. And I, dear children, am the sacrificial lamb." She saluted the air and downed the vodka in one gulp.

"Is there some cosmic meaning to that, Diana?" asked Cordelia. She eyed Curt who was still looking at Theo. His expression had turned angry.

"Why, don't you know? My life has become a sacrifice on the altar of human progress. The good of the group at the expense of the individual. Thanks to Theo, my life now has greater meaning. The world is a better place, the air sweeter. Only problem is, my career's in the toilet. But then, who needs to eat when the fucking group needs *spiritual* sustenance."

"Don't be so cryptic," growled Curt.

"Why honey, that's no way to talk to a role model. I'm deeply . . . wounded." She flapped her eyelashes seductively.

"You've been acting cool to Theo ever since we got here," he continued. "Maybe you better explain yourself so we can all understand."

Suddenly, the sound of breaking glass drew everyone's attention to the front. Through the smokey haze, Cordelia could see Orson and Theo shoving each other. The pitcher of Coke next to them had shattered. Liquid was pouring over the side of the counter, spilling onto the stools.

The room became silent as the crowd tried to hear their words.

"You're making some awfully quick assumptions," said Orson. He was inches from Theo's face. "If I were you, I'd back off."

"God, you're full of hot air," snapped Theo. "You haven't changed a bit."

"And you're still a fool. I never should have listened to you."

"You owe me, you overweight weasel. You owe me big."

Orson lunged at him. "Who owes who is a matter of definition."

Theo pushed him away, knocking the pipe out of his hand. "Still Mr. Erudite. Always in control. Well, I happen to have principles too, and unlike you, I'm not afraid to fight for what I believe."

"That's your trouble. You don't know when to *stop* fighting."

Theo took a swing at him, left hand to the stomach, right to the jaw. He was an experienced brawler. Orson folded like a paper doll. He crashed back against the bar and slid to the floor.

In an instant, Curt, Annie and Cordelia were all on their feet, shouting for the two of them to stop. But before they could reach the front, a burly, middle-aged man stepped out of the crowd and grabbed Theo by the arm, twisting it roughly behind his back. "Just calm down," he ordered.

Theo winced with pain.

"Orson? You all right?" asked the man.

Orson felt a lump on the side of his jaw. After examining the inside of his mouth with his tongue, he took the hand being offered him and got up. "I think I'll live."

The man let Theo go. "You wanna press charges?"

Theo rubbed his knuckles. "Yeah. I do."

"Not you," said the man. He glanced at Orson. "Say the word and this guy spends the night on us."

Orson's smile was smug. "I'd like you all to meet Matt Hesslund. Our local sheriff. He also happens to be an old friend."

Theo grunted. "Lucky me." He began brushing off his tux.

"Of course he doesn't want to press charges," said Diana, lurching to a stop in front of the bar. She held the empty glass in her hand. "There's been a mistake. Just go away now. Let us handle it."

"I think there has been a mistake," said Orson, his voice thick with anger. "And Theo's the one who made it." He turned to the sheriff. "Matt, after deep reflection, I think I'll take you up on your offer. This man assaulted me." Turning to Theo, he added, "Do you get the point *now*?"

Theo looked from face to face, but said nothing.

Diana yanked Orson's arm. "Just stop it, will you? This is a party. We're all supposed to be having a good time."

"It's all right," said Theo, straightening his tie. He was attempting to regain some of his damaged dignity. "I'm no stranger to jail. Besides, I'll be out in a flash."

"Don't count on it," said Orson.

As the sheriff handcuffed him and then led him through the crowd and out the front door, Cordelia sank down into a chair. The smoke that circled her head felt like a toxic cloud. This reunion was getting worse by the minute. She wondered, with a growing sense of dread, just what else could go wrong.

11

"Me again."

Jane let out a deep groan.

"Here with your nightly update." Cordelia held the phone in one hand, a cold chicken leg in the other.

"This is a plot, right? You're trying to deprive me of sleep so you can get me to admit to a crime."

"A minor change in your will would suffice."

As soon as Theo had been carted off by the police, the party began to disintegrate. A simple brawl wouldn't faze a big city crowd, but in Summer Green, the locals quickly said their goodbyes and drove off into the cricket-infested night. After another hour, Diana had to admit the obvious. The party was over.

Once back at the parsonage, everyone had gone directly up to bed. No one wanted to dissect the evening over a nightcap. Not even Diana.

"Do you know what time it is?" asked Jane.

"No, dearheart, but I'm sure you're going to tell me."

"You know, Cordelia. My aunt doesn't even ask anymore when the doorbell or the phone rings in the middle of the night. She *knows* who it is."

"I'm glad I can bring some constancy—one might even call it a sense of ritual—into your days, Janey. It helps give life meaning." Cordelia could hear Jane's bed squeaking.

"Where are you?"

"Sitting on the front porch with the cordless phone. Do you want to know what I'm wearing?"

"I want to be allowed to sleep."

Cordelia put her feet up on a wicker footstool. "I don't know how you can sleep when I'm so upset."

A small shriek.

"You'll never guess what happened tonight." When Jane didn't respond immediately, Cordelia sat up very straight. "Well, don't you have any curiosity?"

"Of course, Cordelia. Tell me, what happened tonight?"

Cordelia knew she was being *handled*. She didn't care. "Orson and Theo got into a fight at a local bar. It was at the party after the performance."

"And?"

"Orson had Theo arrested."

"Seriously?"

"He's in the slammer even as we speak."

"That's awful."

"Damn straight."

"What was the fight about?"

"No idea. I heard one of them say something about principles. They argued briefly over who owed the other. But on the way home, Orson wouldn't say a word."

"Do you think it has anything to do with that business last night? The bald guy? Theo asking Orson for money?"

Cordelia had wondered the same thing. "Maybe."

"So what's going to happen to the intervention? If Theo's in jail, will that change things?"

"I don't know." Cordelia took a bite of the chicken leg and chewed thoughtfully. "Diana is furious. She can't believe Orson would try to ruin the reunion over something so petty."

"I doubt it's a plot. Besides, maybe it isn't petty."

"God, I wish I knew more."

"I wish you did too. What's on the agenda for tomorrow?"

"Just a day to relax, I guess. Diana's planned a Labor Day picnic for Monday."

"Cordelia?"

"Hum?"

"What are you eating?"

"A chicken leg."

"Do you think I could go back to bed now?"

"I suppose."

"Goodnight, Cordelia."

"Goodnight, Jane."

"Oh, and one more thing?"

"Yes?"

"Let me sleep tomorrow night. Please."

12

Early Sunday morning, Diana phoned her lawyer in Green Bay and demanded that she find a way to get Theo released from jail. Orson remained adamant. He wouldn't say what the argument had been about, and he refused to drop the assault charges. He seemed perfectly happy to see Theo cool his heels behind bars for a few days. To eliminate any further conversation on the matter, he'd driven into town after lunch.

By four in the afternoon, Diana was fuming. Cordelia found her pacing the floor in the kitchen, waiting for a phone call. Curt was having a cup of coffee, keeping her company. No one had seen Diana take a drink all day. Her attention was completely focused on freeing Theo.

"Any word yet?" asked Cordelia, scrambling to get out of Diana's path—more like her war path. She sat down next to Curt.

"Nothing. I thought we'd hear something before this."

Without being asked, Curt poured Cordelia some coffee and pushed the mug toward her. His eyes warned her it might be a long wait.

"I just can't understand why Orson is being so hardheaded," continued Diana. "It's not like him. He won't listen to reason." She stopped and glared at Curt, then at Cordelia. When they said nothing, she turned around and kicked the refrigerator. "You two act like you agree with him."

Cordelia could see what was happening. Diana needed a punching bag for her growing frustrations. Since the refrigerator didn't exactly work, and Orson was nowhere to be found, Curt and Cordelia were elected. Cordelia had seen her do this many times. She found it childish. But before she could say anything, the phone interrupted them.

Diana leapt to the counter. "Yes," she said, her voice almost breathless as she held the receiver to her ear. "Oh. Annie." She slumped onto a stool. "Right. I'm glad you called. How's it going? Did you find some decent school clothes for Amity?" She tapped her nails on the table and looked out the window. "Well, tell the kid she can't wear that sort of thing here. This isn't New York." A pause. "Then find her size, buy it and we'll discuss it later. Right. Thanks again. I just couldn't deal with shopping today. I'll see you when you get back. Oh, and tell Amity somebody named Chickie called. Right. See you tonight. Bye." She got up and dropped the receiver back on the hook.

"I take it Annie took Amity to buy some new school clothes," said Cordelia.

Diana grabbed her hair, pretending to pull it out by the roots. "What am I supposed to do with a teenager? She's used to Manhattan. How the hell is she going to deal with the Radish Hill Mall?"

And what was she going to do while Diana was in treatment, thought Cordelia? Another complication. One that would have to be worked out in a way that didn't make Amity feels like a yo-yo. "Amity said she wasn't getting along with her grandparents."

Diana sighed. "She ran away. After Jill died, her grandmother insisted Amity come to live with them in Montana. It's what Jill would have wanted. You know me. I've never been much of a kid person, but even I could see that taking her away from the only home she'd ever known was a bad move. We got along okay. She was really close to Jill. I thought about fighting it in court, but my life was crumbling in New York, and I had no idea where I'd end up. So, I just let her go. We wrote. Talked on the phone. She came out to see me here during spring vacation. Stayed for a week. I knew she was unhappy—she hates Billings—but I thought she was going to stick it out. Last Thursday, she simply appeared. I came back from rehearsals, and she was sitting on the couch. One suitcase. Hardly a dime left in her pocket. I called her grandmother right away so she wouldn't worry, and do you know what that old bat had the gall to say? *Good riddance.* She washed her hands of her. So, I guess I'm back in the kid business. Unfortunately, this time, it's without Jill. I don't know what the hell I'm going to do." She began pacing again.

"Where's her father?" asked Curt.

"The original deadass dad."

"Don't you mean dead*beat*?"

"That too. He runs a greenhouse out of his basement. Occasionally does some general contracting. But basically, he just screws around. Goes to a lot of movies. Doesn't make much money, or if he does, he's learned how to hide it. He hasn't wanted to see her since she was five. He doesn't like strong women. Five years old is about his limit."

Cordelia shook her head.

Again, the phone rang.

Diana jumped at it. "Yes," she said, her voice hopeful. She listened. "Great. When?" Another pause. "No problem. We'll be there to pick him up. Thanks. You're a lifesaver, Donna." She hung up and turned around. Her expression was intense, though distracted. Even more strange, she didn't look the least bit happy. But she did seem vindicated. "I knew we'd get him out."

81

"When will he be released?" asked Cordelia.

"Around six." She looked at her watch. "I've got to make one more phone call, and then we can all take a glass of lemonade, or whatever, and go sit out on the porch. I've hardly had time to talk to you two since yesterday. Too much going on." She dialed the number. Several seconds later she said, "Hello, Hilda? This is Diana. I need you to do me a favor. I know it's your day off, and this is kind of short notice, but I was wondering if you could pick up some food at the grocery store and cook us one of your fabulous dinners? You can. Wonderful. Let's see. How about your pan-fried Walleye with that lime butter sauce? I'll leave the rest to you. Great. See you in an hour." She hung up and turned around. This time, her smile lit up the room. "What do you say we go find those drinks?"

Diana sat at one end of the formal dining room table, Theo on her right, Cordelia on her left. At the other end sat Orson. Annie and Curt faced Amity. The conversation was subdued during the first course—a cold yoghurt and cucumber soup (which Cordelia thought contained entirely too many minced radishes)—but picked up slightly over the salad. Since no one was able to settle on a wine, Diana had scattered several bottles around the table. She knew, even with fish as the main course, Orson preferred Italian reds. Theo liked the sweeter German wines, so she'd given him his own bottle of Riesling. Cordelia and Curt sipped from their glasses of white Zinfandel. Only Annie refused the bottle of California Chardonnay set in front of her. Cordelia could tell she didn't have the stomach for it tonight.

Thankfully, neither Orson nor Theo had made any mention of last night's fight. Perhaps they'd called a truce. Instead, the dinner conversation centered around the next production Diana was going to mount, once *Blithe Spirit*'s run had ended. She had several plays in mind, but hadn't yet decided.

"You know Diana," said Orson, giving Amity a confidential

wink, "you built this playhouse just so you could get some decent parts."

Everyone laughed. Everyone except Diana. Her voice defensive, she said, "You're right. There are some women I'd like to play."

"Like who?" asked Theo, pouring himself another glass of Riesling.

Diana laid down her fork and folded her hands over her plate. With her eyes fixed on Theo she said,

Naught's had, all's spent,
Where our desire is got without content:
'Tis safer to be that which we destroy,
Than, by destruction, dwell in doubtful joy.

She held his eyes for a long moment and then resumed eating her salad.

"Lady Macbeth," said Cordelia, intrigued by the brief performance.

Theo seemed shaken by Diana's choice of quotes. He downed his glass of wine and then poured another.

"Kind of morbid," said Amity, playing with a tomato slice.

Curt smiled. "Yeah, and besides, it's bad luck."

"What do you mean?" she asked.

"To actors," replied Orson, wiping his mouth with a napkin, "even the mention of the name Macbeth is considered very bad luck. It goes way back. I'm not even sure of the origin."

"Haven't a lot of people died while acting in the play?" asked Annie.

Theo put his hand on his chest and coughed several times.

"You okay?" asked Curt.

"Fine. Just fine."

"I don't know," said Orson, considering the question. "That could be."

"What's wrong?" asked Cordelia. She saw a frightened look

pass over Theo's face. He seemed to be having trouble breathing.

Diana patted him on the back.

"God," said Theo, doubling up in pain. He started to gasp.

"What is it?" demanded Diana.

Theo slipped off his chair and fell to the floor.

"Help him, somebody." cried Annie.

Orson got up and knelt down next to him. "Are you choking?" he asked.

Curt's face had gone white. "Do something."

"Try the Heimlich maneuver," blurted Cordelia.

Theo shook his head.

"I'll call 911," said Orson. He jumped up and raced out of the room.

"Give him some air," called Cordelia. In a flash she was by his side. His breathing was rapid and shallow. His color still looked normal. Perhaps a good sign.

As if in a trance, Diana inched to the liquor cabinet and removed a bottle of vodka.

Indignantly, Annie grabbed it out of her hand. "Not now. For god's sake, get a hold of yourself."

"They'll be here any minute," said Orson, returning to the room. "How is he?" He rushed to Theo's side.

Theo's eyes were shut. His body seemed to have relaxed. Cordelia bent down close and listened. "Theo, can you hear me?" she asked. Looking up she said, "He's still breathing, but I think he may be unconscious."

Backing into the table, Amity knocked over Theo's wine glass. "Sorry," she said, her eyes pleading for forgiveness.

Annie put her arm around the girl. "It's all right."

Curt stood looking down at him, unable to move.

"I think he said something once about a heart condition," said Orson. "It was just a couple of days ago. He'd come over to the Blackburn Playhouse in Shoreview, and I'd asked him to help me lift an old trunk off the stage. I thought he was kidding—that he simply didn't want to get his clothes dirty. "

"He was in Minnesota?" repeated Diana. "He never said anything to me about that."

Orson realized he'd put his foot in it. He had to cover. "Yeah. He stopped on his way here."

"Here's the ambulance." cried Curt, nodding to the window. He bolted into the hall to open the front door.

Cordelia got to her feet and waited for the two men to make their entrance. They carried a stretcher, two boxes resting on top of it.

"Hello Orson," said one of the men. He was dressed in a shirt and tie. The other man had on bib overalls. They were obviously volunteers.

Orson nodded. "Ted."

The man named Ted asked everyone to get back. He immediately checked Theo to see if he was breathing. He was. He popped his jaw forward to make sure there was a good airway. Next he felt for a pulse. "Slow and irregular," he said to the man in overalls, the one who looked like a farmer. He then checked his eyes with a small stick of light. "Reactive. Good. Let's get him on oxygen."

Cordelia watched the men work. They seemed to know what they were doing. Hilda slipped into the room just as they lifted Theo onto the stretcher. She stood flush against the wall, her chicken-hawk eyes missing nothing.

After they covered Theo with a blanket, Ted walked over to Orson. "He's stable. What happened?"

Orson explained that they were having dinner when Theo clutched his chest and fell to the floor.

"Any history of heart problems?"

"I'm not sure. We haven't seen him recently. He did say something jokingly a few days ago, but I thought he was just trying to get out of doing some work."

"Is he on any medication?"

Orson looked around the room. "Not that I'm aware of."

"Any history of drug abuse?"

He shook his head.

"What about allergies?"

"Sulfa drugs," said Curt, his voice wooden.

"Anything else?"

No one responded.

"His blood pressure's low," called the other man.

"We've got to get him to a hospital right away. I need a phone," said Ted.

"Right down the hall," replied Diana, weaving to the door and pointing.

"Thanks." He left the room. "Is he going to be all right?" asked Cordelia. She stood next to the stretcher now, holding Theo's limp hand.

"He's stabilized," said the farmer. "That's all I can say. We'll take him over to the hospital in Binghamton. Summer Green's only got a clinic. He needs an emergency room."

Ted returned to the room. "I got space in the cab for one rider. You want to come along, Orson?"

Orson seemed to hesitate. "All right. Sure." He turned to the others. "I'll call you as soon as I get any news."

"But—" Annie clearly wanted to come too.

"Really, there's nothing you can do right now," said Ted, quickly folding his stethoscope into a small bundle. He glanced at the wine bottles littering the table. "Besides, I don't want any other emergencies tonight if I can help it."

They all got the point.

As Theo was wheeled out, Diana grabbed the bottle of vodka back from Annie. "This is my house and I'll do what I damn well please."

Cordelia could see a look of shock mixed with disgust pass over Annie's face. "Just terrific. One of your best friends is on his way to the hospital, and all you can think to do is drink yourself into a stupor."

"You don't understand *anything*."

"No? I understand more than you think."

Diana narrowed her eyes. "What do you mean by that?"

"Put that bottle of vodka away and I'll tell you."

She seemed to consider the request. She knew everyone was watching. "Screw it," she said finally. "I'm not interested in any of your moral superiority."

Annie stared at her for a moment and then tossed her napkin on the table and stomped out.

"Bye Annie," said Amity to her retreating back. The words were mumbled.

Cordelia felt terribly sorry for the kid.

"Hilda," continued Diana, her voice taking on an imperial quality, "you can clear the table. We're done." She swept the room with her eyes. "I'm going up to my room. Please call me when you know anything more." Swaying slightly, she made a stab at a dignified exit.

13

Cordelia was the first to grab the phone in the front hall when it finally rang.

"He didn't make it," whispered Orson's voice. He was crying, almost choking. "I don't know what happened. He was doing fine. Even Ted said so."

Cordelia felt her mind disconnect from her body.

The others gathered around.

"We were on our way out of town when he seemed to have another attack. They did everything they could, but it didn't help. Ted called the local coroner, and he just got here. He pronounced Theo dead." Orson could hardly speak through his sobs. "God, what am I supposed to do?"

"It's all right," said Cordelia, trying to comfort him. Though she knew nothing was all right. "You did everything you could. Were you . . . with him when it happened?"

"Yeah." His voice cracked.

"I'm sure he knew that."

"I don't know. He kept trying to say something. I have to believe it was important, but he never actually looked at me. I couldn't understand a word of it."

Cordelia looked up at her friends' faces. By their stunned expressions, she knew they understood.

Orson broke down again. Cordelia could hear him put his hand over the phone.

A few moments later he returned. "Are you still there?"

"Right here," said Cordelia.

"Arnie—the coroner—owns the funeral home in town. He said we could bring the body over there. What do you think? I can't make this decision all by myself."

What the hell did Cordelia know about funeral homes? Very gently she said, "That's a good idea. Are you going to ride over in the ambulance?"

"I guess so. I'll have to talk to someone about the . . . arrangements. He doesn't have any family to speak of. Just a brother he hasn't seen in years."

Of course. There would have to be a funeral. A lot of decisions would have to be made.

"What happened?" said a thick voice from the stairway. Diana, looking like a crumpled bed and clutching the railing for dear life, eased herself down the steps to the first-floor landing. "Is that Orson?" Her head wobbled from side to side, and her pronunciation was too precise for normal speech.

"Yes," said Cordelia, holding her hand over the phone. She motioned for Annie and Curt to help. Diana could barely stand up.

"Is Theo all right?" she demanded.

"He's dead," said Cordelia. She knew her voice was cold, but she couldn't help herself. She was furious with Diana and her drinking, and she wasn't going to hide it.

"Dead," she whispered, as if examining the word for its exact meaning.

Cordelia resumed her conversation. "Listen Orson, we've got kind of a . . . situation here."

"You mean Diana?" he asked.

"Yes. I think Curt and I should stay here and help her up to bed. Give me the directions, and Annie can drive over and pick you up."

"Fine."

Cordelia found a pen and note pad next to the phone. She wrote as legibly as she could under the circumstances. Her hand was shaking. She knew the catastrophe hadn't sunk in yet. She'd never see Theo again. Never. It was too much. "I've got it," she said into the receiver. "Orson?"

"What?"

"Are you okay?"

Silence. "No. Are you?"

"No," she said softly. She was starting to cry. "I'll see you soon."

After hanging up, she took several deep breaths. Then, turning resolutely, she entered the parlor. Diana was propped up on the sofa, Annie and Curt on either side of her. Amity was in a chair all the way across the room. Her back was to them, but Cordelia could see she was staring out the front window. What a horrible time for her to arrive.

Diana held her head in her hands and was sobbing and babbling at the same time. Her words came out in fits and starts, none of it making much sense.

"Annie, Orson would like you to pick him up at the funeral home. I've got directions."

"Okay," she said, wiping the tears from her eyes.

Curt's eyes were dry. "I'll stay with Cordelia and make sure Diana gets up to bed. Are you all right to drive?"

"I'll be fine," said Annie. "Don't worry." She flicked her eyes to Amity, giving Cordelia a *what should we do?* look.

Cordelia shook her head.

As if sensing that the lull in the conversation had to do with her, Amity said, "I've seen her drunk lots of times." She didn't turn around; she merely sat in her chair and looked straight ahead. "Once in a while Mom and I would have to go get her from a restaurant or something. We'd take a cab. Only, it didn't happen so often back then. She's really . . . sick now. "

Cordelia bit her lip. God, what she must have seen in her young life.

"But I did love him," said Diana, her voice projecting as if she were on stage. "You all know . . . that. I didn't . . . mean . . . he was a good . . . and I never meant—"

"Let's take her upstairs," said Cordelia, motioning for Curt to lift her up.

Annie stood with them, her eyes still on Amity. "Are you going to be all right while we're gone, Amity?" Her voice was kind.

"Fine. No problem."

Nobody was fine, thought Cordelia. But she couldn't handle any more right now. She grabbed Diana's other arm and helped Curt carry her out.

"Just put her on the bed," said Cordelia, looking around the messy room. Diana hadn't changed much since college. She still liked clothes.

"Do you think she's going to get cold?" asked Curt, trying to disentangle a sheet and pull it over her.

"Yeah, maybe. I'll see if there's a blanket." Cordelia kicked a pair of shoes out of her way as she moved across the room.

"God, she's really plastered," said Curt.

"I know. She didn't have time to drink that much. Her liver must not be processing well at all anymore. That's a very scary sign." She moved to the closet and lifted down a quilt from the top shelf. Turning back to the bed, her calf brushed against something hard. She bent down to take a closer look and saw that a knife had been thrust through a *Minnesotans for Choice* button. Cordelia had sent it to Diana last spring. Behind it was a picture. "Holy shit," she muttered, her eyes opening wide as she realized it was an old college photo of Theo.

"Need some help?" asked Curt. He was closing a window Diana had left wide open.

"No," said Cordelia. "It's nothing." She felt bad for lying, but how could she tell him Diana had stuck a knife into Theo's chest—even if it was only pretend? After all, a picture wasn't a human being. But it was such an angry, violent thing to do. Almost as if she wanted to see him— "*Dead*," she whispered.

14

"How are my cats?" sniffed Cordelia. She was sitting up in bed, a heavy quilt pulled over her head, a flashlight held in one hand, the cordless phone in the other. The house was dark and silent.

"I waited up for you tonight."

"Did you? What a dear human being."

"You're late."

"Am I?"

"And you sound strange."

"I have to be quiet."

"Why?"

"It's a long story." Again, she sniffed.

"Why don't you ever call Mugs at three a.m? She's the love of your life. Destroy her sleep patterns for a change."

Cordelia felt warmed by the reference to her newest tootsie. Lately, she had begun to use the term *consort*. Not only did she like the word—with its smutty Elizabethan connotations—but she liked every modern definition. *A harmony of sounds. One ship traveling with another.* Cordelia had no difficulty seeing herself as a ship.

"So?" said Jane. "You've got thirty seconds. After that I'm hanging up and going to sleep."

"Fine. As long as you set an alarm."

"Why should I set an alarm?"

"You have to be down to the Greyhound depot by five. I've already called to check out the times. Your aunt Beryl can drive you. The bus leaves at five-fifteen. Gets in here around one. The picnic starts at three, so don't worry about missing a thing."

A long pause. "Cordelia . . . what are you talking about?"

"At first I thought you should just drive up, but I don't think that car of yours would make it past the city limits."

"I'm dreaming. This is just a bad dream."

"I suppose you could rent one, but if you take the bus, you can use my car while you're here. We can drive home together."

"Cordelia."

"Shhhh."

"Will you tell me why I should take a bus to Summer Green? If that's what you're actually suggesting."

Cordelia lowered her voice even further. "It's Theo. Janey, I don't even know where to begin." She grabbed a fresh Kleenex. "He's . . . dead."

"Dead."

"Just listen. Tonight at dinner, he sort of clutched his chest. Before we knew what was happening, he'd fallen to the floor. I tried to get him to talk to me, but he couldn't. That's when Orson called 911. These two volunteer paramedics came and took him away in an ambulance. About half an hour later, Orson called and said he was dead. The first attack didn't kill him, but the second one did."

"This just happened tonight? Out of the blue?"

"Yes." She could feel the panic rising in her chest again. She had to stay calm. Get through this. "He was drinking some wine, eating his salad, and he just . . . keeled over. I guess he had a heart condition, though he never told anyone." She blew her nose. "Then again, he was so ridiculously private about his life, it doesn't surprise me."

"I'm really sorry, Cordelia."

"Thanks. The funeral will be Tuesday or Wednesday. The actual date hasn't been set yet."

"And . . . you want me to come?"

"I do. But not just for that."

"What about the intervention?"

"Orson is going to call the doctor in the morning. See what she thinks. We talked about it some when he and Annie got back from the funeral home tonight. I think we were all in agreement that it should be postponed until after the funeral."

"But why should *I* come?"

Again, Cordelia took a deep breath. "Janey, I'm not sure Theo's death was . . . natural."

A long silence. "You think Orson had something to do with it?"

"No—I don't know. It's too awful to contemplate. But see what you think. After the paramedics took Theo away, Diana went up to her room and proceeded to get totally plastered. When we got the news of Theo's death, she came down the stairs and started babbling and crying. Meanwhile, Annie drove over to the funeral home to pick Orson up while Curt and I stayed behind to help put Diana to bed. While I was getting a blanket out of her bedroom closet so she wouldn't freeze to death, I noticed a knife sticking out of the door. Jane, the knife had been thrust through a Choice button—"

"Abortion rights?"

"Yes, but behind it was an old college publicity photo of Theo. The knife went straight through his heart."

Again, Jane was silent. After a long moment she said, "And you think this means Diana murdered him?"

"I don't know. I realize it's not proof of anything, but what the hell was it doing there?"

"Good point."

"It got me to thinking. I decided to go downstairs. You know how my mind works. I started wondering if someone had put something into Theo's food—or his wine."

"Who had access to it?"

"Any one of us, really."

"You know, Cordelia, there are poisons that react in the body like a heart attack. I was just reading something about that recently."

"For your next cookbook?"

"Don't be snide."

"Anyway, I waited until no one else was around and then I ducked into the kitchen. Hilda—she's Diana's part-time cook and bottle washer—was still doing dishes. I asked her for the bottle of Riesling—that's what Theo was drinking tonight, and I hasten to point out, he was the only one who liked such sweet wine. Everybody knew it. Anyway, Hilda said she'd left all the bottles on the buffet in the dining room. I thought that was a good place to start, so I checked." Her voice grew low and thrilling. "It wasn't there."

"Really?"

"And I know he hadn't finished it. There was at least a third of a bottle left."

"That is odd. But I'm not sure any of this constitutes foul play."

"I know, but Janey, you have to understand. I have this awful *feeling*. I just *know* something isn't right."

"You have a feeling."

"Right. You've got to come and help me figure all this out. Theo's body is being cremated in the morning."

"Cremated? Did they already perform the autopsy?"

"Nothing was said about an autopsy. Annie remembered that Theo had said once he wanted to be cremated when he died. Curt thought he remembered something about it too. So, since directory assistance couldn't find Theo's brother in the Los Angeles phone book—that is, if he's still living there—and there was no one else left to contact, Orson just said to go ahead with it."

"That's kind of fast. Normally, they have to wait forty-eight hours. But back up a minute. I don't understand why the coroner didn't order an autopsy. I think it's pretty standard in cases of sudden death. If Theo's body is cremated, there's no hope of further testing."

"Are you saying someone might be trying to cover up . . . a murder?"

"Maybe."

"Should I try and stop it?"

"I'm not sure you could. Since neither of us knows all the facts, we're in no position to suggest anything. The coroner makes those decisions. He should know what he's doing."

"He also runs the funeral home."

"You're kidding."

"That's what Orson said. It happens in small towns."

"Seems rather—"

"Inbred?"

"I was thinking of the word *convenient*, Cordelia."

"Whatever."

"But you're right. This is a strange situation."

"Then come to Summer Green. You liked Theo. If someone murdered him, we have to find out who did it and why."

"Even if it's one of your friends?"

Cordelia knew it came down to that. Unless it was Hilda or Amity, and what would their motives be? Come to think of it, what was anybody's motive? None of this made sense. "All I know is, if I leave here and this isn't settled in my mind, I'll never have another night's rest."

"I know what that feels like."

"You have to come, Janey. I realize I'm asking a lot. But who better than you to figure this out. After all, you're the Jane Marple of the Midwest. The Sherlock Holmes of the wild prairie."

"And you're full of crap."

"Can I take that as a yes?"

More silence.

"Janey, I'll never . . . make fun of your car again."

"How kind of you."

"And I'll never call you cheap."

"Because I'm not."

"Right. And I promise to . . . get you front-row seats—all comps—to this season's new plays at the Allen Grimby."

"And?"

"What else do you want."

"Just seeing how far you'd go."

"Bring something other than jeans and high-top tennies. The funeral will be rural, but tasteful."

"Cordelia."

"You won't change your mind, will you?"

"No . . . I'll come. If for nothing else, than for your peace of mind. And also for Theo. I liked him a lot."

Cordelia could feel herself beginning to crumble. She knew it would be a long, sleepless night. "You can stay here at the parsonage. There's lots of room. I'll talk to Diana about it in the morning."

"What time did you say that bus left?"

"Five-fifteen."

Jane let out a muffled shriek.

"I think it stops at the Sunburst Motel just south of town. I'll be there to pick you up."

"You'd better be"

"You're a lifesaver, Janey. See you anon." Cordelia clicked off the phone, switched off the flashlight, and uncovered her head. Sitting now in the chilly blackness of her bedroom, her eyes readjusting to the dark, she contemplated a trek to the medicine cabinet in search of an antacid. As she was about to get up, she heard a soft knock on the door. "Come in," she whispered.

A dark form entered and moved quietly to the foot of the bed. It hovered there, not saying a word.

Cordelia felt her skin prickle with a cold anticipation. Remembering the flashlight in her hand, she switched it back on.

"Turn that goddamn thing off." ordered Diana, covering her eyes with her arm.

Even in that brief second, Cordelia could see enough to know Diana looked terrible, her eyes red and swollen. "What do you want?" she asked, knowing her tone wasn't exactly friendly.

Diana eased herself onto the edge of the bed. She was trembling. "No one came and told me. How's Theo doing?"

Cordelia was momentarily lost. "But we—"

"I must have fallen asleep. Jesus, Cordelia, I'm not a princess. Why didn't someone wake me?"

"Don't you remember coming downstairs?"

"I . . . what?"

"While I was talking to Orson on the phone. You came down the stairs. We explained everything. "

"Oh . . . uh, sure." She ran a hand through her hair. "I must have . . . you know. I just woke up." She attempted a smile. "Everyone's a little fuzzy when they wake from a sound sleep. Just . . . tell me again." The smile faded.

She was obviously lying. And there was only one logical explanation for her behavior. Diana had had a black-out. Cordelia wondered if she would even remember this conversation. "He had another heart attack in the ambulance on the way to the hospital. He was pronounced dead by one of the paramedics."

"Dead?"

Cordelia could feel her draw away.

"His body was taken to the DeLappe funeral home."

Diana sat very still, her head tilted up toward the open window. The weak moonlight filtering in through the sheers made her face look bleached. Drained of all blood.

"Are you all right?"

Without a word, Diana got up and left the room.

Humph, thought Cordelia. Just charming. She could at least have said *something*. *I'm sorry*, would have been nice. *Gee that's too bad*. Or, *tough luck*. Anything. Cordelia could hear a door shut farther down the hall. She wondered if she should go to her. Make sure everything was okay. But something prevented her normal empathy. Too much was unknown. Too much unsaid. Instead, she got up and moved to the window, looking out at the playhouse.

It was a windy night, the trees rustling in the distance. As her eyes fell to the parking lot, she heard a motor start. A second later, a car backed out of a parking space and drove to the edge of the highway. With its lights still off, it turned left and began its climb over the rise and out of sight. Cordelia froze as she realized it was the same car she'd seen the other night. The white Cadillac.

15

By ten the next morning, Cordelia had already done her morning exercises—five sit-ups and a minute and a half of running in place—and dressed in a comfortable cotton caftan. She trudged down the stairs to the first-floor parlor feeling like a zombie.

Orson was already up. Since the morning was cloudy and cool, he'd built a fire in the fireplace and was sitting in front of it, reading the paper and sipping from a mug of coffee.

"Morning," she mumbled, dumping herself onto the sofa. "Where is everyone?" Orson looked up from the paper, his eyes blinking rapidly as he gazed into the fire.

Cordelia could see he'd been crying.

"Diana's still in bed," he said, wiping a hand across his mouth. "Curt went out for a walk a few minutes ago, and I'm not sure about Annie. She's probably in the kitchen making herself some breakfast."

"And Amity?"

"Still in bed. She had kind of a late night."

"What do you mean?"

"Some kid came over here about eleven. Chickie Johnson. Apparently, they'd met last spring during Easter vacation. He and Amity left together. She didn't get back until after one."

Cordelia wondered what Diana's rules were. Surely she and Jill had enforced many while they lived in New York. Amity was older now, but she couldn't be allowed to run wild. Someone had to keep track of her for her own safety.

"I didn't say anything to her about a curfew," continued Orson. "I'd never allow my fourteen-year-old to stay out that late, but last night I just let it pass. I couldn't deal with it anymore. What I'm really worried about is what's going to happen to that kid after the . . . you know." He didn't want to say the word *intervention*.

Cordelia had already registered the same thought. She hadn't come up with a solution.

Just then, Annie walked into the room, a half-eaten English muffin held in one hand, a glass of orange juice in the other. Theo's death had obviously not affected her appetite. "Did you ever get hold of Theo's brother?" she asked Orson, sitting down next to Cordelia.

Annie's thick red hair was loose around her shoulders today. For years, she'd never worn it any other way than pulled back tightly into a bun. It gave her an air of professionalism. Competence. Something she no doubt needed in her job. But this morning, she looked ten years younger. More relaxed. Even the way she moved her body seemed different. Cordelia had forgotten what a strikingly lovely woman she could be. Giving the air a surreptitious sniff, Cordelia also noticed that Annie was wearing a light scent of roses. In some strange way, she felt as if she were witnessing a transformation. Orson seemed to notice it too. He stared at her for a long moment before speaking. "I talked to James about half an hour ago."

"James?" repeated Cordelia.

"Theo's brother."

"Right. But I thought you weren't able to locate him in the L.A. phone directory."

"I wasn't." Orson looked a little sheepish as he explained, "I was in Theo's room earlier this morning and I noticed an address book on the nightstand next to his bed. So I checked to see if his brother was listed. He was. He's living in Sacramento now."

"Is he coming?" asked Annie.

"Yes. But he asked if we could hold the funeral off until Wednesday. It's just two days. I didn't think it would be a problem."

"What about Dr. Bernson?" asked Cordelia. "The . . . *you know what* was supposed to happen tomorrow morning."

"I talked to her too," replied Orson, taking a sip of his coffee. "She agreed with us. It should happen after the funeral. So we've rescheduled for Thursday. "

"Rescheduled what?" asked Diana. She slunk into the room, a bathrobe pulled haphazardly around her satin nightgown. She looked awful, her hair a stringy mess.

"The . . . ah . . . our final breakfast together, " smiled Orson, standing as Diana entered.

Under the circumstances, Cordelia felt Orson's genteel formality was ludicrous. The day was starting out in cartoon-land once again.

"Oh. Right," said Diana, lurching a bit further into the parlor. "Well, I've got a solution for that. You must simply all stay in Summer Green. Orson, you can run the playhouse. Cordelia, you can direct. Curt can do the lighting and the stage managing, and Annie—" She hesitated. "Well, Annie can do what Annie does best." An eyebrow rose slowly as she eyed Annie's hair. "What the hell happened to you?"

"I beg your pardon?"

Diana waved the matter away. "Then it's settled."

Cordelia wondered if she'd already been drinking. Her

behavior had that unmistakable alcohol-induced imperiousness.

"Hilda." barked Diana. "Breakfast."

"She's not here," replied Orson. "She's over at the playhouse helping prepare for the picnic this afternoon."

"God." She flopped down on a chair. "I'd forgotten about that. Horrible timing."

Cordelia assumed this was finally a reference to Theo's death. Not that she'd even so much as mentioned his name.

"Yeah," said Orson, looking deep into the fire. "The worst. A woman called this morning while you were sleeping. She wanted to know if the plans were still on."

"What did you say?"

"I told her yes, unless they heard from you directly."

"Good. I've invited the entire goddamn town. Also some big shots from Appleton and Green Bay. It's a good way to publicize the theatre. All my actors will be there. I can't cancel."

"Everyone will understand," said Annie.

"Yeah." Diana rubbed her eyes.

Still, thought Cordelia, no one spoke Theo's name.

"Well, I'd better get back upstairs," muttered Diana. "Take a shower and slip into some clothes." She stood to leave. Before she got all the way to the door she stopped. "Oh," she said, not turning around, "What about the . . . funeral?"

"Wednesday afternoon. At three," said Orson.

Diana nodded.

"One other thing," said Cordelia. She watched Diana's back grow rigid.

"What?"

"You remember Jane Lawless?"

"Sure. Why?"

"She'd like to come for the funeral. Can she stay here?"

"Fine." Diana dismissed the question with a wave of her hand and proceeded out the door.

After she'd gone, Orson turned to Cordelia and asked, "When is she arriving?"

"This afternoon. The bus gets in around one."

"Why's she coming so early?" asked Annie.

"Jesus," said Orson. "That bus leaves Minneapolis at five a.m."

"Five-fifteen," Cordelia corrected him.

"You must have called her in the middle of the night."

"I needed to talk."

"About Theo?"

Cordelia nodded. "It's a lot to deal with."

"I know." His eyes fell to the floor. "I called my wife before I turned in. She won't be able to come, but she sends her love to all of us."

"She never knew him," said Cordelia, trying to be comforting.

He turned his head away. "How are we ever going to get through this?"

"Together," said Cordelia, reaching for his hand.

Annie just sat and sipped her orange juice.

16

Jane glanced at her watch, realizing the bus was already half an hour late. Cordelia was probably sputtering around the Sunburst Motel's parking lot, contemplating a long, scathing letter to the bus company. She was a stickler for punctuality.

For the last two hours, the deep green fields whizzing past Jane's window had been bathed in a delicate mist. Trees looked indistinct, the landscape permitting no sharp lines of any kind. It was a perfect day to reflect on the subtleties of life. Perhaps even the subtleties of death. All morning, Jane had thought of little other than Cordelia's phone calls. Even though she hadn't known Theo well, his loss seemed to touch a place deep inside her. He was a figure from her past. Since she hadn't seen him since college, in her mind's eye he would forever remain that passionate young actor, handsome, living on the edge, doing the inexplicable. What kind of man had he grown up to be? And would the questions surrounding his death shed any light on his very private life?

Over the past few years, Jane had lent a hand in solving several unexplained deaths. Some silly people were even starting to think of her as a sleuth. Even though Jane considered these incidents as completely out of the ordinary, one-time occurrences, she did have to admit she had a certain facility when it came to ferreting out the truth. Because she had recently hired a new day manager for her restaurant, initially so that she would have more time to publicize her new cookbook, taking a few days off to visit Summer Green presented no problem to the Lyme House. Jane's Aunt Beryl, who had come from England two years ago to live with her, could take care of their home—and Cordelia's cats. So, if this trip would help ease Cordelia's mind, it was certainly worth the trouble.

Up ahead, Jane could see a sign which said, Welcome to Summer Green. The bus began to slow. Stuffing the paperback she'd brought with her—but never looked at—into her backpack, she readied herself for the end of her journey. She slipped on her leather jacket and touched her hair, making sure everything was in place. Jane was a handsome woman in her late thirties, with deep blue-violet eyes and a great smile. She'd always felt the smile was one of her best features—and her nose, one of her worst. It was too large. Then again, perhaps it was a cosmic message. With a nose like hers, what else could she be other than a snoop? Might even make a good logo if she ever had business cards printed up. If you need the police, call them. If you're looking for a good PI, try the Yellow Pages. But if you want a trained Nose, call Jane Lawless. Yes. It had a certain ring to it.

When the bus came to a full stop and the driver announced the name of the town, Jane grabbed her suitcase and swung into the aisle.

Cordelia was waiting for her, leaning against the hood of her car. Even from a distance, Jane could see she looked tired. A little more make-up had been used to give her cheeks some color. Jane had never worn make-up herself. She couldn't be bothered.

But Cordelia had never met a lotion or a cream, a blush or an eyeliner, or even a lipstick she didn't like. All her life, she'd been experimenting with different looks. It was part of the fun of being alive she always said. Jane had to hand it to her. Cordelia never tried to squelch a natural inclination for a political reason. All during the seventies and eighties, she'd steadfastly worn her make-up, even though she got some nasty looks from women who felt she was a sellout to the patriarchy. Now, as time and luck would have it, Cordelia was probably considered on the cutting edge of the new dyke-chic. But whatever, Cordelia just kept on doing what came naturally. No matter who it annoyed.

"Not a great day for a picnic," said Jane, striding up to the car and letting her suitcase hit the dirt with a thunk. "Don't I get a hug?"

"Of course you do," said Cordelia, her eyes brimming with tears. "I'm so glad you're here."

Jane felt the breath being squeezed out of her. "Are you all right?"

Cordelia stepped back. "I've been better. But I think I'll live." She opened the trunk. "One suitcase. A small one at that. You amaze me, Janey. You truly do." Even her attempt at humor seemed strained.

Jane could feel a light drizzle begin to fall.

"Get in," said Cordelia. "They've decided to hold the picnic in the church basement—I mean, the playhouse basement—because of the weather. No one wanted rain-soaked radish casserole."

"I beg your pardon?"

Cordelia patted Jane's hand. "I shall explain everything on the way."

"So this is what Diana's been working on for the last year," murmured Jane, admiring the arched double-doors as they entered. The vestibule was small, a rose-and-emerald Oriental covering the floor. At one end, a stairway led to the basement. Moving into the main part of the building, Jane took in the stage. It was built in the shape of a wide V. The set was still in place from the opening performance. She looked up and saw a huge metal grid filled with spotlights. What this church had undergone was nothing short of a transformation. Then again, since only the rear of the structure had been rebuilt, it felt like she was standing in some strange hybrid. Half sanctuary, half theatre. An interesting marriage. "How was the opening performance?" she asked, following Cordelia down the center aisle.

"It was fabulous. Except, Diana had been drinking. She muffed some of her lines, but the audience ate it up. Thought it was all part of the show."

Descending the concrete steps at the right of the stage, they entered an underground hall. The basement, once the domain of church suppers and wedding receptions, had now been turned into the costume shop and prop area. Today, everything had been pushed to the side and covered. It was already filled with people. Bright pink and blue balloons were affixed to the walls. One long table in the rear was loaded with fried chicken, steaming corn-on-the-cob, beans—the standard picnic fare.

On the ride over in the car, Cordelia had warned Jane to stay away from the locally grown radishes, explaining that they contained an hallucinogenic substance which reduced the townspeople to incoherent puddings. In response, Jane suggested that perhaps she should drive. Cordelia gave her a nasty look. The subject was dropped.

"There's Orson," said Cordelia. She waved at him, unable to get his attention. "And Annie and Curt are over by the coffee urn, talking to John Hubble—he's the director. Let's go join them." She grabbed Jane's hand and dragged her though the crowd.

"Jane." said Annie, turning as they approached. She gave her a small peck on the cheek. "It's good to see you again."

Curt smiled his hello.

They were still a handsome couple, thought Jane. Annie

looked particularly wonderful. "Good to see you, too."

"Did your bus just get in?" asked Curt.

"It was late," grumped Cordelia. She turned to a lanky, sandy-haired man with a blond beard and said, "John, I'd like you to meet my old friend, Jane Lawless. She's also from the Twin Cities."

He held out his hand. "It's a pleasure. Do you work at the Allen Grimby with Cordelia?"

"No," said Jane, "I own a restaurant on Lake Harriet."

"Ah." He nodded and then smiled. "I've never been to Minnesota. I'm originally from New York. Spent the last ten years in L. A."

"A long way from either coast here in Summer Green," said Jane.

"Yeah." The smile faded. "I thought this was going to be my big break. A chance to work with the great Diana Stanwood. I even signed a two-year contract. Now I wish I hadn't."

"Why?" Jane wondered if his tone held anger, or merely disappointment.

"No one told me Diana was a drunk." He glared defiantly at Cordelia, and then at Curt and Annie. "I know she's your friend, but she's going to single-handedly sink the next two years of my life."

"Do others in the company feel the same way?" asked Jane.

"Most everyone," he said, "though I'm the only one who was asked to sign such a lengthy contract. I've done some sitcoms. A *Matlock* episode. Several *Knot's Landing's*. So I have more of a name than anyone other than Diana. That also means I have more at stake. And I'm also the only one with enough guts to say out loud what we're all thinking. The rest of the sheep feel matters will improve now that the stress of opening night is past. That's crap, if you ask me."

"I'm sorry to hear that," said Jane. Though, she wasn't surprised.

"You do have *understudies*, don't you?" asked Cordelia. "I

mean, in case someone gets . . . sick?"

Jane assumed this was a veiled reference to the intervention.

"Of course we do. That might be what saves the season." He folded his arms over his chest. "If Diana would just come down with a small but potent case of the flu— let's say, for the next two months?—we'd probably do okay."

"That's unlikely to happen," said Curt, cutting him off. He had apparently taken a dislike to the director and wasn't interested in hiding it.

"You never know," said John.

"Who's that with Orson?" asked Cordelia. She stretched her neck to get a better view.

"Beats me," said Curt. He didn't even bother to look. Turning to Annie he said, "I have to go back to the parsonage. I can't handle this today."

She nodded. "I'll come with you."

"No, really. I'll be fine by myself."

"Don't be silly." She turned to Jane. "Will we see you this evening?"

"You bet."

"Good. We can talk more later."

Jane could tell Curt wanted to be alone. She found it curious that Annie didn't take his hint. Or, maybe she felt it best that he not be by himself today. Whatever the case, it wasn't much of a day for celebration.

"I better shove off too," said John.

"Do you live in town?" asked Jane, curious where the people in the company were staying.

"For the time being. I made a deal with the guy who owns the Sunburst Motel. I got a pretty good monthly rate. Unfortunately, there aren't many choices around here."

Jane didn't have trouble believing that. "Well, nice meeting you."

"Yeah." He hesitated. "I don't suppose—"

God, he wasn't going to ask her for a date.

"There's a roadhouse just south of town. Would you like to have a drink with me later tonight? It would be nice to have some female company." He moved a bit closer. "It gets pretty lonely around here."

"I don't think so," said Jane.

He looked at Cordelia, who was still straining to see who Orson was talking to. "Oh, sure. I get it. You two—"

She shook her head. "Not exactly, but you got part of it right."

"You're gay."

She nodded.

"No problem. But that doesn't change things. I'd still enjoy the company."

"Maybe another time."

"Suit yourself." He turned and walked away.

After he was gone, Jane continued her perusal of the room. She could see Diana working the crowd, talking to people, shaking hands, patting some on the back. She looked older than she had the last time they'd met, but her charisma hadn't dimmed with age. She was holding a beer in her left hand, but she didn't seem high or unsteady.

Jane turned to Cordelia. "What *are* you staring at?"

"That guy talking to Orson. I've seen him before."

"So?"

"Remember I told you about the white Cadillac?" Cordelia closed her eyes for a moment to review the scene in her mind. "Well, I'm almost positive that's the bald man. The one I saw talking to Theo."

"Why would he be at the picnic?"

"Good question." She crooked her neck again, trying to get a better view. "Damn. They're gone." She bolted for the stairs. "They must have gone outside," she shouted over her shoulder.

Jane followed. She raced up the steps and out the back-stage door. "Jesus, is this a cemetery or a movie set?" she asked, coming to a dead stop.

Cordelia stood a few feet in front of her, her eyes sweeping over the misty countryside. "There they are," she whispered, pointing to a weeping willow about a hundred feet in the distance.

Jane could barely make them out. The weather lent a sinister quality to their conversation. "What are you going to do?"

"I don't know. I'd sure like to hear what they're saying. Come to think of it, why should I give a rip? Come on, Janey." She strided off toward the tree.

Jane shrugged. At this point, Cordelia knew more about what was going on than she did. She quickly picked up the rear.

As they approached, Jane saw that Orson was doing most of the talking. Cordelia's advancing form must have caught his eye because almost immediately he stepped away from the tree and called, "Cordelia. And Jane." He sounded entirely too pleased.

"Orson." replied Cordelia, matching his tone. "Haven't seen you in, gosh, it must be two hours."

His smile disappeared. "What do you want?"

She flicked her eyes to the man by the tree.

"Not now," he growled.

"Why not?"

"It's personal."

"Don't be trite."

"Cordelia, this is none of your business. Why don't you take Jane back to the parsonage and fix some fresh coffee. I'll join you there in a few minutes."

"I am *not* your secretary. I do not make coffee."

"I wasn't suggesting you were."

Cordelia lowered her voice to a whisper. "I demand a full explanation."

"No explanations. This is none of your business."

"I beg to differ. Anything that has to do with Theo's death *is* my business."

Orson's eyes opened wide, but he recovered quickly. "Get out of here," he said, his teeth clenched. "This is not your concern."

"It's a free graveyard. I can stay if I want."

Jane watched the face-off with interest. Orson and Cordelia

were standing nose to nose, neither blinking. Two huge bears on the verge of a roar.

"I'm going, Orson," called the man, moving from behind the willow. Dressed in an expensive dark suit, he looked well past middle age. His face was lean and intelligent. "If I need to, I'll find you later."

Orson's body seemed to deflate. "Fine."

Cordelia waited until he was out of earshot and then said, "I demand to know who he is."

"Drop it." Orson started to walk away. Cordelia blocked his path. Pinching the bridge of his nose, he said, "I'm going to say this one more time. Who that man is, is none of your goddamn business. You can scream your bloody head off, but that's all you're going to get on the subject." With that, he marched off toward the playhouse. He'd only gotten a few yards when he stopped, swiveling around. "Where are my manners?" he muttered. "Welcome to Summer Green, Jane. I'm sure we'll be seeing more of you."

"You will."

"Wonderful." His voice held no warmth. Again, he turned, this time, heading for the parsonage.

17

Cordelia knocked softly on Jane's door and then poked her head inside. "You ready?"

"All set," said Jane. She was sitting on the bed, paging through a copy of the *Summer Green Gazette*. Theo's death had made the front page. So had a picture of Orson.

"Just be quiet. Diana's downstairs in the parlor with everyone else. Dinner will be served in fifteen minutes, so I doubt she'll be back up before that. But we can't take any chances."

Jane followed Cordelia out into the hall. As they walked to Diana's room, Jane eyed some of the framed awards Diana had won. They were hanging in a row on the long wall. She stopped in front of the largest.

"Come on." urged Cordelia in a barely whispered voice.

"I didn't know about—"

"Diana has won three Emmys and a Tony. Plus everything you see there. Now get over here." Jane took one last look and then crossed to the closed door. She waited for Cordelia to enter.

"You've got to see this for yourself," insisted Cordelia, leaving the door slightly ajar. "If you do, you'll understand what I meant last night. It's really bizarre. But remember, we have to listen for footsteps."

Jane nodded. She didn't like any of this. They should have waited until everyone was out of the house.

Diana's room was neat. The bed was made and fresh flowers brightened her bureau. The windows were wide open, letting in the scent of rain. A rumble of distant thunder made Jane wonder if Summer Green wasn't in for an evening storm.

Cordelia swept to the closet and opened the door. "Oh shit."

"What is it?"

"It's gone."

Jane moved closer.

"It was right here." Cordelia bent down and ran her hand across the painted wood. "A knife that big would leave a mark. I don't get it. I don't feel a thing."

Jane touched the wood herself. "You're sure it was here?"

"Positive."

She got down on her knees and examined the surface more closely. In the dimly lit room, the new paint wasn't all that apparent, but she found it. "Look, Cordelia. Someone touched up this spot. They probably filled it with wood putty first. If you get real close, you can smell it."

Cordelia put a hand on her hip. "Diana must have done it."

"Probably."

"That means she was scared someone would see it."

"A good guess. But didn't she notice you looking at it last night?"

Cordelia shook her head. "She was too out of it."

"You're sure?"

"She didn't even remember Theo had died."

"Right. Good point. Describe it to me again."

"Well, it was an old college photo of Theo. Publicity for

some play, I don't remember which one. A kitchen knife was stuck through a button right into Theo's chest."

"Weird."

"I know."

"Describe the button again?"

"It said 'Minnesotans for choice.' Diana made a sizable contribution to the Minnesota Abortion Rights Council so I sent her a couple of them."

"Interesting. You mentioned she was cool to Theo the first couple of days. Did she ever say why?"

Cordelia shook her head. "When she's been drinking, she becomes rather cryptic. Sometimes I don't have a clue what she's talking about. I'm not even sure she does."

"I think we should get out of here," said Jane.

"Say, come to think of it, she did do one odd thing."

"What?"

"The night Theo died, we were all sitting around the dinner table. She quoted from Macbeth. She was staring straight at him when she said it. It seemed to make him uncomfortable."

"What was the quote?" Cordelia closed her eyes, holding up her hand for silence.

Naught's had, all's spent,
Where our desire is got without content:
'Tis safer to be that which we destroy,
Than, by destruction, dwell in doubtful joy.

"Lady Macbeth. I don't remember the act or the scene. Sorry."

Jane considered it for a moment. "Sounds like maybe she thought Theo had hurt her in some way. Is that possible?"

"Jesus. I don't know how."

In her mind's eye, Jane saw the abortion rights button with a knife thrust through it. "You know, Cordelia, this doesn't make any sense."

"I know." Suddenly, from down the hall came the sound of a door creaking open.

"I thought you said everyone was downstairs," rasped Jane, scrambling to her feet.

"I thought they were." Before they could make a move to hide, a hand knocked softly.

"Diana?" came Curt's voice. He stepped into the room. "Hi," he said, glancing around. "Where's Diana?"

"That's . . . uh, what we were wondering," said Cordelia, attempting a smile.

"Come on, let's go find her," he said. "I think it's about time for dinner."

"Right," agreed Cordelia. "Good plan."

As Jane walked past him, she couldn't help but feel he knew they were lying. They had no business alone in Diana's room. She wondered why he hadn't called them on it.

18

So," said Diana, passing Jane a basket of homemade rolls, "How was the bus trip?"

"Uneventful," answered Jane. She took a bite of her Caesar salad. This cook, whoever she was, was excellent.

"And what did you think of our playhouse?" Diana lifted a glass of weak looking orange juice to her lips. Jane assumed it was mostly vodka.

"I was very impressed."

"We'll be having Wednesday, Thursday, Friday and Saturday night performances until Thanksgiving."

"Except for this Wednesday," Orson corrected her.

She looked at her drink, setting it down next to her plate. "Of course. You don't have to remind me." A shaky hand moved briefly across her eyes. "Have you made all the . . . arrangements yet?"

He nodded. "Theo's body is being cremated, but the remains

will be buried. We thought it was best to do it in the church cemetery out back. He never really stayed in one place long enough to call it home. I think he'd like to be here—with you."

Diana's face flushed.

"Have you picked out a spot?" asked Curt.

Again, Orson nodded. "It's all been handled."

"I'm . . . glad you've taken the initiative, Orson," said Diana, her words slurring slightly. She'd been drinking all day, but this was the first time she sounded high. "I've been . . . unable to deal with some of this. You all understand how hard this has hit me. I'm not one to talk about my feelings openly." Another drink of vodka. This time a gulp.

"We understand," said Annie.

Diana's head wobbled backwards as she attempted to straighten her sweater. "I just think it would be good if we all . . . spent some time talking about it."

"We have been, Diana," said Cordelia. The irritation in her voice was apparent to everyone. Except Diana.

"Don't get me wrong, Theo and I had our differences." Another sip. "I don't know why he felt he could—" She stopped.

"Could what?" asked Jane. Suddenly, Diana burst out crying.

Everyone was momentarily stunned.

Annie shot Jane a cautionary look. "Diana, I think perhaps you need to rest."

"Everybody always knows what's best for me." she shrieked. "Theo thought that too. I'll never forgive him."

"Calm down," said Curt. His voice was impatient.

"Why should I?"

"Because he's dead, that's why. There's nothing more you can do."

She folded her arms over her chest and began to rock. "I know," she sniffed. "I never wanted it to end like this."

Jane and Cordelia exchanged glances.

Hilda came to the door. "Are you all finished with your salads?" she asked.

No one responded.

"Would you like me to take the plates away?"

As if aroused from a deep sleep, Diana's body jerked. An unconvincing smile replaced her tears. "I'm being a terrible hostess. Yes, all done, Hilda. Bring on the . . . beef, or whatever."

"Roast duckling," replied Hilda, moving into the room and removing the plates to a stand near the buffet. Every so often, she would steal a glance at Diana.

Diana's head tilted confidentially toward Jane. "Quack," she muttered soulfully.

Jane raised an eyebrow.

"Seems like we should have a toast," said Diana, rousing herself from the vestiges of her melancholy. "To what?" asked Orson.

"To...our memories of Theo. Does everyone have some wine?"

No one did.

Diana didn't notice. She raised her vodka high, and the rest raised their water goblets. "To Theo."

"To Theo," everyone responded.

"May he rot in hell."

"Diana." exclaimed Orson, his face frozen in surprise. "Jesus, get a goddamn grip on yourself."

Ignoring him, Diana finished her drink. "I think Annie's right. I need to rest." Lurching out of her chair, she muttered, "Catch you all later. Maybe we can build a bonfire and sing camp songs. You all make me sick." Everyone was silent as Diana shambled out of the room. A few moments later she began singing "Kumbaya" as she climbed the stairs.

"Lord," said Curt, pushing back from the table. "I can't take much more of this."

Annie laid her hand gently on his arm.

"We've got to hold together until Thursday," said Orson. "We have to remember the Diana we all love. Keep that in our minds. I know it's not easy, but we have to try.

Curt tossed his napkin on top of his silverware. "Of course. You're right. "

"Let's talk about something else," said Cordelia.

"Like what?" asked Annie.

"Oh, I don't know. Politics. Religion."

"Let's keep it light." Jane shook her head. "Where's Amity tonight? I haven't met her yet."

"She had dinner up in her room," answered Annie. "She said she had a headache."

"Who doesn't?" grumped Curt.

Hilda entered the room with the main course."What happened to Miss Stanwood?"

"She wanted to find her guitar. Practice some old John Denver songs, " answered Cordelia.

Hilda humphed. She set the plates down in front of everyone and then said, "When are you people going to do something to help her."

"We're trying, " said Orson.

"Not very hard if you ask me." With a nasty backward glance, she left the room.

"Charming woman," said Curt.

Annie picked a piece of parsley off her potatoes. No one was very hungry.

"Cordelia tells me that Jane was instrumental in solving a murder last year. Something about a women's club in Minneapolis."

"Right," said Orson. "I read about that in the Minneapolis paper. You're getting a reputation for being quite the detective."

Jane smiled. She was glad for the change of subject; she just wished it was another topic.

"Maybe you can figure out why Diana was so pissed at Theo," said Curt. He wasn't even making an attempt to eat.

"I am curious about one thing," said Jane "The night Theo died, Cordelia tells me the coroner never ordered an autopsy. Do you know why?"

"Why would they need an autopsy?" asked Annie. "We all know how he died. A heart attack."

"But normally," explained Jane, "in cases of sudden death—especially when the person is considered healthy— an autopsy is ordered."

"But he told me he had a heart condition," said Orson.

"That's not enough. He could have been kidding."

"What are you suggesting?" asked Annie. "That someone was trying to cover up. . . what? A murder?"

"Of course not," said Orson, patting his mouth with the edge of his napkin. "How could he have been murdered? We were all in the same room with him. We saw what happened. I even rode in the ambulance. The paramedics didn't see anything unusual. Neither did I."

Annie wasn't convinced. She glared at Jane. "You actually think one of us killed him, don't you."

"I didn't say that," said Jane.

"No, but it seems pretty clear to me."

Curt put his hand on the back of her neck. "Don't get so excited, honey."

Annie looked as if he'd just slapped her across the face.

"I was simply wondering about the autopsy," said Jane, trying to keep her voice neutral. "I wasn't accusing anyone." Boy, were these people jumpy. She'd have to be more careful.

"See," said Orson. "The question was entirely innocent. Besides, Jane's father is a defense attorney. She would know about these things."

"Well, not really," said Jane.

"YOU don't have to be modest," continued Orson. "But, in this case, even though your curiosity is understandable, I think your concern is unnecessary."

Jane nodded. She was suddenly very tired herself. She'd been up since four.

"I've got to get some air," said Curt. "I feel like I'm suffocating."

"It's pouring rain outside," said Annie.

"I don't care." He pushed away from the table. "Sorry. See you all later."

"Later," said Cordelia. She and Orson were the only ones who had eaten any of their duck.

Cordelia elbowed Jane in the ribs. "Come on. You need your strength."

To be honest, Diana's little *quack* had really gotten to her. She knew she needed a long night's rest. But Cordelia was right. She also needed food.

"So," said Orson attempting to pick up the pieces of an otherwise ruined evening, "What aspect of religion would you all like to argue about?"

19

Shortly after Annie and Cordelia had left for an evening of fun and frolic at the new Radish Hill Mall—they insisted they couldn't stick around the parsonage one moment longer and maintain their tenuous grip on sanity—Jane came down the stairs in search of cup of tea before bed. It was only eight-thirty, but she was exhausted. As she was about to enter the kitchen, Orson came barreling out, nearly knocking her down. He was wearing a raincoat and a tweed hat, and carrying an umbrella.

"Going somewhere?" she asked.

"I'm meeting a friend in town for coffee. I grew up here, you know. I've still got some buddies. I figured I might as well see them while I'm visiting. There's nothing else to do."

"Sure. Have a nice time."

"Right." He touched his hat and steamed off down the hall.

After making herself a mug of Earl Grey, Jane strolled back into the foyer. The house felt pleasantly quiet after such a stressful dinner. Before heading upstairs, she noticed Curt stretched out on a rug in front of the fire. The scene looked so inviting, she walked into the room. He didn't hear her so she cleared her throat, hoping she wasn't ruining a private moment. He turned his head. "Jane. Hi. I thought you'd gone to bed."

"I'm on my way," she said, holding up her mug, "but I just can't pass up such an inviting scene. Do you mind if I join you for a few minutes?"

"Not at all," he smiled. He got up and moved two chairs closer to the hearth. "I'd enjoy the company. I thought I'd wait up until Amity got home. She starts school tomorrow. I don't know how she's going to like it. She didn't sound too thrilled when she found out she had to be bussed to another town. Summer Green has a grade school, but the high school is over in Pine Creek."

"From what Cordelia's told me, she's really been bounced around since her mother's death."

"Yeah," he said, shaking his head. "It's a rotten shame. She's a nice kid."

Jane made herself comfortable, enjoying the added warmth. It was a cool night. Autumn was definitely on the way. As they sat in companionable silence, Jane took a moment to study Curt. At dinner, and earlier at the picnic, his blond hair had been combed straight back, flat against his head. But tonight, after his walk in the rain, he'd towel-dried it and simply left it natural. He now looked more like the Curt she remembered from college. He was a good-looking man—tall, well-built, prominent nose, strong chin, full lips. Yet he'd always struck her as somewhat distracted, as if he continually had something on his mind which kept him from living fully in the present. She wondered if he was happy.

Out of the blue, Curt said, "You didn't come for Theo's funeral, did you? You came because Cordelia asked you to." It was less a question than a statement.

"I don't—"

"It's all right. You don't have to explain. But it surprised me. She must feel pretty strongly that Theo's death wasn't . . . natural.

I suppose she has a right to her opinion."

Since he'd brought it up, Jane decided to run with the ball. "What do *you* think?"

He rubbed his chin, giving himself a moment. "Who of us does Cordelia suspect?"

Not an answer, thought Jane. Even so, she had to respond. "You have to understand. She's not accusing anybody. "

"So, what you're saying is she suspects nobody. And everybody."

"Well—" he had a point.

"Why were you in Diana's room earlier this evening?" Before she could say anything in her defense, he said, "Let me guess. Cordelia wanted you to see the photo of Theo that Diana had hung inside her closet door."

Jane was aghast. "How did you know?"

"Cordelia took a little too much time getting that quilt last night. I saw her looking at the door. Since she was so secretive about it, I came back later and took a look myself."

Jane sipped her tea. "And what did you make of it?"

"Diana was upset with Theo. I knew that from the moment we walked in the door."

"Do you know why?"

He shrugged. "With Diana, it could be anything. Big or small, you never know. She's got a terrible temper, but I hardly think she wanted to murder him." When Jane didn't say anything, he added, "She's not an easy person to figure, I'll grant you that. But when she accepts you as a friend, she's your friend for life. She writes Annie and me faithfully. We used to get a letter a month, no matter what she was doing. She's been a real encouragement to me over the years. Helped me with jobs. And she's an incredibly generous person. Ask anyone here. They all have stories. She came to speak to Annie's university class several times. Once she took the entire theatre department to a play in downtown Chicago. Made quite a splash. When Annie's mother died four years ago, she flew out and spent a week with us. Even though it was a sad time for Annie, having Diana there meant the world. The thing is, when it comes to alcohol, it's like she's been on a greased slide all her life. And now she's fallen off the edge."

Jane had never known Diana the way the rest of them had, but for five people to drop everything in their lives and come to a small town in Wisconsin, well, she had to be someone very special. There was a lot of love here. Jane knew how much it hurt Cordelia to even think one of her friends had harmed Theo. Perhaps, in the end, they would find nothing amiss. But for Cordelia's peace of mind, Jane felt compelled to search a bit deeper. "The night Theo and Orson got into that fight, were you at the roadhouse?"

"Ah, now we're moving on to Orson. It was just a fight, Jane. They've had many."

"But had Orson ever pressed charges before? Had they ever come to blows?"

Curt shook his head. "That was a fluke. An old friend of Orson's just happened to be at the bar. After Theo decked him, Orson couldn't pass up the chance to teach Theo a lesson. There was always a rivalry between them. If you ask me, someone should have ended the competition long ago."

"But what actually happened that night?" asked Jane. "What were they arguing about?"

"Don't know. I was across the room. Didn't hear the argument until the very end. I don't even remember what they said."

"All right." She took another sip of tea. "So Theo hits Orson, he goes down. The officer comes over, and Orson has Theo arrested."

"That's about it. They pull Theo's arms behind his back, slap on the handcuffs and haul him out to the squad car."

"That's everything you remember?"

"Well, yeah. Everything until . . . later."

"Meaning?"

He hesitated. "It's kind of personal. But I suppose it doesn't matter if you know. Theo sent me a note."

"How?"

"Through Orson."

"What kind of note?" Curt raked a hand through his hair. "Theo and I had had a conversation the day before. It ended with me getting pretty hot under the collar. I suppose he wanted to clear the air. While he was in the squad car, he wrote down a message and asked Orson if he'd give it to me."

"What did it say?"

Curt felt in the pocket of his jeans. "You might as well read it for yourself." He handed it to her. Jane opened the piece of yellow stationery. In pencil, Theo had written:

Curt—Sorry about yesterday. It was all my fault. I think we need to talk. I don't know how long I'm going to be in jail, and I don't want to put this off. Could you come down tomorrow morning? I'm sure they'd let me have a visitor—I'm not an ax murderer. Please come. I'll be waiting.

Theo

Jane looked up. "Did you go?"

Curt turned his head away.

Jane could tell he was struggling with his emotions. "Are you all right?" she asked gently.

After a long moment, his chin began to quiver. He put a hand to his forehead, covering his eyes. This was a fresh wound.

"God, I was so mad at him. I thought he was jerking me around again. Same story, different chapter. He'd never give me a straight answer to anything."

"So you didn't go?"

"Annie saw me reading the note. She demanded to see it. Needless to say, she was furious. She thought he wanted to . . . did you know Theo and I were . . . lovers in college?"

Jane nodded.

"Annie felt terribly threatened by him. We've had a few problems in our marriage. But I love her. I told her that. I want things to work between us. It's just . . . I needed to have Theo tell me the truth just once."

"So, did you go?"

"No," he said, his voice barely audible. "I promised Annie I wouldn't. And to be truthful, I thought it would hurt Theo if I didn't come. And I *wanted* to hurt him."

Jane could see the pain in his eyes. "Did you talk when he got back on Sunday night?"

He shook his head, biting a trembling lower lip. "There wasn't time."

"Listen Curt," she said, turning the mug around in her hand, "you couldn't have known he was going to die. You probably thought you had all the time in the world."

He squeezed his eyes shut.

Jane wanted to touch him, to reassure him, but Curt wasn't the kind of man you could approach easily. Even though they were talking intimately, he seemed to have a wall around him.

"Do you realize," he whispered, "that I don't even know why Theo went to prison."

"I thought he'd impersonated an IRS agent."

"Oh, I know that part, but *why* did he do something so stupid? He wasn't that reckless. When I asked him, he always made a joke of it."

"I'd heard he'd stolen fifteen thousand dollars. Maybe he needed the money."

Curt eased back into his chair. "On that point, Theo was adamant. From the very first, he insisted he hadn't taken a penny. He maintained that the head honcho at that widget company, or wherever it was he went, was probably embezzling funds and that Theo's arrest gave him an opportunity to blame it on someone else."

"Do you believe him?"

"I do." His gaze dropped to his hands.

Jane could tell that he was moving away from her. Perhaps it was time for bed. She quickly finished her tea.

Wearily, Curt stood and tossed a couple more logs on the fire. As he moved them around with the poker he said, "You're going to have a hard time coming up with a murderer from this group."

Jane wasn't so sure. He may not have realized it, but he'd revealed some rather intense emotions during their brief conversation. People had been killed over far less.

"Besides, what was the murder weapon?" He turned and stared at her.

"I don't know."

"No. That's because there wasn't one." He resumed his seat.

Jane's eyes felt like gravel. Her mind was shutting down. "Well, I think I'll turn in," she said, getting up. "I'm pretty bushed."

"Right," said Curt, his attention fixed on the fire. "Hope you sleep well."

"Thanks." As she walked up the stairs, she had the vague sense that something he'd said hadn't rung true. Unfortunately, she was too tired tonight to do any more thinking. It would have to wait until morning.

20

Jane didn't wake the next morning until after ten. She quickly showered and dressed, knowing the day was going to be a busy one. She had only forty-eight hours before the intervention. She hadn't slept well. Instead, she'd spent the night going over everything she'd learned. Cordelia had been right to think something was amiss. Jane's conversation with Curt last night had confirmed it. What she must do now was simply follow the threads to see where they led.

As she moved silently down the upstairs hall, she noticed that most of the doors were still closed. Only Orson's was open and empty. She didn't knock on Cordelia's door, she merely entered, lifting the shade slightly to allow some light into the room before sitting down on the edge of the bed.

"You don't need to get up," she said softly.

The covers rustled. Cordelia was completely buried in them.

"Just tell me where your car keys are."

"Why?" came the muffled response.

"I want to drive over to the funeral home. Check it out."

"Without *me*?"

"I didn't think you'd want to get up. I know you had a late night at The Mall."

An eye appeared. "Cute."

"So where are they?"

"When are you leaving?"

"Fifteen minutes, maybe. I thought I'd run downstairs and grab a bite to eat first."

"Make it twenty and I'll meet you out in the parking lot."

"Don't you want any breakfast?"

"I went a little berserk last night at the frozen yoghurt stand."

"I got it." She stood. "See you in twenty minutes."

As Jane passed the parlor, Hilda was running the vacuum cleaner over the carpet. The fireplace had already been cleaned. Newly picked daisies adorned the coffee table, and the smell of freshly baked bread told Jane that Diana's one person staff didn't let her mornings get away from her.

She entered the kitchen. Orson was sitting at the center island, having a cup of coffee. He was bent over a newspaper.

"Good morning," she said, getting down her own mug.

He didn't look up. "Morning."

"Something interesting in the paper?"

He nodded. "Theo's obituary."

"Oh . . . sorry."

He took a sip of coffee and then leaned back, scratching his unshaven chin. "*The Summer Green Gazette*. All the news that's fit to swat deer flies with."

Jane slid onto a stool.

"If you're up for it, Hilda made some rhubarb coffee cake. It's quite good. Heavy on the nutmeg and brown sugar."

"Thanks," said Jane. "This is fine." She poured herself some coffee. "How was your evening?"

"My evening?"

"You were meeting a friend in town."

"Oh. Yeah." He folded the paper and pushed it away. "It was okay. I suppose you went to bed early."

He'd changed the subject rather quickly. She wondered why. "Around nine. Where is everyone this morning?"

"Diana's still in bed. She never gets up before noon. And I assume Curt and Cordelia are still asleep too. Annie was up pretty early. She wanted to help Amity get ready for school. When I came down, they were leaving for the bus."

"That was nice of her."

"Annie's a great person."

"Where is she now?"

"Well, after Amity was safely on her way, she got in her car and drove off."

"Did she say where she was going?"

He shook his head, refilling his cup.

Jane's attention was drawn to the window as Hilda marched past it, a shovel over one shoulder. "You know, she's like a one woman army."

Orson turned to look. "Good description. She has the same energy level as my twelve-year-old. And the same annoying curiosity." He sighed, touching his graying temples.

Unlike yesterday, the sun was beating down on the cemetery in the distance. It was going to be a hot day. Jane was glad she'd brought some cool clothes along. "How long did you live in Summer Green before you left?" she asked.

"Nineteen years. Until I went to college."

"I suppose your family's happy to see you."

He shook his head. "They're all gone."

"I'm sorry. I always thought it would be great growing up in a small town."

"It was. My dad ran the local hardware store. Only problem was, I had a lot of interests I couldn't share with anyone. That's why I had to get out."

"But you probably come back often to see friends."

"Not really."

"I'm curious. How did you know about the church next door?"

He stood and walked to the refrigerator, lifting out a pitcher of orange juice. "It was kind of the town mystery. Friends mentioned it in letters."

"Really?"

"No one ever figured out why it burned. There were no electrical problems. Nothing wrong with the furnace. The insurance company wasn't going to pay off because they thought the fire was set."

"By whom?"

"The pastor, or someone in the congregation. They'd been trying to sell the building for years. They wanted to erect a new church on the other end of town—closer to the mall. This one was getting too small. Problem was, no one wanted to buy it."

"But couldn't the authorities prove something, one way or the other?"

He shook his head, grabbing two glasses and returning to his seat. "Want some?" he asked, nodding to the juice.

"Sure."

He poured Jane's first. "The pastor vehemently denied that he or any member of his church had anything to do with the fire. He told the insurance company to either prove their contention that it was arson, or pay up."

"And?"

"They paid up. Eventually. The church sat idle for almost a year."

Interesting, thought Jane.

"It was a stroke of luck for Diana. She got it for next to nothing. I've always thought that church would make a perfect theatre. Except—" His expression sank. "It didn't help. I hoped beyond hope it might. I thought Diana could get it together if she just had some focus to her life."

"It was a good try. It might be just the thing to help pull her through—after the intervention I mean "

He put a finger to his lips.

"Sorry." She tried the juice. It was fresh squeezed. "I wanted to tell you how sorry I am about Theo."

"Thanks."

"Funny how things work out."

"Yeah." He looked up. "What do you mean?"

"Well, that you'd be unfortunate enough to get into a fight with him one day before his death." She knew the comment was insensitive, but she wanted to see how Orson would react.

"Are you trying to draw some conclusion from that?"

"No. I just think it's sad."

"It's more than sad. It's tragic."

Maybe it was her mood, but she didn't believe him. "What was the fight about?"

"It was personal."

"Oh. I see."

"No you don't. You couldn't possibly. But I can't explain it to you."

"You mean you won't."

"Quite frankly, Jane, I don't care what you think of me. But you should understand one thing. I loved Theo like a brother. I would never hurt him."

"But you had him arrested."

"I mean hurt as in *murder*. That's what we're talking about, isn't it?"

She shrugged. "Maybe."

"I hardly think being knocked down in a bar is a reason to kill someone."

"I never said it was."

He studied her openly. With his growing anger held carefully in check he said, "Back off, Jane. Your insinuations are the last thing we need around here right now."

She finished her juice. She wasn't going to let him intimidate her. Besides, she was in Wisconsin. Her *Minnesota Nice* internal programming wasn't functional this far from home. "I'm not insinuating anything, Orson. I'm merely asking some questions."

He glared at her.

Cordelia chose that exact moment to breeze into the room. "I'm ready," she said, her eyes drawn like a magnet to the coffee cake. "I thought I smelled nutmeg."

Jane stood, glad for the interruption.

"What's wrong?" asked Cordelia, noticing Orson's scowl.

"Nothing. Jane and I were just . . . clearing the air."

"I didn't realize it was cloudy."

"Don't forget the unveiling this afternoon at three," said Orson.

"What unveiling?" asked Cordelia. She inched over to the counter.

"Oh. I forgot. You two weren't in the parlor last night before dinner. Diana got a call from an artist she commissioned in Chicago. Seems she's been sitting for a portrait. It's going to be hung in the vestibule as you come into the playhouse. The official unveiling is this afternoon." He added, rather ominously, "It's a command performance. Everyone is to be there."

Cordelia broke off a piece of the cake. "Black tie, or can we wear our grungies?"

"Something in between," he said, his scowl mellowing a bit.

"It's a date." She turned to Jane. "Ready?"

"Where are you off to?" he asked, trying not to sound too interested.

Before Cordelia could respond, Jane said, "Just some exploring."

"Think of us as local prospectors," grinned Cordelia. "Tapping away at the cow-infested hillsides, searching for gold, precious jewels. Lost farm machinery."

"Don't dig too deeply," he said, his scowl returning. "You may not like what you find."

21

The DeLappe Funeral Home was on Myrtle Street, just south of the library. It was an old two-story brownstone that had once been the home of the town's mayor. A tasteful black and gray sign hung high over the front door announcing its current occupants.

Jane led the way into the grand foyer, now turned reception area. No one was behind the desk. In fact, no one seemed to be around at all.

"Come here," whispered Cordelia, motioning Jane over to what appeared to be a chapel. Two fake marble pillars stood on either side of the archway. "Look at all the plastic flowers. I feel like I've died and gone to K-Mart."

Jane had to agree. The decorations were ghastly.

"And look at that podium," said Cordelia, trotting over to take a closer look. "Decals." she gushed. "Little blue and white angels."

"Can I help you?"

Jane turned to find a short middle-aged woman with a blue smock and orange hair—very heavy on the make-up—staring at her. "Yes," she smiled, backing up several steps. "I'd like to talk to the coroner. I understand he owns the funeral home."

The woman eyed Jane's hair, touching an errant wisp that had slipped out of her French braid. "Great texture. I could do you up nicely."

"Excuse me?"

"Sorry, I should introduce myself. I'm Cora DeLappe—Arnie's sister. I do the corpses."

"You do the—" Out of the corner of her eye, Jane saw Cordelia's head ooze from behind one of the pillars.

"Corpses?"

"Right," said Cora, her voice matter-of-fact. She moved behind the desk and sat down. "You know. The hair. Make-up. Nails." She took out an emery board from the top drawer. "I do it all. Used to be a hairdresser in Chicago, but I couldn't stand the pace. This is better."

Jane didn't doubt it.

"Except, I always say, the tips aren't as good." She laughed, catching sight of Cordelia. She gave a little wave. "I suppose you want to see my brother."

"Is he the coroner?" asked Jane.

"For the last eight years."

"Is he also a physician?"

She shook her head. "Coroners are elected officials here. He appoints a real doctor to work with him as his assistant, but Arnie's just . . . a regular guy. I'll go get him. He's in the back, arranging a cremation."

"You do cremations?" asked Jane.

"Nah. We send the bodies over to Appleton. I'll be right back." She crossed to a door at the rear of a short hall and disappeared.

Cordelia inched a little further into the room. "I'll bet she decorated the chapel."

"Good guess," said Jane. She took another moment to look around. "No Smoking" signs were plastered everywhere, so much so that she had the urge to light up, even though she loathed cigarettes.

A few seconds later, Cora came out of the back room, followed closely by a stocky man of approximately the same height. They could have been twins, except the man's hair was brown. "Good morning," he said, his voice low and calm. "Arnold DeLappe."

Jane could see a mixture of curiosity and sadness pass across his solid face. He obviously wasn't sure why they were there and he didn't want to seem too chipper in case Uncle Bob had just bought the farm. At least he wasn't rubbing his hands together. "I'm a friend of Theo Donati's," said Jane. Was it her imagination, or did the man's expression tighten.

"Yes. Your name is—"

"Jane Lawless. And this is my friend, Cordelia Thorn."

"Nice to meet you both." He shook their hands. "Mr. Donati's remains are just being taken to the crematorium as we speak. We generally hold them for forty-eight hours, but in this case, we had to rush a little. The service is set for three tomorrow afternoon."

"I know."

"Are you familiar with cremations?" He looked at Cordelia for an answer.

"Familiar? No."

Most people aren't. Fire has been used to dispose of our dear departed since prehistoric times. The Greeks started using it around 1000 B. C. Even the Bible talks about the cremation of King Saul. I know the Jewish religion forbids it, but the Catholic church—are you Catholic?"

Cordelia blinked. "No. "

"Neither am I. But as I was about to say, even the Catholic church has removed its ban. Did you know that in Great Britain fewer than one third of all bodies are buried?"

Cordelia was becoming annoyed. "Fascinating."

"It is, isn't it. You learn something new every day."

"Actually," said Jane, "I was hoping you could answer a couple of questions for us."

"Why certainly," he smiled, again sadly. "Would you like to sit down?" He swept his hand to the folding chairs in the chapel.

She shook her head. "This shouldn't take long."

"All right." He waited, a pleasant look on his face.

"Did you sign the death certificate?"

"I did. One of our volunteer paramedics called me from the ambulance right after your friend—Theo—had passed away. I was on the scene in a matter of minutes."

"Do you have a copy of it here?"

"The death certificate? No. Sorry. You'll have to go over to the courthouse for that."

"I'm just curious. Why didn't you order an autopsy?"

Arnie DeLappe jutted out his somewhat weak chin. "But there was no need. It wasn't an unattended death. Three people witnessed the trauma. The body was pronounced dead by a police officer who was called to the scene shortly before I arrived. One of the witnesses suggested the man had a history of heart problems—confirmed, I might add, by a bottle of prescription heart medication I found in his pocket. I did order a blood test. The findings are in the case file with the death certificate and police report. Nothing was amiss. Orson Albern, an old friend, was also present. You can ask him if you have any lingering doubts about the manner of Mr. Donati's death."

"He's not a physician."

Arnie blinked several times. "I don't quite understand your concern, Ms. Lawless. Are you suggesting Mr. Donati's death wasn't . . . entirely natural?"

"I'm not suggesting anything. However, the fact that no autopsy was performed does give me pause."

He squared his shoulders. "I have been the coroner in this county for many years, Jane. May I call you Jane? And never *once* has one of my death certifications been called into question."

"I'm not attacking your honesty."

"I should hope not."

She knew she had to give him the benefit of the doubt. Besides, small towns did things differently than big cities. "Did the blood test reveal anything unusual?"

"Absolutely nothing out of the ordinary. He'd apparently been drinking, so that was recorded. You can look at the findings yourself if you go over to the courthouse." He puffed out his chest, such as it was.

"What about this heart medication?"

"Aldomet. Yes. Apparently he hadn't been taking it. No traces were found in the blood. That could be why he had the problem that night."

"What about his personal effects?"

"I have them in the back room. Since you're staying at the parsonage, you might want to take them with you." He stepped to a door off the chapel and returned a moment later with a small plastic suitcase, handing it to Cordelia. "It's all included in the cost of the cremation."

Cordelia held it up, pointing to the words DeLappe Funeral Home written in black gothic script across the front of the case. She gave Jane a sickly smile.

"By the way, who's paying for all this?" asked Jane.

"Orson Albern and Annie Whittig. At least they signed the forms. You just missed Mrs. Whittig."

"She was here?"

He nodded.

"Do you know why?"

Cora DeLappe, who had been sitting quietly behind the reception desk filing her nails, answered, "Oh, she brought by a map. She wanted to give us the exact location of the cemetery plot—where the cremains will be buried."

"I see." Jane didn't feel entirely satisfied. Still, she couldn't think of anything else to ask. "Well, I guess you've answered my questions."

"I sincerely hope so," said Arnie, his official tone tinged

with a certain reproof. "You mustn't worry, Ms. Lawless—Jane. Everything is being handled properly."

"Thanks. I suppose we'll see you tomorrow."

"You will," he said, his voice once again sad.

As they got out to the car, Cordelia put a hand on the door handle and then stopped.

"What is it?" asked Jane.

"Just answer me one thing."

"What?"

"How did he know we were staying at the parsonage?"

Jane cocked her head. "Did he say that?"

"He most certainly did. All we told him was that we were friends of Theo's."

Odd. "Maybe he assumed."

"Quite a leap of faith."

Or maybe he was warned, thought Jane. "Who could have told him we were coming?"

Cordelia held up her hand and ticked the names off one by one. "Orson, Annie, Curt or Diana. They all know you came to Summer Green for one reason, and one reason only. To find out if Theo was murdered."

"You think this DeLappe guy was lying to us?"

"How should I know. It makes me sick to think one of my friends might be involved in Theo's death. All I've got to go on are feelings—impressions. A knife in a door. A guy driving a white Cadillac. A fight in a bar. What the hell am I supposed to think?" She turned her back to Jane and took several deep breaths. "Maybe I'm just neurotic. Don't answer that."

Jane gave her a moment to calm down. "I'm sorry this is so hard on you."

"Last night I thought maybe we should just give it up. Leave well enough alone."

"Is that what you really want?"

Cordelia held Jane's eyes. "No," she whispered. "I want to know the truth."

Jane's heart went out to her. "I can't lie to you, Cordelia. I think your impressions are accurate. Something isn't right here. I just need more time."

"We haven't got much."

"I know."

"The problem is—" She kicked a rock across the lot. "—I always tell people that . . . well, that I've had a large part in helping you solve some of these mysteries."

"Is that right," said Jane. "I was under the impression you told everyone I helped you. Minimally, of course. "

"Well . . . I suppose I might have said that. I will admit to a certain penchant for hyperbole."

"That's good of you."

"But I'm desperate here. The truth is, when it comes to solving crimes, I'm a dud."

"No you're not."

"I am. You're my only hope."

"Don't say that. Besides, you've helped me a great deal."

"I have?"

"Sure. For instance, let me ask you this. What part of our conversation with Arnold DeLappe do you think was a fraud?"

Cordelia closed her eyes and shook her head, leaning back against the car door. "I don't know. It all sounded plausible to me. I mean, what the hell do I know about autopsies? You're the real sleuth, for chrissake. You tell me."

Jane could feel her teeth clench. "Don't wimp out on me now, Cordelia. We've *both* got to use our heads."

"Right."

"Get in." She opened the driver's door.

"Why?"

"You'll see."

22

Jane and Cordelia drove to a small park directly across the street from the First Bank of Summer Green. Since it was now nearly noon, and Cordelia needed a dose of saturated animal fat to keep her going until dinner, they'd stopped at a hamburger stand on the way and bought some lunch.

"Nice spot," said Jane, setting the DeLappe Funeral Home suitcase on one of two picnic tables. She was anxious to examine the contents, but first things first. Swings and an old-fashioned teeter-totter nestled against a stand of pine. Since school had now officially started for the year, the park was empty of children. One lone dog trotted across the grass, heading for the woods which bordered the property.

"Very bucolic," replied Cordelia, dumping the white food bag on the table and sitting down. She unwrapped one of the burgers. "This is yours. I ordered extra mustard, no pickle."

"Thanks." Jane sat down on the other side. "These look

pretty good."

"Try the cole slaw. The sign said they're famous for it."

"Are they also famous for onion rings?" She fingered the hefty sack.

"Janey, you *know* I've been searching for the perfect onion ring all my life. Of course, it would be just my luck to find them at Mannie's Hamburger Heaven—since I come here so often."

Jane tried one. "Not bad." She took a bite of her hamburger while Cordelia did the same. "Tell me something. Has Diana been drinking pretty steadily ever since you got here?"

"She's usually got something in her hand, though most of the time she doesn't seem all that high. It's generally in the evenings when she starts showing the effects."

"Like last night at dinner."

"Exactly. Her attitude changes. She becomes more confrontational. More—"

"Obnoxious."

"Well, sort of."

"Refresh my memory. Does she have any brothers or sisters? Are her parents still alive?"

Cordelia took a sip of Coke. "She's an only child. Her mom and dad live in St. Paul. They've never gotten along very well. I don't think Diana has kept in contact with them."

"That's too bad. Do they know she's a lesbian?"

"God, no. I forget you don't know Diana very well. She's a very closeted person. She's always maintained she needed to be because of her career."

"Is that true?"

Cordelia took another bite of her burger, thinking the question over. "Yeah, I suppose in some ways it is. Not so much with the theatre, but certainly on TV and in film. There are lots of gay and lesbian actors who are very secretive about their sexuality. Things leak out, but you never know for sure. Maybe the nineties will change some of that. Still, up until now, specific knowledge could easily hurt or even ruin somebody's career. For some reason, when you think about a woman doing a love scene with a man, you realize the audience wants to believe they really are watching a piece of reality. Even if the two people in question can't stand each other, even if the guy's got halitosis from hell, or she's a rabid racist or he's a hopeless sexist, the fact that this interaction *could* be true carries the audience along. When one of the actors is gay, it removes that possibility. Of course, we also see lesbians and gay men kissing and mauling each other all over the place in movies and on TV—and, I might add, very realistically—we just don't *know* that's what we're seeing."

Jane shook her head. "What crap."

"It is. In many ways, by keeping our identities in the dark, we're perpetuating the notion that gays or lesbians can't act any role that's given them. After all, that's the bottom line, isn't it? It *is* acting."

"What about Theo? Was he pretty out in college?"

"He and I both were—unlike you, my dear, who never told a single soul in that godawful sorority you belonged to."

Jane wiped her hands on a napkin. "Coming out is a process, Cordelia. Everyone does it at their own pace and in their own way."

"And some people never do it at all."

"Meaning what? You think people should be *outed?* Forced out of the closet by some sleazy exposé in a magazine or a newspaper?"

Cordelia shrugged, popping an onion ring into her mouth. "Theo thought that."

"Seriously?"

"Orson told me he and Diana had a big argument about it once. Diana said people had a right to their privacy. Theo agreed—in principle—but in today's world, he insisted we all needed to do our part, no matter what the cost. Claim our identities and our rights. We can't do that hidden in a closet . . . and other stuff like that." She took another bite of burger.

Jane had heard the arguments before. "I always love it when

other people make decisions for my life."

Cordelia raised an eyebrow.

"What does Curt think about it?"

"Curt's about as private as they come. If I had to guess, I'd say he'd agree with Diana. He's spent the last twenty years with his hand on the mute button."

"He is a quiet man."

"That's an understatement."

"But is it possible he's the kind of person who keeps everything bottled up deep inside until one day it explodes?"

Cordelia finished her burger. "Sounds a little too slick to me."

"What do you mean?"

"We all keep stuff bottled up inside. They're called memories."

Jane smiled. "Thank you Dr. Bradshaw."

"You're welcome."

"Come on," said Jane, stuffing the remnants of her lunch back into the paper sack, "Let's look at that suitcase."

Cordelia grabbed the last onion ring before Jane whisked everything away. She sipped her Coke as Jane removed Theo's clothes. Jeans. A shirt. A sweater. "Are you looking for something specific?"

"His wallet. And that heart medication DeLappe said he'd found." Jane felt a certain revulsion, pawing through a dead man's effects. Still, it had to be done. "Here it is," she said, finding the wallet at the very bottom. She opened it, slipping out his driver's license. "Hey, will you look at this. "

"What?"

"It's Theo's picture, but the name on it says Rob Wilson."

Cordelia scrunched up her nose. "Come again?"

"And didn't you tell me he was living somewhere in Florida."

"He is. Was. At least, that's what Orson told me."

"This is a Texas license."

"Let me see that." Cordelia grabbed it and read out loud: "Rob Wilson, 4837 Freemont Way, Houston, Texas. It expires in January." She looked up. "I don't get it."

"He was using an alias."

"Obviously. But why?"

Jane shook her head. "Did any of you know?"

"Not to my knowledge."

"What did Theo do for a living?"

Cordelia looked a bit startled by the question. "You know, I've got no idea."

"You never asked him?"

"Janey, I haven't seen Theo since he was in prison. He never came back to Minnesota—at least, not that I knew of—and according to Orson, he never gave away his address."

"But I thought he visited Diana in New York."

"He did. Orson saw him there once. And he visited Curt and Annie right after he got out of the slammer. Spent a couple of months in Chicago, but then he disappeared."

"And during the first two days of his stay here, no one ever asked him about a job?"

"I didn't. I guess maybe I thought it might embarrass him. Just in case times were tight."

"Isn't that his new Acura in the parking lot?"

Cordelia nodded.

"Times weren't too tight."

"Well, whatever. Maybe someone else talked to him about his work life. But I wasn't in on it."

Jane shook her head. "It doesn't matter. I doubt he would have told the truth anyway." She retrieved the wallet from Cordelia and continued her search. "Everything's in the name of Rob Wilson. Credit cards. A library card."

"Let's see the picture of the Shevlin Underground."

"What picture?"

"The one Theo showed us the other night. He said he always kept it in his wallet. In the money flap. It was taken of the six of us in the fall of our sophomore year. He was arrested the next spring."

Jane emptied the pouch of cash and then looked behind the

flap. "Nothing." She held it out for Cordelia to see.

"I don't understand."

Jane searched the rest of the wallet, but found nothing other than a paper clip, two stamps and a folded newspaper article.

"Do you suppose someone stole it?"

Jane shook her head. "Why?" Then again, her gut feeling told her it was gone for a reason. "You're *sure* he kept it in his wallet?"

"Positive. I saw him put it away." Cordelia tossed a piece of hamburger bun to a squirrel. "What's that newppaper clipping about?"

Jane opened it up. "It's from the *Chicago Sun Times*. A small piece about the opening of the Summer Green Playhouse. Someone must have interviewed Diana." Jane read down the column. "She mentions all of you by name. Talks about your directorship of the Allen Grimby. Mentions Orson's ownership of the Blackburn Playhouse. Talks a little about Annie and Curt. And then it just mentions Theo's name. Says you'll be attending the first performance."

"That was nice of her," said Cordelia absently. "Oh yeah, it was a press release."

"Hum." Jane finished reading it. "I wonder why he saved it?"

"Sentimental reasons, I suppose."

"And here's the heart medication," said Jane, finding a small orange plastic bottle in one of the suitcase's side compartments. She read the printed matter on the front. "RX 498205—Dr. Smith. Rob Wilson. Take one tablet daily. Aldomet. 0.625 MG. Net—34 tablets. No refills. 08/15/94."

"Sounds legitimate enough."

Jane turned it over, trying to picture what her own prescriptions looked like. "Something isn't right."

"Be more specific."

"There's no pharmacy name or address. No phone number." She removed the cover, shaking one of the pills into her hand. It was small, round and white. She showed it to Cordelia.

"Looks like an aspirin."

Jane held it closer. "It says APAP on the front."

"Oh, sure. I take APAP all the time for heartburn."

"Be serious."

"How the hell should I know what APAP is?"

"One way to find out."

"And that is?"

"See that drug store over there—next to the bank."

"I have eyes."

"I'll lay you odds they have a pharmacy. All we have to do is walk over and ask."

"I'll bet it's Aldomet."

"Put your money where your mouth is."

Cordelia stood up and started putting Theo's belongings back into the case. "An ice-cream cone. You buy if I'm right."

"You're on." Jane scrambled to her feet.

"God, I feel . . . guilty."

"Why?" Jane knew, even before Cordelia said the words. She watched her zip up the suitcase and then cradle it lovingly in her arms. "We're here talking about ice-cream cones, and Theo's—"

"I know," said Jane. "It's not fair."

"Maybe he's having an ice-cream cone wherever he is."

"Maybe."

"I hope so. With a cup of coffee. He loved coffee." She sighed. "Come on. This day doesn't have enough hours in it. We still have to get over to the courthouse."

Jane was glad for the show of enthusiasm. If they kept up the pretense of movement, maybe she wouldn't be depressed by the realization that she didn't know what the hell she was doing.

23

Jane walked directly back to the pharmacy at the rear of the store and waited while a clerk standing in front of the cash register broke open a new roll of nickels. The building was long and narrow, with scuffed wood floors and a high, neon pink ceiling. Jane spied a row of condoms *behind* the counter. Great place for them, she thought as she examined a bottle of mouthwash. When the woman was done and had closed the register, Jane asked, "Could you help me?"

"Certainly." She moved closer. "Do you have a prescription?"

"No," said Jane. She handed over one of the pills. "Can you tell me what that is? I was told it was Aldomet—a heart medication."

The clerk put on her glasses which had been hanging by a black cord around her neck. "Offhand, I'd say you were misinformed. But, wait a minute. I'll show it to the pharmacist." She stepped behind a door.

Jane could hear a muffled conversation. A minute later the

woman returned.

"I was right," she announced. "It's not Aldomet. It's acetaminophen."

"What's that?"

"It's like Tylenol. This is just a generic form." She handed the pill back and readjusted her glasses, eyeing Jane a bit more critically.

Jane nodded her thanks. So, she'd been right.

"If someone thinks this is a heart medication," continued the woman, "they need to be warned." Her face was full of concern.

"It's nothing like that," said Jane. "But thanks for the information." She turned and headed back to the front of the store. Cordelia was standing near the soda fountain, reading a list of ice-cream flavors posted on the wall.

"You owe me a double dip," said Jane, moving up beside her.

"What was it?" asked Cordelia.

"A generic form of Tylenol."

She whistled. "No kidding. Somebody was trying to pull a fast one." She sat down on a stool. "I wonder why?"

Jane had already formed a couple of theories. For now, she decided to keep them to herself. She glanced up at the wall. "Let's see. I'll have a scoop of the praline cream and one of the chocolate brownie."

"You took the words right out of my mouth," smiled Cordelia. She placed the order.

A few minutes later as they were about to exchange the cool interior of the drug store for the sweltering interior of Cordelia's car, Jane pulled her to a stop.

"What's wrong?" Cordelia licked a major drip off the side of her cone.

"Look over there," said Jane, pointing to a silver Honda which had just parked across the street next to a red truck. "Isn't that Curt and Annie's?"

Cordelia squinted. "Since Curt and Annie are getting out of it, I'd say that's a good guess." She took another lick. "Doesn't

Annie look nice with her hair down like that? I'd never tell her this to her face, but she looks ten years younger."

Jane watched them stroll casually into a restaurant several doors down. She read the name on the dark green awning. "Johnson's Bar and Deli." On the side of the building she saw another sign which said, "On Sale/Off Sale Liquors. Biggest selection in the county."

"I don't blame them for wanting to get away from the parsonage for a while," said Cordelia, biting into a caramelized nut. "It's beginning to feel like a prison."

Jane glanced to her left and was surprised to see Orson come out of the bank building right next to them. His eyes darted furtively both ways down the street as he stuffed an envelope inside the pocket of his sport coat. "And look there," she said, dragging Cordelia further into the shadows. "Brother Orson. I wonder what business he has at a bank."

"Probably something monetary," offered Cordelia.

Jane closed her eyes and shook her head.

Orson gave the street one last perusal and then trotted across to the same restaurant Curt and Annie had just entered.

"A meeting in town?"

"I'd say it's a conspiracy to have lunch," replied Cordelia, elbowing Jane in the ribs. "Just a little joke."

Jane's eyes rose to the sky.

"And pay attention to your ice cream, dearheart, or it's going to turn into a disgusting puddle."

She licked off the biggest drips.

"Come on. Let's go. We've still got to hit the courthouse. And remember, we promised to be back at the playhouse before three."

"You go get the car. I'll wait here," announced Jane.

"Why?"

"Just get it, will you? Let me watch for another minute."

Cordelia gave an exasperated snort. "I think we're about to cross the border into paranoid-land, Janey."

Jane glared at her.

"Sorry. Just an observation."

Jane returned her gaze to the restaurant.

"Right. Well. I'm off. Miss me." She sauntered slowly across the street. Her Le Sabre was parked in a lot on the other side of the park. At her current pace, it would be a ten-minute stroll.

As Jane continued to watch, licking her ice-cream cone somewhat absently, the minutes ticked by. Just as she was about to give up her post, Orson appeared in the restaurant's doorway. Again, he looked both ways down the street. It was clear to even the most amateur observer that he was being very careful. Since he hadn't been inside long enough to have a meal, Jane wondered what his purpose was for meeting Curt and Annie. Maybe it was a chance encounter. Or maybe it wasn't. She watched him get into his car. Just at that moment, Cordelia roared up. She might walk with the casual insouciance of a bored tourist, but she drove like a maniac.

Jane hopped in. "You're not going to believe this next request."

It was Cordelia's turn to glare. "Which is?"

"See that light blue Lincoln over there?"

"That's Orson's car."

"Right. Follow it."

Cordelia crunched the last bit of her cone. "Why?"

"And don't be too obvious. I don't want him to know he's being followed."

"I am not a New York City cab driver."

"Good. Then perhaps we'll survive the ordeal."

"I despise chase scenes.""

"This isn't a chase scene. I just want to know where he's going."

Orson's car pulled out into the street and turned west on the highway which led out of town.

Cordelia eased in behind him, keeping a safe distance.

"Now," continued Jane, "if he stops somewhere, just keep

going. We can double back after a couple blocks."

"There are no blocks in the country."

"Fine. Then turn around at the second cow."

"You're mocking me."

"How could you think that?"

Orson's car was beginning to slow.

"You have to admit, there *are* a lot of cows around here," sniffed Cordelia.

"Wisconsin is the dairy state."

"Thank you for that civics lesson. Perhaps we'll have time to visit a creamery while we're here."

"Say, there's that motel," said Jane. "The one where the bus dropped me off." She couldn't miss the horrid turquoise siding even from a distance.

"Ah yes. The Sunburst Motel. I remember it fondly. Probably Summer Green's version of the No-Tell Motel."

"Isn't that where that director is staying? You know, John Hubble?"

"I empty my mind of such trivia as soon as I hear it."

The blue Lincoln turned into the dirt lot in front of the motel and kicked up a cloud of dust before pulling to a stop.

"Keep going," said Jane.

"I know what I'm supposed to do." Cordelia pressed the accelerator and sped down the highway. About a quarter of a mile up the road she spied a fruit stand. "Want a watermelon?"

"Just turn around. When we get back to those trees just this side of the motel, pull off."

"You're sure you don't want a cantaloupe?" She wiggled her eyebrows.

"Cordelia."

"Just checking." She turned the car around.

"I wonder what business he could have at a motel?"

Cordelia shrugged. "Is that our hiding place?" she asked, nodding to a thickly wooded spot on her right.

"It's perfect. He won't be able to see us, but we can see him."

Cordelia drove slowly in between two huge elm trees. She slipped the car into neutral and let it idle. "Now what?" she asked, tapping an impatient finger on the steering wheel.

"We wait."

"For how long?"

"Until he comes out." Jane swept her eyes down the long row of rooms. Only two other cars were in the lot. Summer Green wasn't a particularly busy spot for adultery, or anything else. As they sat and waited, one lone truck passed them on the highway.

"Can I turn on the radio?" asked Cordelia.

"You won't find anything other than polka music."

"My, aren't we into stereotypes."

"All right. See what you can get." Jane had already tried the radio back at the parsonage. This far from a large town, the selection was pretty slim.

Cordelia switched it on, adjusting the controls until she found a station. Polka music blared from her four, perfectly balanced speakers. Gasping, she lunged for the off button. "Okay," she growled, "be smug. See if I care." She turned her head away and started humming.

Thankfully, their wait didn't turn out to be long. Less than ten minutes later, a tall dark-haired woman came out of the last room on the right. She got into her car and sped off without a backward glance. A few moments later, Orson reappeared. Once again, he surveyed the country-side, looking both ways down the highway. Apparently satisfied that he wasn't being watched, he got back into his car and started the engine.

"Looks like he's renting a room," said Jane.

"If he's cheating on his wife again." erupted Cordelia, "I'll strangle him with my bare hands."

"I didn't know Orson—"

"He and Ingrid were having some problems a while back. He said it was just a brief encounter. It didn't mean a thing. But this."

"I don't think you have anything to worry about."

"How can you be so sure?"

Jane was beginning to put a few of the pieces together. It looked like one of her theories might just hold water.

"Quick," she barked, "or we'll lose him."

Cordelia pulled back onto the highway. "He's heading out of town. Where the hell is he going?"

"Don't let him get away."

Orson's car picked up speed. In fact, as Cordelia's Le Sabre barreled around a steep bend about half a mile down the road, the Lincoln seemed to have disappeared.

"Keep driving," said Jane. "He's trying to ditch any tail he might have picked up. I'm sure he's moving as fast as he can."

"He's going to kill himself on one of these curves," she said, trying to keep her own car in the proper lane.

"Just drive."

About five miles out of town, the road straightened and the land became flat. They could now see for miles.

"He lost us," said Jane, banging her hand on the dashboard. "Damn it."

"Where do you suppose he is?"

"He could be anywhere. He could even be at that goddamn fruit stand eating a peach."

Cordelia slowed the car to fifty-five. "What are we going to do?"

Jane had to think. "Listen, Cordelia. I want to go back to that motel. I have to know for sure if Orson's rented a room."

"So what if he has? What does it tell us?"

Jane rolled her window down all the way and let the fresh country air rush over her. "It tells us, Cordelia, that Orson is up to something. And I'll bet the farm it has to do with Theo's untimely demise."

24

"Pull up over there by that last room," said Jane, pointing to the spot where Orson's Lincoln had just been parked. The motel's office was all the way at the other end of the building. She wondered if Orson had chosen this room with privacy in mind.

"What do you expect to find?" asked Cordelia.

"I'm not sure." Jane slid out of her seat, glad that so few people were around. It would make this a lot easier. Stepping up on the sidewalk that ran in front of the units, she crossed to number twelve's picture window and peeked through a crack in the heavy drapes. Inside, the room was dark. She could make out a bed, a TV set, two chairs, a nightstand and a dresser. Nothing very fancy.

"Is anyone in there?" asked Cordelia, coming up behind her.

Jane shook her head. "It's quiet." She turned around, her eyes readjusting to the brilliant afternoon sunlight.

"So? Do we break in?"

Jane smiled at her enthusiasm. "No. Now we go talk to the manager."

"Oh goody."

Halfway to the office, a door opened and out stepped John Hubble. "Afternoon ladies," he said, a look of mild surprise on his face.

Jane took in the cashmere jacket, brown tam and dark glasses. He wasn't even pretending to look like one of the locals. "Hi," she smiled.

"To what do I owe such an unexpected visit?"

So, he thought they'd come to see him. Jane decided to play along. "Did you know about the portrait of Diana that's going to be unveiled this afternoon at the playhouse?"

"I certainly did. I'm on my way right now to pick up a couple of the actors."

"Now?" said Jane.

He checked his watch. "It's nearly two-thirty."

"My, how time flies when you're eating ice cream," chirped Cordelia. She shielded her eyes from the sun.

He fished inside his pocket for his car keys. "That was nice of you two to drive all the way over here."

"We were in the neighborhood," said Cordelia, breaking an awkward pause. "Searching for watermelon."

"Watermelon?"

"Say," said Jane, "as I think of it, perhaps you could answer a question for me."

"Anything," he smiled.

"Do you know the man who's renting the end room here?"

"You mean your friend, Orson Albern?"

It was Jane's turn to be surprised.

"I think people have a right to their privacy. He doesn't bother me, and I don't bother him. As far as I can tell, we're the only two people here."

"Do you see him come and go a lot?"

He shrugged. "Only once. The first and last time was

yesterday evening. He drove in just after dark." So Orson hadn't gone for coffee with a friend as he'd said. Jane wondered what he'd been doing here.

"I'd better get moving," said John, feeling in his back pocket for his wallet. "If we're late, Diana's going to have our hides—and perhaps other, more essential parts of our anatomy. Come to think of it, if I don't show up, maybe she'll fire me."

"You want out of that production pretty badly, don't you," said Jane.

"That's an understatement." He seemed to grow uneasy. "Alas, duty calls. I gotta run." He dashed to his car. "See you two at the playhouse."

Jane waited until he'd driven off before continuing on to the office. "Seems like a nice enough guy," said Cordelia, puffing to catch up.

Jane didn't respond. She was already thinking about what she would say to the manager. Before they got to the door, she stopped. "Have you got a twenty?"

"Dollar bill?"

"We may need to bribe her . . . or him."

"This is Summer Green, Janey. Wouldn't a five do?"

"And you call *me* cheap?"

Glumly, Cordelia reached into her front pocket and drew out a money clip. She pulled off a twenty, handing it over.

"Let me do the talking."

"While I do the paying."

"Shhh." As she opened the door, a wave of musty, rancid smelling air rolled over her. Cordelia began to choke.

"Get a grip," whispered Jane. She approached the counter. No one was around. The furnishings were about what she'd expected. A study in '60's grotesque-right down to the dark blue shag. The only thing missing was a lava lamp. She rang the buzzer.

Out from the back room came a middle-aged man. He was wearing shorts and a T-shirt. "Yeah?" he said, a cigarette dangling from the side of his mouth.

"I've got a couple of questions."

"So?" Jane put the twenty down on the counter top.

"What about?"

"The man in number twelve."

He looked her up and down. Then he eyed Cordelia. "What do you wanna know?"

"When did he check in?"

The man's eyes flicked to the twenty.

"I'm not allowed to give out that kind of information."

"Fine," said Jane. She picked up the money and turned, starting for the door.

"Just hold your horses," he said, removing the cigarette from his lips and tapping the ash into an ashtray. "Bring that back here." He pointed to the bill in her hand.

She slid it onto the counter.

He quickly slipped it into his pocket. Then, opening a plastic file sitting on the counter next to him, he removed a small card. "The guy's name is Able. Martin Able. Said he's from Duluth. He checked in on the fourth. That would be Saturday afternoon."

"How long is he staying for?"

The man put the cigarette back in his mouth. "He left that open."

Jane looked at Cordelia, dropping her eyes to the pocket where Cordelia kept her money clip. She rubbed her fingers together.

Cordelia got the message. Reluctantly, she removed it again and handed it to Jane. "I want to see inside the room."

"Impossible."

She pulled off another twenty.

"If you get caught, it's my butt that's in the sling."

Another twenty went down on the counter.

"Nobody will catch us," said Jane. "This is how we're going to do it. Is the room next to number twelve connected by an inside door?"

"Yeah." He scratched his shoulder.

"Let us in that one like you're showing it to us. Then unlock the connecting door. I'll go in and look around—it'll only take a minute. Then we're out and gone. And you're sixty bucks richer. What do you say?"

He continued to scratch his shoulder. "Yeah, well . . . I guess so. That sounds okay."

"Great." Jane swept to the door and held it open.

The man grabbed a set of keys off a hook and followed her out and down to the next to the last room. Cordelia brought up the rear. She'd completely lost her enthusiasm.

As they entered unit number eleven, Jane was once again struck by the awful smell. Centuries of cigarette smoke. She waited while he unlocked the connecting door.

"Make it fast," he mumbled, moving over to the drapes and looking outside. "If I see anyone pull up, I'll holler—quietly, that is. I expect the two of you to get out of here pronto. You got it?"

Jane nodded. She let Cordelia go first.

Once inside, Jane found a light switch that turned on a dim lamp on the nightstand next to the bed. She couldn't believe people would actually spend time in a place this filthy. The rug looked like it hadn't been washed since the Crusades. Cigarette burns were everywhere.

"What are we looking for?" whispered Cordelia.

"Anything," said Jane. "And everything." She crossed to a closet and opened the door. It was empty. One crooked hanger dangled from a hook. Same with all the dresser drawers. All empty. "He's using this place for something."

"Like what? Cheap sex? I'd rather do it in a feed bin in central Iowa."

"You read too many romance novels," said Jane.

"So what if I do?"

Standing in the center of the room and searching it with her eyes, Jane saw an answering machine next to the phone. "That's it."

"What's it?"

"He's getting private calls here." She moved over to the bed and sat down. "This isn't the kind of place that offers amenities like an answering machine."

"You got that right." Cordelia backed away from the dresser. She didn't seem to want to touch anything.

Jane pushed the playback button. After a few clicks, a woman began speaking. "The train arrives at one thirty. I can't *wait* to see you." The voice was breathy. Seductive. "Bye."

"I was right." roared Cordelia.

"Shhh." Jane was confused. She waited for another message, but that was it.

"Time's up," called the manager. He sounded like he meant business.

"We better hit the bricks," said Cordelia, checking her watch. "We've got exactly ten minutes to make it back to the playhouse."

"What about the courthouse?"

"It's going to have to wait." Cordelia made a swift but dignified exit.

As Jane got up from the bed, she realized she was more confused now than she'd been before. Maybe what she needed was a break. If she gave her mind some time to work this all though, she was sure she would come up with an answer. Well, pretty sure, she thought as she switched off the light.

25

"Step on it," said Jane, glancing at her watch as they sped out of town. "We're going to be late."

"No, we aren't," Cordelia assured her. "If Diana said three, she meant in the vicinity of three. She's not known for her punctuality." She slowed for a truck driving erratically along the dirt shoulder.

"Watch it." cried Jane. The truck veered suddenly into their lane. As Cordelia slammed on the brakes, a hard object hit Jane's foot.

"Fucking moron." shouted Cordelia as the rusted heap lumbered in front of them and then turned onto a country road.

Jane bent down and picked up an empty wine bottle. "A little late night party?" she asked, waving the evidence in front of Cordelia's nose.

"Where did you get that?"

"When you braked, it rolled out from under the seat."

Cordelia grabbed it from Jane's hand, her eyes growing wide. "This is the wine bottle I told you about. The one I couldn't find. See? It's a German Riesling. The very same one Theo was drinking from the night he died."

Jane held it at arms length. "How'd it get in your car?"

"Good question." Their eyes met briefly.

Jane removed the cork and sniffed the contents. A tiny bit remained in the bottom. "Smells like regular old wine to me. Nothing out of the ordinary." She dipped her finger into the top.

"Don't taste it."

"Why not? A little won't hurt me."

"You don't know that, Janey. Just leave it alone."

Jane gave an exasperated sigh. "Do you realize how toxic it would have to be to—"

Cordelia gripped the steering wheel. "Don't argue. Just do as I say." Her lips pressed together tightly. "Look, I'm sorry, but I've really had it with this entire situation. I'm . . . on overload, okay? You're just going to have to put up with me." She relaxed her grip a bit. "Maybe we should have it tested."

"I doubt they have the facilities to do that sort of thing in Summer Green. We'd have to drive to Green Bay. It would take a while to get the results back. We'd never have them before it was time to leave."

Cordelia shook her head. "This is all happening too fast."

"I know." Jane turned the bottle over and read the back. "Look at this. It was bought at Johnson's Liquors. Remember that place we saw Orson, Annie and Curt go into at lunch time? It was a restaurant, bar and off-sale liquor store. I wonder if Diana buys all her liquor there?"

Cordelia shook her head, braking as she saw the playhouse's spire come into view. "I'm pretty sure Diana has everything sent from a store in Appleton. Summer Green is a little too provincial for her tastes."

"Then why was this bought at Johnson's?"

She shrugged. "Maybe Diana didn't buy it."

They both realized the importance of Cordelia's words at exactly the same instant.

"Let's not leap to any conclusions until we know for sure," said Jane.

"Right. I never leap. I have weak ankles."

Jane could see Orson's car already parked in the lot. Curt and Annie's Honda was next to it. Where had Orson disappeared to? Wherever it was, it wasn't far away. She knew it wouldn't be smart to grill him on the subject, but maybe she could think of some low key way to bring it up.

Once inside the playhouse, Jane and Cordelia found others milling about, waiting for Diana to arrive. The canvas had been placed on an easel in the center of the stage, a white sheet tossed over it, covering it from public view.

Curt strolled up, holding a glass of champagne. "Kind of a lot of folderol if you ask me. But then Diana loves the dramatic moment."

"Where'd you get the booze?" asked Cordelia.

"On a table behind the stage. A bunch of the actors are already back there. That's where the party's going to be after the unveiling." He drained the glass. "So, what have you two been up to all day?"

"Just seeing the sights," smiled Jane.

"I'll bet."

"We noticed you and Annie go into Johnson's restaurant in town."

"Really? Spying on us?"

"No," snapped Cordelia. "For your information, we were just coming out of the drug store across the street. We felt an irresistible urge for a double dip. Praline Cream and Fudge Brownie. Very hush-hush stuff," she added with more than a hint of sarcasm.

"Were you meeting Orson there for lunch?" asked Jane, trying to sound casual.

"No. Annie and I saw him come in, but we were sitting

towards the back. The place was full so he didn't see us. I think he walked up to the bar and ordered a beer. He drank it pretty fast and left." Curt ran a hand through his hair. "Actually, Annie and I wanted some privacy. We needed . . . to talk."

Jane would have liked to ask what about, but didn't want to seem too nosey.

"What about?" asked Cordelia.

Jane turned and glared at her.

"Oh, you know. Everything that's been going on. Theo's death. Diana's . . . drinking. This waiting around is really getting to me. Even though I know it's important, I was never really looking forward to the intervention—but several days ago I felt more prepared. Almost psyched. Now, I'm sort of losing my nerve. I hate confrontation."

"I know how you feel," said Cordelia.

"Hey, here's Amity," said Curt, his scowl changing to a smile. She had just come through the front entrance. He waved her over. "So, how was your first day at school?" he asked.

She gave an indifferent shrug.

"Not much of an answer."

"Not much of a school."

Another teenager accompanied her. He looked about the same age and was as thin as the proverbial reed. Amity introduced him to everyone as Chickie Johnson.

"Johnson," said Jane, smiling pleasantly. "Any relation to the Johnsons who own the restaurant in town?"

"Yeah," he said, his voice unusually deep for someone his age. "That's my parents." He took a look around the theatre. "Seems kind of strange to be back in here again. This used to be our church."

"Really," said Curt. "What denomination was it?"

"First Church of Christ."

"Sounds like a bank," muttered Cordelia.

Jane stuck a discreet elbow into her ribs.

"Yeah, my dad's a deacon. He was one of the leaders who

wanted to build a new church. A bigger one. Over on the other side of town. God, they were having one hell of a time getting rid of this turkey." He put his hand over his mouth. "Sorry."

"And there was a fire?" said Jane.

He nodded, then looked away.

"I was told the police never found out why it burned," said Curt.

"Yup. That's right." Again, his eyes darted away.

"Chickie's got a band," said Amity, obviously bored with the subject.

"Is that right," said Cordelia. "Marching?"

"What?" He bit his thumb nail. "No. Heavy metal. A little reggae sometimes."

Jane saw Orson waving at them from one of the front pews. He shook hands with the person he was talking to and then dashed to the back of the hall where they were standing. "Where's Diana?" he asked, a bit breathless.

Jane glanced at her watch. It was nearly three-thirty.

"Maybe someone should go back to the parsonage and see what the trouble is?" he suggested, his gaze coming to rest on Cordelia.

"I suppose that means I'm elected," she grumped.

"Do you want me to go?" asked Amity. "I don't mind."

"No, that's all right. I'm sure Diana's just . . . just lost track of time," offered Cordelia.

"Right." Orson nodded his agreement.

"I'll be back in a flash."

Famous last words, thought Jane.

Cordelia entered the parsonage and looked first into the parlor. She was in luck. Diana was standing in front of the fireplace, both arms resting on the mantle, staring at herself in the mirror.

"So, you've finally sent out a search party, have you?" she

said, seeing Cordelia's reflection enter the room. A large vodka and tonic rested on the coffee table behind her.

Cordelia's eyes fell to the drink. "Consider me the cavalry."

"Well, I'm *coming*," she declared, smoothing an eyebrow with her little finger. "By the way—" She hesitated. "Tell me the truth. Do you think . . . I'm still attractive?"

This was hardly the time for a discussion of physical disintegration. Then again, maybe it was the perfect time. Cordelia sensed a reticence in Diana, as if she didn't really want to go over to the playhouse at all. "Are you apprehensive about seeing the painting for the first time?"

She whirled around. "Don't be silly. It was just a simple question—requiring a yes or no answer."

Cordelia didn't care for the acid in her voice. Yet, by saying nothing, she knew she'd made a big mistake.

"Never mind. I know what I see when I look at myself. A beautiful . . . woman."

Cordelia was sure it killed Diana not to be able to put the word young in the sentence. Youth meant so much on TV and in the movies. Except for that rare exception, women didn't get leading roles without it. Just thinking about such inequity made Cordelia furious. But Diana had had to live in that make-believe world. She'd simply caught the same disease which afflicted so many others. Cordelia felt sorry for her, knowing at the same time that it was the last emotion Diana wanted to elicit.

"Have you ever considered . . . a little cosmetic surgery?" asked Diana, picking up her drink.

"You mean like a face lift? No. I haven't."

"Ah, always the good little feminist."

"Don't patronize me, Diana. If you want to have one, you don't need my permission."

She sat down. "You're right, I don't."

"Don't you think we should get over to the playhouse? Everyone's waiting."

"There's plenty of champagne. The troops won't mind if I'm

late." She sipped her drink. "I suppose you think age looks good on people. Gloria Steinem is a role model."

"What's the point, Diana?"

"We all go to pot in the end."

"Yeah. And I'm as vain as the next person."

"I'm glad you admit that about yourself." She closed her eyes and leaned back against the couch. "It's true. We all crumble. Unless something gets us first—in our prime, so to speak."

"You mean like self-pity?"

Diana leveled her gaze. "I don't want to grow old, Cordelia. And, unlike all you sober folk with your sensible opinions and your appropriate behavior, I've got the guts to say it out loud." She stood once again and moved a little unsteadily back to the mirror. "I want an answer. Do you think I'm still in my prime?"

"Yes," said Cordelia, knowing not to hesitate this time. Besides, it was true. She was in her prime—or, at least she should be.

"I think so too." Diana leaned closer and examined one eye. "Do I look dissipated to you?"

"A bit."

Her entire body stiffened. She turned. "Thank you for that vote of confidence."

"Do you want lies?"

"Yes." she roared. "I want all my mirrors to lie."

"I'm not a mirror."

"Of course you are."

They stared at each other. "Diana, we've got to go. We can't make those people wait all day."

"Why not?" She finished her drink. "And you know what? I had a plan. I was going to put that portrait in my attic and have *it* age—not me."

"That's a story, Diana. It's not real."

"Did it ever occur to you that I don't want reality?"

Many times, thought Cordelia. "All right then. Let me take back what I said and start over. What I meant to say was that the gallons of booze you've guzzled over the last twenty years have left your skin, your hair, your eyes, your voice, *and* your mind completely untouched. Not to mention your liver."

Diana charged past her. "Get out of my way," she growled, stumbling into the foyer and out the front door.

Cordelia felt rooted to the floor. In the silence of the empty house, she couldn't seem to move. She knew she'd handled this badly. Her patience was just about gone. All in all, it had been a miserable day.

Lurching ever so slightly, Diana entered the playhouse near the stage and clapped her hands for attention. "Let's all gather in the main theatre," she shouted, her eyes searching the crowd. "There you are," she called to a man seated in the front pew. "Ethan, I'd like you to introduce yourself and then present the portrait."

Jane sat down next to Annie and Amity and waited while the tall lanky artist in jeans and a Cal State sweatshirt took the stage. He waited for everyone to be seated. Diana had hopped up next to him and was standing on the other side of the easel.

"My name is Ethan Burgess," the man began, "and I live and work in St. Charles, Illinois, just outside of Chicago. Diana contacted me last spring and asked if I'd be interested in doing her portrait. We got together several times over the summer, and what you see here today is the result of those meetings." He swept his hand to the covered canvas.

Everyone clapped.

"Shall I uncover it, or would you like to?" he asked Diana.

"Please," she said, deferring to him. Carefully, he slid the sheet off the portrait and dumped it behind him on the floor.

Jane kept her gaze fixed on Diana, not realizing for a moment why the audience was silent.

Diana stood back from the easel. "Is this some kind of joke?"

The audience began murmuring.

Jane's eyes moved to the painting. "Jesus," she found herself whispering. There was nothing there—nothing except a large piece of heavy cardboard.

The artist moved around to the front. "What the—?"

"Explain this." demanded Diana.

"I . . . can't."

"This is fraud. I paid you nearly twenty thousand dollars for that portrait."

"It was right here. I put it here myself this morning. I don't understand."

Diana took in the assembled crowd. She seemed disgusted, accusing, as if it was their fault. Her eyes rose to Cordelia's face as she came through the back door. "Somebody's playing games with me," she whispered.

Orson rushed up on stage. "I'm sure it's just a mix-up," he said, taking her by the arm. "Why don't we just go back to the house and—"

She broke free of his grip. "I'm not a child. I don't need a keeper." With one last angry glance around the room, she bolted to the back curtain and disappeared stage left.

Orson held up his hands for silence. "I'm sorry about all this," he said, waiting while everyone quieted down. "I don't know what happened, but I'm sure we'll locate the portrait very soon and you'll all be able to enjoy it hanging in the front entrance. In the meantime, there's lots of food and drink. Please. Enjoy yourselves." He took out a handkerchief and wiped his damp forehead. Then, ignoring the artist and everyone else's confused stares, he turned and ducked behind the curtain in search of Diana.

26

Half an hour later, Jane was on her way back into town. She had just enough time to make it to the courthouse before it closed for the day. She wanted to take a look at Theo's case file. She wasn't sure what she was looking for, but for Cordelia's peace of mind, and for her own, it had to be checked.

Cordelia wanted to remain at the parsonage. After the unveiling—such as it was—Diana had stomped out of the playhouse and returned to her bedroom where she had not only slammed, but locked the door behind her. Annie had tried to talk to her, but Diana insisted she wanted to be alone. Cordelia felt confident Diana had stolen the portrait herself, and what they'd witnessed on stage was just another one of Diana's little dramatic moments—as well as some rather unconvincing acting. Jane, on the other hand, wasn't so sure. She'd been watching Diana's face when the sheet was removed. From what she could tell, Diana had been genuinely shocked. Then again, if Diana hadn't taken the canvas, who had? And for what reason?

Since Jane didn't have any immediate answers, she shook the questions out of her mind as she pulled into a parking space just down the street from the courthouse. Walking up to the two-story building, she could see the facade was constructed of brown bricks and white painted wood. Two thick pillars on either side of the front entrance gave the structure a kind of historic formality, though it was obviously a new building.

Once inside, she crossed to the front desk and waited while the man behind the counter finished a phone conversation. He appeared to be in his late sixties and was wearing a dark business suit, complete with red silk handkerchief in the vest pocket and a white carnation in the buttonhole.

After hanging up, the man asked somewhat superciliously, "May I help you?"

Jane nodded. "I'd like to see the case file on Theodore Donati."

He looked her up and down. "May I ask why?"

"It's a public record, isn't it?"

"Yes."

"Then I'd like to see it."

He studied her for a moment longer and then stepped to the end of a long row of filing cabinets and pulled out a white folder. "Would you care to use a conference room to look at this?"

Good idea. She didn't want him in her face while she examined the documents. "Yes. That would be great."

He led the way down a side hall to the third room on the right. Switching on the light, he said, "I'll be at the desk if you need any further assistance."

"Thank you," she replied, matching his preciseness. She shut the door, knowing he was still standing on the other side. Perhaps she should make some odd noises, hum the theme from *Twin Peaks*. Give him some small conundrum on which to dwell while she was out of sight, but not out of mind.

Hearing his footsteps finally recede, she turned to the

table and sat down in the nearest chair. She placed the folder in front of her and stared at it for a second before pulling out the contents. On the top of the pile was a series of black-and-white photographs taken of Theo the night he died. They were all from different angles. He was lying on a stretcher, his eyes closed, his body limp. He appeared to be inside the ambulance. In one, she could make out Orson's face in the background. He looked devastated, the palm of one hand held flat against his forehead. Jane was glad Cordelia hadn't come with her. These would have been hard to take.

Laying the pictures aside, she found a small card with Theo's fingerprints on it. She studied it briefly. Next was a property receipt for his wallet and clothing, as well as the contents of his pockets. Since she'd already seen this first hand, and nothing on the list seemed to be missing, she went on to the police report. It had been filed by a Sergeant Steve Bossing. Jane found his comments clear and to the point. He had arrived on the scene shortly after Theo's death. He'd made a note that the volunteer paramedics had done everything they could to save his life. He pronounced Theo dead at exactly 8:47 p.m., Sunday, September fifth. Jane was surprised to find a copy of Theo's prison record included in the documents. Something like that probably followed a person everywhere. No wonder he'd used an alias, also noted by the sergeant in his comments. Lastly, the coroner's report. Sure enough, it was signed by Arnold DeLappe. She pushed everything else aside and studied the report more closely.

She read through all the information on the decedent. Name. Date of birth. Place of death. Marital status. Race. Educational Background. Religion. When she came to decedent's occupation, she saw that someone had written Contractor in the space provided. Next to it were the words, Blandin Builders, Houston, Texas.

Jane took out a small note pad from her pocket and wrote it down. It might be important. Evidently, Orson had not only known where Theo lived, but what he did for a living. Odd that

Orson should be privy to such a wealth of information about Theo when everyone else was almost totally in the dark. Under the heading, Parents, each space was blank. Under Informant, Orson had signed his name. She read through to the bottom. The report seemed to be in order. As she looked up from the pile of papers, she felt an empty feeling deep in her stomach. It was such a cold act, this picking over the legal remains of a man's life.

Stuffing everything back into the file, Jane opened the door, switched off the light and walked back to the front desk.

"All finished?" asked the man.

"Yes." She handed him the file.

"Did you know Mr. Donati?"

"I did."

He took the folder back to the cabinet. "It's a sorry business," he muttered, shaking his head. "Well, have a good day."

She nodded her thanks and tried to walk as calmly as she could to the door. She realized with a sinking sensation, that seeing the photos and reading the coroner's report had made Theo's death all too real—much more so than she'd ever wanted it to be. All she could think of now was breathing some fresh air.

After a short walk to clear her head, Jane remembered she had one more stop to make before she returned to the parsonage. She needed to check out Johnson's Bar and Restaurant. It might not prove anything, but she had a couple of questions she wanted to ask.

Walking two blocks south along the business district, she caught sight of the building half a block down on the other side of the road. Since it was a little early for dinner, very few cars were parked in front of the restaurant. Jane waited for a stoplight to turn green and then sprinted across the street, removing her sunglasses as she entered the dark interior. Instead of going into the bar, she made a hard left and walked straight into the liquor store. A middle-aged woman in a bright pink sun dress stood behind the counter, paging through a magazine. She looked up as Jane entered.

"Can I help you?" she asked.

"I hope so. I'm . . . staying at the old parsonage out on County Road C, and—"

The woman took off her bifocals and gave Jane a hard once-over. "You one of Diana Stanwood's friends?"

Jane smiled. "I guess you could say that."

"My son's a friend of Amity Scarbourough."

"Oh. Sure. You must be Mrs. Johnson. I met Chickie earlier this afternoon."

"That right?" She closed the magazine. "We had Amity over to dinner the other night and I don't mind telling you, I'm worried about that child's welfare."

"Really? Why?"

"We had that Stanwood woman checked out before she moved into town."

"We?"

"My husband's a deacon at the First Church of Christ. People around here like to know who's moving into the area."

"I see."

"You probably know all about it, since you're a friend of hers."

"Well, really, I'm just here for a funeral. I can't say I know Diana all that well."

The woman hunched her shoulders and bent closer. "She's one of them *gays*."

Jane backed up a step. "Really?"

"It's true."

She was surprised by the woman's knowledge. From what Cordelia had said, Diana was very closeted about her sexuality. She was sure nothing had ever been printed on the subject. "Who'd you hear that from?"

The woman gave a knowing nod. "Jack—he's my husband—drove over to that big library in Appleton. Got everything he could on the woman. There was an article in the Greenwich

Village Sentinel about her relationship with some personal secretary. I assume it was Amity's mother since they had the same last name. Anyway, ever since we found out I guess you could say we haven't been too thrilled with the idea of her living out there. We never would have sold her the building if we'd known."

The woman acted like the church was her personal property. "But I'd heard you were desperate to get rid of it. You needed the sale to finance the new church you were building over by the mall."

Mrs. Johnson squared her shoulders. "Well, not that desperate."

Jane picked up a bottle of Merlot and examined the label. "The scuttlebutt around town is that someone in your church set the fire." There. She decided to chuck that little pebble into the pool of their somewhat one-sided discussion. See what the ripples looked like.

"Who told you that?"

"Lots of people."

"It's a lie. Nobody in our congregation would do something so . . . wrong."

Jane shrugged. She wasn't going to let the woman off the hook that easily. "Maybe."

"You tell those people *from me* to mind their own business. That's always the best policy. People should keep their noses in their own nests."

Jane was pretty sure the woman didn't find any irony in her statement. "I'm curious. Does Ms. Stanwood order much wine or spirits from your store?"

The woman shook her head. "When she first arrived, we sent out a few cases, but I suppose she found another supplier." Pulling up a stool, she added, "She did order a bottle of German Riesling from us about a week ago. I took the order. She said she had a guest coming who liked sweet wine."

So the bottle had been purchased by Diana. So much for jumping to conclusions.

"How come you want to know?"

Jane set the bottle of Merlot down. "No reason, really. Just making conversation."

"You're not from around here."

"No, I'm from Minneapolis. I own a restaurant on Lake Harriet."

The woman scrunched up her face in thought. "The Lyme House?"

"That's the one."

"We've been there. Jack and I loved it."

Jane grinned. "That's kind of you to say."

"No, I really mean it. The food was great. I loved the way you could sit out on the balcony and hear music playing from the bandstand way across the lake."

Another customer entered the store.

"I wish we could have sold that church to someone like you," she continued. "Maybe one day you'll decide to expand. Summer Green is a growing metropolis, you know."

"I'll remember that."

"It was nice meeting you, Miss—?"

"Lawless. Jane Lawless."

The woman stuck out her hand. "A real pleasure."

Jane shook it and then leaned closer. In a confidential whisper she added, "By the way, Mrs. Johnson, just for your information, I'm one of them *gays* too."

27

Except for Diana and Amity, Jane found everyone gathered in the parlor when she got back to the parsonage. Wonderful aromas filled the house. Jane could see Hilda dashing about in the kitchen, preparing dinner. Across the hall in the dining room, the table was already set with Diana's favorite bone china.

"What smells so good?" she asked, sitting down on the sofa next to Cordelia.

"It's Cornish game hen," said Orson. He was sprawled in an easy chair reading the paper, his feet up on a footstool. "I was just in the kitchen getting the particulars. Seems Hilda marinates it in orange juice, garlic, capers, brown sugar and cinnamon. She serves it as a hot salad—sort of Niçoise—over fresh sautéed green beans and slivers of red potato. Oh, and just a tad of chopped tomatoes and shallots."

Jane looked to her right and saw Cordelia trying not to drool.

"Where did Diana *find* that woman?" asked Curt. He was

lying on his stomach next to the cold fireplace, a couch pillow propped under his chin. "She should be the executive chef at an exclusive restaurant."

"I second that," said Annie who was sitting on the floor next to him, paging through one of Diana's many scrapbooks.

"Where's—" Jane's eyes rose to the ceiling. She didn't want to say Diana's name out loud.

"In her boudoir," answered Cordelia, twisting an auburn curl around her finger.

"Is she okay?"

"She hasn't sent out for another case of vodka, so at least she's content."

Jane grimaced. "Has anyone seen her since . . . this afternoon?

Orson shook his head. "She's probably just asleep. We'll wake her before dinner."

"Hey, remember the summer we took that stage craft practicum?" asked Annie, turning a page in the scrapbook.

"I'll never forget it," muttered Cordelia, covering her face with her hand.

Jane was intrigued. "What happened?"

"It was just the six of us," said Orson, putting down the paper. "We were the only ones taking the class. The professor, what was his name?"

"Pelty," snickered Curt. "Lambert Pelty."

"Right. He really had it in for us right from the start."

"Why?" asked Jane.

"I m not really sure," said Orson. "He knew we were all good friends."

"He also knew we thought pretty highly of ourselves," replied Curt, "and he was going to take us down a notch or two."

"He wouldn't have had the chance if it hadn't been for me," said Cordelia, lowering her head. "It was so incredibly stupid."

"It was funny," said Curt. "He simply overreacted."

"What'd you do?" asked Jane.

"Well, it was during a break. Pelty had gone upstairs to get a cup of coffee, and so I took the opportunity to hop up on stage and continue teaching the class from his notes on the blackboard. With a few of my own additions, of course."

"Of course," nodded Jane.

"She could really mimic him," grinned Annie. "It was hysterical."

"Did he catch you?" asked Jane.

Cordelia shook her head.

"Then what happened?"

"It was what she wrote," said Curt, a slow grin forming. "During one of her digressions—Pelty liked to digress—she wrote *and blah blah blah* after every one of his points."

Orson started to laugh. "I know it was childish, but we were just doubled up it was so funny."

"When Pelty got back," continued Cordelia, "he went berserk. He demanded to know who'd done it."

"And did you tell?"

"God no," exclaimed Cordelia. "I thought he'd have my hide."

"That's when he said that if we didn't offer up the guilty party, he'd flunk us all," said Orson.

"Could he do that?" asked Jane.

"He was the professor," said Annie. "I think we all thought he could."

"But no one ever told?"

"Well," said Curt, "after he threatened us, Diana raised her hand. She got up and very meekly replied, 'Mr. Pelty, I cannot tell a lie. It was me.' Then she just stood there, in utter contrition, her head bowed. Needless to say, Pelty didn't know what to think. He just glared."

"Then," said Orson, "I stood. I couldn't let Diana have all the best lines. I said that in good conscience, I mustn't allow a friend to take the heat for something I'd done. I promised to write *I shall never annoy Lambert Pelty again* five hundred times on his blackboard."

Jane began to laugh.

"Then Theo stood," said Annie. "He started to cry. He squeezed his baseball cap in his hands and said that his parents had never paid any attention to him when he was a child. That's why he'd done it. He thanked Orson and Diana for attempting to shield him, but he was ready to pay the price. He suggested that he crawl from Scott Hall to Northrup on his hands and knees at midnight during a rainstorm. By this time, Pelty's expression had turned sort of glassy-eyed."

"That's when I got up," said Curt. "I said my friends were just being noble. I'd written the heinous *blah blah blah* on the board and I was ready to take my punishment. Of course, I also mentioned that my father was a close friend of the president of the University. And I pointed out that he played handball every Wednesday afternoon with several of the regents, but what the heck, punish away."

"We all got up eventually," said Annie. She cast an amused eye at Cordelia. "Even the real culprit."

"So what did he finally do?" asked Jane.

Orson put a finger to his cheek. "I think we confused the poor man. He simply got up, picked up his pointer, and continued on with the day's lesson."

"Thanks to Diana's quick thinking, my college G.P.A. was saved from total ruin," said Cordelia.

"And with a little help from your friends," winked Orson.

Jane could tell they needed this story tonight. It reminded them of who they had once been, and what they still wanted to be to each other.

After a few seconds Jane asked, "Where's Amity?"

As if roused from a sleep, Annie looked up and said, "She's out with that boy." She pushed the scrapbook aside and drew her legs up to her chest, her back resting against Orson's chair. "Chickie. But she'll be back for dinner. I told her seven."

"What kind of name is Chickie?" asked Orson.

"He wants to be a rock star," said Annie, as if that explained everything.

"I'd say the name's inspired more by his *rural* background," offered Cordelia with a smirk.

Curt glowered. "Cut the kid some slack, will you?" He got up and crossed to a table where Hilda had set out a pitcher of lemonade and some glasses. She'd also fixed a plate of cheese and fruit, but no one had eaten any. "Is everything all set for the funeral tomorrow?"

"As far as I know," said Annie. "I drove over to the funeral home this morning and dropped off the exact location for the grave site. Just so there wouldn't be any confusion."

An awkward silence followed. No one knew quite how to pick up the conversation.

"Well," said Curt finally, taking a chair by the fireplace. "How's the murder investigation coming, Jane?"

Annie and Orson turned and glared at him.

"Just making conversation."

"Drop it," said Orson.

"Why? I have a right to know." He stared at Jane. "Do you still think one of us murdered Theo?"

The doorbell sounded.

"I'll get it," said Orson, looking like he had just been released from prison.

Jane was about to answer when she heard Orson exclaim, "We're so glad you're here. Please, come in." A moment later he appeared in the doorway accompanied by a man who looked a great deal like Theo, only taller, beardless and much younger.

"This is James Donati," announced Orson. "Theo's brother."

Everyone stood.

James looked curiously from face to face. "I've never met any of you, but I know you all." His smile was warm.

"Come in and sit down," said Orson.

"Okay. Sure, for a few minutes." He made himself comfortable in a chair opposite the couch.

"Can I get you anything?" asked Orson.

"A brandy would be great. This has been kind of a long day."

"I'll only be a second." He left the room.

"So," said Annie, picking up the conversational threads, "How was your trip?"

"Fine. Too long." His eyes took in the parlor. "This is a nice house. Kind of old fashioned."

Orson returned with his drink.

James took a sip. It seemed to relax him. "You know, while Theo was in jail, he wrote me so many letters. I still have most of them. I was pretty young when he left for college, so we didn't know each other all that well." His eyes stopped at Curt. "You must be Curt Whittig." He took another sip. "Theo thought the world of you, though I'm not sure I'm telling you anything you don't already know. He wrote about you so . . . affectionately."

Curt was stunned. "He wrote to you about me?"

"Many letters. At first, they were almost *all* about you. How talented you were. How much fun you'd had together."

"I . . . didn't know."

"But you certainly were aware of how much he cared about you."

Curt shook his head. "I wasn't . . . sure." He looked at Annie. Strangely, her eyes were full of tears.

"And you must be Cordelia," smiled James, moving on. "Theo wrote lots about your midnight conversations. You used to sit on the counter in your apartment with your feet in the kitchen sink."

"He wrote you that?"

"Theo thought you had a totally weird mind. He was sure someday you'd be recognized as a theatrical genius."

Cordelia raised her chin. "The boy had taste."

Again, James moved on. "And, of course, you're Annie. The woman with the fiery red hair. Theo said you were the kindest person he'd ever met."

Annie put a trembling hand over her mouth.

"We all loved him," said Cordelia.

"I know," said James. "But sometimes I just wish I could have understood him better. After he got out of prison, he simply evaporated. He was going to come and visit my wife and me in Sacramento, but he never did. He wrote every now and then, and occasionally he'd call, but he'd never tell me where he was living."

"Join the crowd," said Curt.

James glanced at Jane. "I'm sorry. I don't—"

"Jane Lawless. I'm not part of the Shevlin Underground. Just a friend."

"Sure. Nice to meet you." He turned to Orson. "You know, Theo told me you were like a brother to him. I don't mind telling you I used to be pretty jealous of that. But when I got older, I guess I was just happy he'd found such good friends."

"Can you stay for dinner?" asked Annie. "I'm sure we've got plenty of food."

James shook his head, finishing his drink. "Sorry. My wife's back at the motel. We're pretty beat. We got up this morning at the crack of dawn and drove the kids to her sister's in Bakersfield. Then we hopped a plane to Chicago and drove up here. I think we're going to pull the shades and hit the sack."

"The funeral is at three tomorrow afternoon," said Orson.

James nodded. "We'll be there." As he got up to go he asked, "I do have one question."

"Anything," replied Orson.

"Well, I was just curious. Who made the decision to have my brother's body cremated?"

Annie slipped her arms around her stomach. "I remembered Theo saying once that when he died, that's what he wanted."

"Really?" James scratched the back of his neck. "That's so weird. When he was a kid, he was almost phobic about fire. It just seemed odd to me that he would say something like that."

Annie looked up at Curt.

"Well, it's done now. No use worrying about it." James turned and crossed into the foyer. He stopped when he saw Diana coming down the stairs.

"You must be Theo's brother," she said, extending her hand

as she got to the bottom.

"I am," he smiled, shaking it warmly. "And you're Diana Stanwood. It's great to finally meet you. I just wish it could have been under . . . you know. Other circumstances."

"So do I," she said, still holding his hand.

Everyone moved in closer to watch.

"I'm sorry, I haven't packed Theo's things yet," said Diana, her voice a bit too regal for normal speech. She took hold of the banister to steady herself.

If James had caught the fact that she'd been drinking, he didn't let on. "That's all right. I can get everything tomorrow."

"And he has a car out in the parking lot," she continued. "I'm sure he'd want you to have it."

James turned to Orson.

"Absolutely," Orson replied. "Diana's right. Theo didn't have much, but I know the car is paid for. It should go to you."

James passed a hand across his eyes. "Thanks. But . . . what I'd like most is to be able to talk to you all. Maybe tomorrow . . . after the service. I need to know more about him. Hear your stories. See him through your eyes."

"Of course," said Diana, putting her arm around his shoulder. "There isn't a person here who wouldn't be happy to sit down with you and reminisce. As far as I'm concerned, it's a date."

He beamed his thanks. "Theo was a lucky man."

Diana nodded. "The sad thing is, we often don't realize how lucky we are until it's too late." Her eyes flicked to Orson, and then away.

"Well," said James, clearing his throat, "I'd better shove off." He moved to the door. "Will there be a lot of people from Summer Green at the funeral tomorrow?"

"I don't think so," said Orson. "Theo didn't know anyone here other than the six of us."

"That's what I thought," said James, shoving his hands into his pockets. "But as I was coming up the front walk, a guy stopped me. He asked if I was Theo's brother. Asked if I was coming for the funeral."

"What did he look like?" asked Orson.

"Bald. Well dressed. After we were done talking, he got back into his Cadillac and drove off."

Diana shook her head. "I haven't the faintest idea who that could be."

"Me either, " said Annie.

"Well, maybe we can ask him tomorrow," said James.

"What a good idea," replied Cordelia, her eyes locking on Orson. "I think I will."

28

After dinner, Jane spent several hours walking in the graveyard. She had a great deal to think about and needed some privacy. After a sweltering day, the evening had turned deliciously cool, a light breeze ruffling her hair as she passed aimlessly among the gravestones. This visit to Summer Green wasn't in any sense a vacation, yet she was enjoying the change of pace. She was glad Cordelia had called her. Glad most of all that she could bring a perspective Cordelia entirely lacked.

Returning to the parsonage around nine, Jane found Cordelia and Orson in the dining room, engaged in a subdued game of cribbage, while Annie, Curt and Amity were sitting over Cokes in the kitchen, talking in hushed tones about a subject which looked quite serious. Jane was curious, but felt it best not to disturb them. Diana had gone to her room directly after the peach cobbler saying she had a splitting headache. No one had any trouble believing *that*.

After reading for a couple hours in the chair next to her bed, Jane switched off the light and slipped under the covers. She closed her eyes and tried to empty her mind, knowing she was still suffering from lack of sleep. But, as she suspected, the events surrounding Theo's death were too much in her thoughts to allow her any rest. Every half hour or so, she could hear someone trudge up the stairs, use one of the two bathrooms and then retreat into their bedroom. Finally, around one, Jane decided to give up and go downstairs in search of a cup of tea. She grabbed her bathrobe and started down the darkened hall. As she passed the end room, she noticed a light on and the door ajar.

She knew Theo had used this room during his visit. She'd planned on exploring it early tomorrow morning before anyone was up. Getting caught once in someone else's bedroom was enough. She'd never seen anyone in this room before, but tonight, Diana was sitting on the bed, a suitcase open in front of her.

Jane hesitated for a moment, watching her fold a pair of pants. "Oh, it's you," said Diana, looking up. "I thought everyone had gone to bed."

Jane opened the door a bit further. "I couldn't sleep."

"A common malady. Come in and keep me company." She fingered a button on one of Theo's shirts. "I promised James I'd have all this packed by tomorrow afternoon. Theo didn't bring much. I started going through his things yesterday, but I just couldn't handle it."

A large drink sat next to her on the night stand. It had no ice in it. Diana's speech was considerably more slurred than it had been earlier in the evening. Even so, she seemed to be reasonably coherent, though Jane knew that with someone under the influence, appearances could be deceiving.

"It's hard to believe I'm never going to see him again," said Diana, taking a deep sip from her glass.

"It takes a long time for a death to feel real."

She picked up his wallet and pulled out the driver's license.

"Did you see this? He was using an alias. What the hell was going on, that's what I'd like to know."

Jane knew Diana wasn't interested in her opinion. Instead, she decided to ask a question. "Cordelia said he visited you once in New York."

She nodded. "For Jill's funeral. It was an awful time. But . . . life goes on." She stared at the license photograph for a moment. "He has a bad haircut in this photo. That's not like him."

"What did Theo do for a living?"

Diana shrugged. "He was always evasive about that. It's hard getting a good job after you've been in prison." She picked up a piece of notebook paper and unfolded it.

"What's that?" asked Jane.

"It's . . . well." She paused, but only for a second before plunging ahead. "Listen to this. *Dear Curt.*"

Jane was a surprised and a bit aghast. "Where did you get that?"

"It was in his suitcase." She looked over at the closet. "Funny. When I was going through his stuff before, I never noticed it."

Jane wondered what condition she'd been in. Depending on how much vodka she'd consumed, it wouldn't have surprised her if Diana had failed to notice a rhinoceros next to the shoe rack.

Diana continued:

I've always written letters when I'm upset—most of the time I've had the sense not to mail them. I guess I've never written to anyone very much, with the possible exception of Orson and my brother, James. But rest assured, Curt, you have been in my thoughts more than you know. I didn't like the way our conversation ended this afternoon, and I don't know what to do about it.

"Do you think you should be reading that?" interrupted Jane, not sure she wanted to be hearing it.

Diana waved the question away and continued as if she had every right in the world to be reading another man's letter. "I'll

192

skip part of this. Here—this is where it gets good.

*Do you remember the book I made both you and Orson read in college—*Beau Geste? *For some reason, it's been on my mind a lot lately. It was my favorite story when I was growing up. I suppose that says more about me than it does about anything else, but still, odd as it sounds, my life has paralleled that tale. It's funny. Life moves in a certain way and it becomes hard—sometimes impossible—to change directions even if you want to. That's what life did to Michael Geste— perhaps to me too.*

Diana took several sips of her drink.

The thing is, Curt, I couldn't be anything to you other than what I've been—someone who loved you once—someone who went away, and for all practical purposes, never came back. You've always had trouble letting go. I saw it years ago in the way you nursed your anger against your parents. They were crummy to you, I realize that. What they produced was a very lonely boy. Perhaps some part of you will always be lonely because, deep down, that's who you are. But for God's sake, Curt, take a long look at your life now. Annie loves you very much, and I know you love her. I'm sorry if it seems I never answer your questions as completely as you'd like. All I can say is, if we meet some day on the other side, I'll happily fill you in on every detail. I've made a mess of many things, Curt, but I hope to God you're not part of that. I'm sad to think ours wasn't the love story you wanted. If it's any consolation, it's not the story I wanted for us either. But we play the hand we're dealt. It's strange. When we all agreed to come to Summer Green, I thought it was going to be a real downer. I've never been a big fan of psychologists or the psychological cure—

"What do you suppose he means by that?" asked Diana.
Jane shook her head. "I haven't the foggiest."
Diana considered it for a moment and then continued:

but I've really enjoyed getting away. It's given me a perspective I didn't have before. Maybe you'll leave too, a more grateful man. I doubt I'll send you this. Maybe I will. Who knows? I think, for now, perhaps we should just try to enjoy the country air. I know how much you like to be outside. Maybe the sun and the somber mists, and most of all, the friendships that have sustained each one of us over many rough moments will continue to sustain you now. When I think of you all, and especially you, Curt, I know my life has been very rich indeed. My love to you always.

Theo

She let the paper fall face up on the bed. "Wasn't that beautiful?"

It was. "Are you going to give it to Curt?"

Diana acted as if she hadn't expected the question. "Well, sure. After all, it's addressed to him, isn't it?" She emptied half her drink.

Jane could see Diana's eyes lose focus as she set the glass back on the table next to the bed. Once again, she began pawing through the suitcase. Unlike a few minutes ago, she was now making more of a mess than anything else.

"Cordelia tells me you picked up his belongings from the funeral home this morning." Diana held up an argyle sock, studying it with great intensity.

"We did," said Jane.

She gave her head a small shake. "Uh. Felt kind of dizzy there for a moment, but it passed." She dropped the sock. "Anyway, what was I saying? Oh yeah. Cordelia was pretty vague about your reason for going over there. I hate it when people are vague."

"Me too."

Diana cracked a smile. "Why did you go?"

Jane shrugged. "I had a couple of questions I wanted to ask the funeral director. I was told he was also the county coroner."

"What questions?"

"Well, I wanted to know why an autopsy was never ordered."

Diana's head wobbled back ever so slightly. She regarded Jane with undisguised suspicion. "Why would they perform an autopsy?"

"As I understand it, it's generally standard in cases like this. If one had been done, any question of . . . foul play could have been ruled out."

"Foul play? You mean like—"

"Like murder," said Jane.

"Ridiculous." Diana dismissed the question and returned to the sock, holding it up again as if she'd never seen it before. "Who would want to hurt Theo? Dear Theo. Saintly Theo. Noble Theo. The little rodent."

Jane wondered if Diana was capable of a real conversation— or if she'd crossed the line into drug-induced la la land. She decided to take a chance. "Why did you have a photo of him hanging on your closet door?"

Diana's face twitched. "What?"

"You'd hung a Choice button on his chest and then stuck a knife through it."

She broke into a smile. "I did that, yes."

"Why?"

"Because it was the perfect statement."

"What does abortion rights have to do with you and Theo?"

"Abortion? No, no, Jane. Choice. That's the crux of the matter. Choice, don't you see? We rant and rave about it all the time when it comes to abortion. Choice is sacred. It's hallowed ground. We shout it from the rooftops. Why can't we see it's the same issue when it comes to other aspects of our lives? We *must* have a choice. No one should take that away from us. Not some anti-abortion group, or . . . some sleazeball with a pencil and a column in a newspaper who can, in the name of some larger purpose, ruin a person's career."

"What larger purpose?"

"The advancement of gays and lesbians, of course. Just ask

195

Theo. He said that we all have to come out of the closet. If we're invisible, then society will never realize we're just human beings like everyone else. Some of us are good, and some bad. Some rich, some poor. You've heard the arguments. But try telling that to a producer. Sometimes I think half the people in Hollywood are hiding. I suppose I could have done that too—stayed married, had a kid, denied the reports, insisted they were slander. But I couldn't. God, I was so naive. I thought I could just keep my private life *private*. Is that so much to ask? But it wasn't enough for Theo. If I didn't announce my identity on cue, if I didn't sacrifice my life on the altar of the greater good, then the rumor press starts pumping. Sooner or later, unless you live in a dark hole, they get you."

Of course, thought Jane—the light was beginning to dawn. It was that article the woman in the liquor store had mentioned. "Someone outed you?"

Diana ran a hand over her face. "Two nights after Jill died, Theo and Orson came to New York for the funeral. We were sitting in a bar, talking to this guy. I knew he was asking a lot of questions, I just never thought Theo would be so stupid as to bring up my real relationship with Jill. I'll never forgive him. Do you think I could get a part after that article appeared? I'd already left the soap. I couldn't stand the grind any more. I was up for a great role in a movie, but interestingly, it fell through. Then another, and another. Then I was offered a leading role in a Broadway show. But that went sour too. And all because of Theo. He deserved to pay for what he did. He took my life as surely as if he'd put a gun to my head."

"Bullshit." said a voice from behind them.

Both women turned to find Orson standing in the doorway. He was fully clothed and he was furious. "Theo never told that man anything."

"Of course he did," sputtered Diana. "How else did the guy know what to print?"

"You told him."

"I what?" She blinked.

"Just like always, you got drunk. But that night, you got really drunk. I knew you didn't know what you were saying. Both Theo and I hustled you out of there as fast as we could, but the die had already been cast. If you want to blame someone for the way your life has turned out, blame yourself."

She swallowed hard, picking up her drink. Her hand was shaking so badly, she nearly dropped it. "I—"

"And that play you're always whining about? It went sour because of your boozing. I talked to the director. I know."

"I beg your pardon?"

"You lost the part because you couldn't cut it. You kept forgetting your lines. Showing up late for rehearsals."

"That's not true."

"It is." He moved further into the room. "I can't listen to your self-pity any more, Diana. I've tried to be patient, but I'm just about out. I know why you were so cool to Theo the first couple of days. I'd heard your argument in New York—the one about being in or out of the closet. I knew where you both stood. And I also knew you blamed Theo for the article when it finally appeared. You couldn't find him, or you would have slit his throat. You didn't see him again until last Friday. He didn't deserve your abuse, Diana. He didn't agree with you, but he respected your privacy. That's more than I can say for you." His eyes fell to the note. "Is that Theo's handwriting?"

"Maybe. So what if it is?"

"Give it to me."

"Why? You want to read it too?" She climbed off the bed but lost her balance and crumpled to the floor.

"Christ," said Orson, bending down, "I think she's passed out." He slapped her face lightly. "She probably won't remember a word I said."

"Don't be too sure," said Jane.

Orson had already lifted her into his arms. "I better get her to bed. I'm sorry you had to see this. Don't take what she said too seriously. She'd never hurt Theo—not in the way you're thinking. She was trying to make him pay by withdrawing her love."

"Are you so sure of that?"

He looked her squarely in the eye. "I'd stake my life on it."

Curious, thought Jane. All these people were so protective of one another. Theo was dead, and even Cordelia couldn't imagine that anyone of her friends could have done it. "Do you need some help?"

"No," he muttered as he swung her out the door. "I think we all just need to get some sleep."

After they were gone, Jane stood and looked at the mess on the bed. There would be time in the morning to clean it up. Before she turned off the light, she folded Theo's letter and stuffed it into her pocket. Tomorrow, she'd give it to Curt. In the meantime, no one else should be reading it.

She felt more awake now than she had half an hour ago. Diana's revelation had been nothing less than a clear and highly charged motive for murder. But had she actually done it? In the cold light of day, had Diana wanted to get back at Theo so badly for a perceived injustice that she'd plotted his murder? Or, even more tragically, had her drinking emboldened her? Had it altered her perceptions enough so that she could give vent to a violent emotion without fully comprehending the results?

Jane mulled over these and other questions as she tiptoed down the stairs. A cup of tea was the best company when she needed to think. As she passed the parlor, she saw someone had built a fire. The room was softly aglow.

"Who's there?" said Curt, standing as he saw a shadow fall across the floor. He'd been sitting in one of the wing chairs.

"I just came down for a cup of tea."

"Couldn't sleep, huh?"

"Don't let me disturb you." She remembered the note in her pocket. "Actually, I have something that belongs to you."

He slipped his hands into the pockets of his bathrobe.

"What?"

"Diana found this in Theo's suitcase." She handed it to him. "It's a letter to you. I thought you . . . might want to have it."

He took it and unfolded the paper, holding it close to the firelight.

Jane watched as he read the first few lines. His face betrayed no emotion. "So . . . I guess that's it," she said, backing out of the room. "See you in the morning."

His eyes remained fixed on the note. Slowly, he sat back down. "Goodnight, Jane. Thanks."

29

Around four in the morning, Jane was awakened from a fitful sleep by the hum of a car motor. Rising from her bed, she stood at the window and looked down on the parking lot between the parsonage and the playhouse. No one was stirring. She counted six cars, all parked in their usual spots, all empty and dark. Perhaps the one she'd heard had been driving by on the highway, and in her sleep she'd misinterpreted the nearness of the sound. But it had seemed too loud to be such a distance away. As she looked again, searching the grounds for any sign of life, she saw a pinpoint of light wash over one of the windows in the playhouse. She held her breath. There it was again. She could feel the hairs prickle on the back of her neck. It was undoubtedly a flashlight. Someone was inside.

Jane dressed and then crept down the hall to Cordelia's room. Even though she couldn't ignore the potential danger, she had to know what was going on.

She leaned over Cordelia and gently shook her shoulder.

Cordelia groaned and turned over.

"Come on." whispered Jane, as loudly as she dared. "Wake up. You've got to help me."

Cordelia's nose twitched. "Hmm?" she said pleasantly.

Jane shook her again. "Roast goose and blueberry pie. "

"What?" An eye opened. "Repeat that."

"I said you've got to get up. Someone's broken into the playhouse. We've got to get over there—see what's going on."

Cordelia rubbed the sleep out of her eyes and then took a better look. "I don't like this dream. Go away."

"Get dressed and meet me downstairs in five minutes. I'll find a flashlight."

"Are you serious? It's the middle of the night."

"Shhh." Jane held a finger to her lips. "What's the difference? You think ten a.m. is the middle of the night."

"True. Why don't you call the police? Let them handle whatever it is."

"Two reasons. First, I'm not sure I trust the police in this town."

"Excuse me?"

"And two, if it's one of your friends over there, do you want the police to find them or do you want us to handle it?"

Cordelia pulled herself back against her pillows. "Good point. I'll be down in a jiff."

"Great. Just make sure you're quiet."

Jane and Cordelia stood in front of the playhouse, wondering what the best plan of attack was.

"First things first," said Jane, handing Cordelia the flashlight. She tried the lock. "It's open," she whispered, a note of triumph in her voice. She examined the door for signs of damage. "They had a key. I knew it."

"Kind of narrows down the number of people who could be

inside, doesn't it?" muttered Cordelia, glancing up at the tall bell tower directly above their heads. In the weak moonlight, it was a forbidding sight, an image straight out of the mind of Alfred Hitchcock.

They moved quietly into the vestibule.

"Where to now?" asked Cordelia.

"Just follow me." Jane led the way up the center aisle, remembering the path the light had taken as she'd watched it from her window. The stage was dark. As they stepped around to the back, she saw the light leading down to the basement had been turned on. She pointed to the stairs and then put a finger to her lips.

They both stood very still and listened. Sure enough, someone was moving around deep in the bowels of the building.

Cordelia mouthed, "What are they doing?"

Jane gave her a perplexed shrug, motioning her away from the stairs. "Listen," she whispered, drawing her close, "is there another way to get out of the basement?"

"There are two stairways. This one, and one that leads up to the vestibule."

"Right. Okay," said Jane, thinking the situation over. "Here's what we do. I'll stay here. You take the flashlight and go back to where we entered. Find a spot to hide and just wait. All I want to know is who's down there. We can figure out the why later."

"Gotcha." Cordelia turned to go but instead tripped on an electrical wire taped to the floor and caught her sleeve on the edge of a pew. The flashlight hit the ground with a crack, shattering the glass face. The light went out instantly. "Damn," she groaned.

Downstairs, the movement stopped.

"Oh, Jesus." said Cordelia. "We've got to get out of here."

Jane could hear running footsteps. "No time."

The light coming from the stairway was minimal, but it was enough for them to find their way up on stage. "This way," whispered Jane. "We can hide behind a curtain."

Cordelia brought up the rear. "I don't think so, Janey. They're pretty sheer."

"Where then?"

"Dive." Cordelia grabbed Jane's hand and dragged her behind a sofa just as the downstairs light went off.

The playhouse was plunged into total blackness.

"Our intruder probably thinks they heard a noise," whispered Jane. "They can't be sure it meant anything."

"God, I can't see a thing."

"Shhhh." Jane heard a loud creak—it sounded like it was above them, but far away, towards the back of the theatre.

Suddenly, the amber stage lights were switched on. Jane felt a searing pain in her eyes. She was momentarily blinded by the intense brightness. "Stay down," she whispered to Cordelia.

More lights were switched on. Red. Blue. It was like a Christmas light show, only orchestrated by a madman.

"How is this happening?" she asked, shielding her eyes as they tried to adjust.

"Someone's in the light booth," said Cordelia. She was lying flat on the floor, her legs sticking out at least two feet from the end of the couch. Clearly, they'd picked a lousy place to hide. "You enter the light booth from the basement. I forgot about that."

More creaking.

"What are we going to do?" asked Cordelia. "I feel confident we've been noticed."

Jane glared at her. "How the hell should I know?" She peaked up over the cushions. All she could see beyond the stage lights was blackness. Summoning all her courage, she called, "We know you're out there."

"Oh, great," shrieked Cordelia, covering her head with a couch pillow. "If you can't intimidate them, kill them with comedy."

"Stick a sock in it." Jane was at a loss. "If they were going to hurt us," she whispered, "they would have done it by now."

"You mean, if they have a gun."

Jane could feel the adrenaline pumping. "Can we talk?" she called, inching away from the non-safety of the sofa. She didn't know what else to say.

The theatre remained silent.

"Try, *let's do lunch*," whispered Cordelia.

"Shut up," barked Jane. She walked to the edge of the stage. "I know you're there. You obviously know we're here. What do you want? What are you doing here in the middle of the night?"

Cordelia's head popped up. She scrambled to her feet. "If it's insomnia, we totally understand. We wouldn't blame you in the least."

Just as quickly as the lights had gone on, they were turned off. Jane could hear a door open. Then, movement in the darkness. Footsteps.

Cordelia found Jane's arm. She held on for dear life. "Let's get out of here," she pleaded.

"You got it." Together, they inched their way to the side stairs and climbed down. Jane knew the pews started a few yards to their left. The basement stairs were farther around the back of the stage to their right. Perhaps they'd lost their pursuer in the darkness.

Suddenly, every light in the theatre went on. Bells began ringing out the hymn, "Blest Be the Tie that Binds." It was so loud, Jane covered her ears.

Cordelia pointed to the ceiling. "It's a recording," she shouted. "It's hooked up to a loudspeaker in the bell tower. Diana showed me the first day I was here."

Remembering the danger they were in, Jane crept a few paces farther into the main hall, her eyes searching the room. Seeing no one, she walked slowly down the aisle, glancing both left and right, making sure no one was hiding in the seats. As she got to the back, she bumped smack into Annie who was just coming through the door.

"What's going on?" she shouted above the pealing bells. They were now well into the second stanza of the hymn.

Cordelia rushed up behind them and threw herself into a pew. "I just checked out the basement. As I suspected, it's empty. And," she bellowed, in as confidential a tone as the noise would allow, "I didn't see anything unusual."

Annie looked confused.

"Out for a late night walk?" hollered Cordelia.

"No," she replied, a bit indignantly. "I was downstairs in the kitchen getting a glass of milk when I saw the stage lights come on over here. I wondered what the hell was going on."

"Kind of a dangerous thing to do on your own," shouted Jane. "Why?"

"We could have been burglars."

"Doing what? Reciting Hamlet? If you were stealing something, why turn on all the stage lights?" After a rather grand yet flat Amen, the bells stopped, the last note lingering in the air like an electrical buzz.

Orson and Curt burst through the front door. Both men were in their pajamas, each wearing a plaid bathrobe.

"It's the MacPhersons." cried Cordelia.

"What's going on?" demanded Orson.

Jane slumped into the pew. What a night. "It's a long story."

"I don't doubt that." He put his hands on his hips. "Well?"

"Don't you appreciate religious music?" asked Cordelia, standing and putting her arm around his shoulder. "A tinkling canticle. A reverent little *pastorale*. Pity. I felt, under the circumstances, that our intruder's musical choice was quite . . . interesting. 'Blest Be the Tie that Binds.' The arch of her eyebrow was pregnant with meaning.

Orson glared. "What intruder?"

Jane knew she had to explain. "It's very simple," she began. "The sound of a car motor woke me about four, so I got up and looked outside. I didn't see anyone, but I noticed a light in the theatre. Cordelia and I came over to check it out."

"And what did you find?" asked Curt.

"Someone was in the basement. We could hear movement."

Curt and Orson exchanged glances.

"But then Cordelia dropped our flashlight and the culprit must have heard."

"That's right. Blame me." She gave an indignant sniff.

"We tried to hide on stage, but the stage lights came on. After a minute or two, they went back off. I didn't know what to do. Cordelia and I were trying to get out when those bells started playing."

"And what about you, Annie?" asked Curt.

"Well, I saw the stage lights go on and came over to see what was going on. I guess I thought it might be Diana, giving an unscheduled performance."

He gave her a hard stare.

Orson looked carefully around the playhouse. "I think it's fair to conclude that whoever was in here is long gone by now. I suggest we all get back to the parsonage and try to salvage what's left of our night's sleep."

"Maybe I should look around the basement first," offered Curt. "I already did," said Cordelia. "Nothing was out of place."

Everyone seemed a bit uneasy, but resigned to the situation.

Following Annie and Curt, Jane and Cordelia trudged wearily across the damp lawn. "I wonder who would know how to run those stage lights," she whispered.

"It's not hard," replied Cordelia. "Everything's labeled."

Not the answer she wanted. "What about the bells?"

"Those are controlled by a panel in the basement. Anyone with some electrical knowledge could do it. You can even put them on a time switch. Diana showed me. She wanted to keep the system intact—she thought she might be able to put it to some use."

Someone sure did a few minutes ago, thought Jane. It was a memorable way to begin a day. The sun would be up in less than an hour. Unless she was sadly mistaken, the bell incident had a distinctly theatrical smell about it. Unfortunately, that realization narrowed her list of possible suspects by exactly zero.

30

Curt crouched next to the rear wall of the parsonage, smoking a joint. The funeral was at three—several hours away. If he ever needed a mellow buzz, it was this morning. He took another toke, watching the huge, puffy clouds float across the sky. A crow sat on one of the tallest gravestones, surveying the graveyard with a wary eye. All in all, it was another beautiful day.

Receiving that note from Theo late last night had really thrown him. It was like reading a letter from a ghost, not that Theo hadn't already felt like a ghost more than once. Curt hadn't said anything to Annie about it, knowing it would only upset her. On the subject of Theo, she had long ago ceased to be rational. Curt couldn't blame her. She'd put up with a lot.

Yet, in Theo's own convoluted and cryptic way, Curt felt he'd finally said something real. That letter was his first genuinely honest attempt at addressing the past and assessing the present. Great timing, now that there was no chance of continuing the conversation. Still, even though what he'd said was incomplete, interestingly, by mentioning the story of Beau Geste, Theo may have given away more than he'd intended. That intriguing aside had occupied all Curt's thoughts since he'd read it. He hadn't come to any conclusions yet, but he was working on it.

"I thought I smelled weed," declared Amity, breezing around the end of the house. She had a small CD player hooked to her belt. A pair of earphones hung around her neck.

For an instant, Curt considered dropping the joint between his legs, but knew it was useless. "You caught me." He gave a weak smile.

"Yeah, well. I guess that makes you a bad influence."

"I guess."

"Just like every other adult."

"I'm . . . not perfect."

"I know. Neither am I." She sat down cross-legged on the grass in front of him. "So what's up?"

"Not much."

She picked up a rock and flipped it from one hand to the other.

"No school today?"

"Annie got me a reprieve because of the funeral."

He nodded. "What are you listening to?" He nodded to the CD.

"Soul Asylum."

"Umm."

"You a fan?"

"Not really." He took another toke. "You know, it's funny. Sometimes I get really down on myself because I think I'm stuck in the past. But, in some ways, all adults are stuck there. Take music. I thought I'd always be up on what was new. I love rock, or at least I used to. But after I turned thirty-five, it was like I fell off a cliff. All I ever listen to now are oldies. The Stones, The Who, Fleetwood Mac, Jethro Tull, The Doors, all the old bands. I wouldn't know Soul Asylum if they walked up and bit me in the ass. Uh . . . sorry."

"Don't patronize me, Curt. I know what an ass is."

He let some ash drop to the ground.

"Maybe you need someone to help you," she said.

"Help me how?"

"Get unstuck."

He smiled. God, she was a great kid. He was sick to think what would happen to her if she stayed with Diana. Not that she *could* stay here. He knew Diana loved Amity, but right now, she wasn't capable of being a parent. If Diana did consent to go into treatment, then Amity would have to find a temporary home. She couldn't go back to her grandparents house. They didn't want her. That left what? A foster family? The streets?

"Sure," replied Amity. "I could give you a list. Let you borrow some of my CDs. I'm sure in, say, a month or two, I could bring you up to speed."

He smiled. "That's a tall order."

"Nah. No problem. You just need to loosen up a little. Relax. Try something new. You and Annie'd get along a lot better if you did." She tossed the rock over her shoulder. "She's a neat lady."

"You think so?"

"Absolutely."

"She likes you too."

"Really?"

"We both do."

Amity's face flushed. "How come you never had any kids?"

"I don't have a good answer for that." He stared at the burning tip of his joint, thinking back to the times he and Annie had talked about having children. "I guess we just never got around to it. We both like kids."

"You think you're too old now?"

"Yeah. Well . . . I don't know, maybe."

"For a baby, you mean."

He glanced at her.

She stretched out on her back. "Do you ever just like to sit and watch clouds?"

"That's what I was doing before you came."

"Funny. You looked more like you were worrying."

"I did?"

"Something on your mind?"

"Well sort of."

"Wanna talk about it?" She brushed a fly away from her face.

Curt looked at his watch. They still had plenty of time before the funeral. "You want to hear a story?"

"What kind of story?"

"It's about three young men."

"I prefer stories about young women."

He laughed. "Try to cope." Sitting down on the ground, he fished a roach clip out of his pocket. He carefully pinched the end of the joint and took another toke. "Okay, here's the story. These three young men were brothers. They lived in England back in the late eighteen hundreds. Michael was the oldest. People called him Beau because he was beautiful and had a noble heart. He had a twin brother named Digby and a younger brother named John. They lived with a very kind woman who had befriended them as children. She was quite rich, though unhappily married. One day, Beau learns something about this woman. Something he keeps a secret for many years. When he and his brothers are fully grown, a priceless jewel is stolen from the woman's house. No one knows who's done it—or why. But Beau disappears late one night, leaving a note behind that says he's guilty. He's taken the jewel and gone off to join the French Foreign Legion. The next morning, Digby is found missing. Another note is discovered. In it, Digby says he can't let his brother take the blame for something he did. He took the jewel, and he's also left to join the Foreign Legion. That evening, John doesn't show up for dinner."

"Another letter's found."

"Right. From John saying he can't let his brothers take the blame for what he's done. He took the jewel and he's off to—"

"Join the Foreign Legion."

210

"Exactly."

"So who stole the jewel?"

"We don't find that out until the very end. But the point is, Beau is the only one who knows for sure what really happened. And he willingly sacrifices his life to protect someone he loves."

"He dies?"

"Yes," said Curt, his voice soft. "He does."

"That's very sad. And kind of romanticized."

"I agree."

"But it sounds like a great story. So tell me what happened."

He shook his head. "No, I think you should read the book yourself."

"Do you have a copy?"

"At home in Chicago. It was Theo's favorite."

She closed her eyes. "It's sort of like you and Orson and Theo. You were like brothers."

"We were."

"And one of you died."

He nodded.

"Did he die to protect someone he loved?"

"I don't know," said Curt, his eyes returning to the clouds. "But I intend to find out."

31

Jane stood with the rest of the group crowding silently around Theo's grave. As the minister intoned a final prayer, a small casket containing Theo's cremated remains was lowered into the ground. Everyone's head was bowed. Diana was leaning on Cordelia's arm. Curt, Annie and Amity stood next to her. Peppered among the assemblage were the members of the Summer Green Playhouse. Hilda stood with James Donati and his wife. And Orson stood alone, off to the side, his eyes wet with tears.

Jane carefully watched the faces of those who had come. In each she saw a reflection of the pain of human loss—each, that is, except for one. Strange that no one else seemed to notice. Perhaps she was misreading the situation, but she didn't think so. She had to be careful. She didn't want to be caught staring.

"Into the depths," lamented the minister. He must like that phrase, thought Jane. It was the fourth time he'd used it. She tuned him out, thinking instead about the last few hours. It had been a trying morning. Orson had awakened Diana at ten, insisted she shower and dress, and then he'd stood over her while she ate some lunch. No alcohol had been allowed. He'd blustered around the house saying he knew he was being controlling, but he didn't care. He wasn't going to allow anyone to ruin Theo's funeral. Diana did look a bit better than she had yesterday, but only slightly.

"Holy Father," said the minister, raising his voice as he looked up, his eyes still closed, "we commend our loved one's spirit into your hands." He paused dramatically. "Amen."

"Amen," repeated the crowd.

Jane breathed a sigh of relief. The service was finally over. Without being directed, Diana bent down and picked up some dirt. Leaning over the hole, she let it slip from her fingers, watching as the wind carried some of it away while the rest drifted onto the beautifully polished wood. Then, standing back, she allowed others to take their turn, ending with Curt.

Finally, Annie stepped out of the crowd and invited everyone back to the parsonage for coffee and cake. "I'm told it's a custom around here," she said, smiling sadly. "And we mustn't break tradition."

The crowd began to drift toward the house.

"Well," said John Hubble, emerging out of the group and walking up to Jane, "Another beautiful day in Summer Green. Too bad it had to be such a sad one."

She was about to answer when a thought occurred to her. "Say that again."

"Pardon me?"

"About the weather."

He cocked his head. "I said it was another beautiful day."

She gave a slow nod. "Right. It was, wasn't it." She looked away, trying to pull it all together in her mind.

"Actually, except for the day of the picnic, the weather around here's been nearly perfect for several weeks."

"Is that right?"

He watched her. "Why all the interest?"

"Oh . . . just making conversation." She smiled. Of course. Why hadn't she seen it before. Then again, this wasn't the kind of clue on which to base an entire theory, but it was something.

"Well, if I may be so bold as to change the subject—that is, unless you want to discuss corn prices. Or radish futures."

Again, she smiled.

"That was too bad about Diana's portrait yesterday. Have they found it yet?"

He adjusted his tie. "No. Orson called the police and they're checking on it. So far, nothing." Jane still wasn't sure how the theft fit into the larger picture.

"Pity." His eyes swept over the graveyard. "I was looking forward to seeing it. Well, perhaps later. Say, who's that guy talking to Orson? The one in the dark shades." He pointed to an oak about thirty yards away. "I've seen him before, I just can't place the face."

Jane held her breath. It was the bald man. "I don't know."

John shrugged. "Well, it's probably none of my business. Unless he's a theatre critic, that is." He gave a small wink.

"I don't think so."

"Are you coming over to the parsonage for cake?"

"In a few minutes."

"Okay. I'll leave you to your private thoughts. By the way, I'm very sorry about your friend, Theo."

"Thanks."

He set off toward the house. Jane wished she could hear the conversation Orson was having with the bald man. Then again, she knew it might be dangerous to intrude. Before she could formulate a plan, she saw Cordelia trudging across the lawn, heading straight for her.

"Diana's finally settled in the living room," she announced, slightly out of breath. "Annie and I saw to it that she got the chair that was most thronelike. She's having a pretty awful time of it."

I'm sorry," said Jane, her voice distracted. Every now and then she would sneak a peak at the distant conversation.

"I've never seen her take something this hard. I wish I understood why she had that picture of Theo in her room. It might explain some of this."

Jane cleared her throat. "Well, actually, she was angry at him because she thought he'd given some personal information to the guy who then outed her in a New York magazine."

Cordelia's eyes grew large. "What? You're kidding."

"Afraid not."

She placed an indignant hand on her hip. "Excuse me, but did I miss something here? How did you find *that* out?"

"Diana told me."

"Is that right. She just tapped you on the shoulder and said, by the way Jane dear, Theo's a snitch."

"Not exactly. I found her going through Theo's things late last night. She was packing them for James. She was pretty drunk, and she just started talking about it."

"Really. How fortuitous."

"Except, Theo didn't do it."

In a very teacherly voice Cordelia asked, "And how do we know that, Jane dear?"

"Orson said so. He was there the night it supposedly happened. Theo never said a thing to the guy. Diana did."

"I beg your pardon? Diana outed herself?"

"She'd had so much to drink, she didn't realize what she was saying—or, more importantly, who she was saying it to."

"How did Orson get into this discussion last night?"

"He must have heard us talking. When we got to the part about Theo and the outing incident, he walked into the room and informed Diana that she was wrong. He was furious."

"This all happened while I was asleep?"

Jane nodded.

"That should teach me to go to bed with the farm animals— figuratively speaking, of course. Janey, what are you looking at?"

215

Cordelia turned to see Orson walking the bald man back to his car. "Hey, there's that guy."

"I think we should leave it alone."

"Not on your life," she growled, stomping away without so much as a backward glance.

"Wait," called Jane, but it was too late. She'd already caught up with them. Jane rushed to her side, hoping that she could temper any angry outburst.

"What the hell are you doing at this funeral?" demanded Cordelia, raising herself up to her nearly six foot height.

Orson took hold of her arm. "This is a private conversation, Cordelia. Please leave us alone."

She ignored him. "Who are you?"

Very calmly the man answered, "A friend of Theo's. Just like you. "

"I doubt that."

"I knew him many years ago, Ms. Thorn."

"Hey. How come you know my name? I don't know yours."

He turned to Orson. "I need to be going. Once again, thank you for your time, Mr. Albern. Please extend my heartfelt sympathies to the Donati family."

"I will," said Orson, still holding Cordelia's arm.

As he walked away, Cordelia wrenched it free. "Who is he?" she demanded.

Orson waited. When he saw the man get into his car he heaved a deep sigh. "He's a judge."

"A judge. From where?"

"Chicago."

"How does he know Theo?"

"I don't know."

"I don't believe you."

Orson drew a heavy hand across his eyes. "That's your privilege."

"Did he have something to do with Theo's death?"

He gave her a hard look.

"Answer me."

Orson started to speak, but then stopped himself.

"Well?"

"Just leave it alone, Cordelia."

"How can you ask that?"

"I can't tell you anything else."

"You mean you won't."

Again, he sighed. "I've got to get back to the parsonage. See how Diana's doing."

"She's fine."

"I doubt that."

They stared at each other.

"All right," said Cordelia, folding her arms over her chest, "Just tell me this much. He wasn't Theo's friend, was he?" She waited.

Orson looked at Jane and then at the hearse which had brought the casket over from the mortuary. "No," he said finally. "He wasn't." In the bright afternoon light, his face looked ashen, his body drained of all energy. "I'm sorry. That's all I can say." Unbuttoning the top button of his shirt and loosening his tie, he walked off toward the parsonage.

"He's exhausted," said Jane.

Cordelia nodded, then exploded. "God, I wish I knew what was going on around here." She flung her arms in the air. "What the hell do you make of that bald guy?"

"He's dangerous."

"Is that a theory or a fact?"

"Both, I suppose."

Cordelia stood for a moment, looking toward Theo's grave. Men were already at work shoveling dirt into the hole. "Am I crazy for thinking someone might have murdered him?"

"We'll know before we leave."

"How can you be so sure?"

"Just trust me," said Jane.

She shook her head. "Somebody's lying."

"No, Cordelia." She lowered her voice. "Somebody's acting."

217

32

Jane sat in one of the four white wicker rockers on the porch and watched two cars pull out of the parking lot. The sun was finally setting on a very long and sad day. After the funeral, James had mentioned again how much he wanted to talk to Theo's friends—reminisce about old times. Diana suggested they do it over a pitcher of beer at Al's Roadhouse. Since no one wanted to make a scene, everyone had agreed. Jane had begged off, saying she wanted to get to bed early. The truth was, since she hadn't known Theo all that well, she felt like a fifth wheel. And also, she had some matters she wanted to check on while there was still time.

After the intervention tomorrow morning, if all went as planned, Cordelia was going to fly back to Minnesota with Diana and the psychologist. Jane was to drive Cordelia's car back to Minneapolis. Orson was staying on in Summer Green for a while to make sure everything ran smoothly at the playhouse. Diana's understudy would have to be ready to go on starting Thursday night. A press release would need to be issued about the reason for Diana's untimely absence from the production. With the exception of Cordelia, no one was more qualified than Orson to take care of such matters. And Annie and Curt were heading back to Chicago. Whatever Jane determined was necessary to finally get to the truth behind Theo's death, it would have to happen before tomorrow afternoon. There wasn't much time left to decide on a course of action.

The first order of business was a long distance call to Houston, Texas. If she was lucky, she had just enough time before the end of the business day to call Theo's place of employment. There were a couple of questions she wanted to ask.

As she entered the house, she could see Hilda bustling about in the kitchen, cleaning up the coffee and cake dishes. Jane grabbed the cordless phone from the foyer and sat down in the parlor. She retrieved a slip of paper from her pocket—the one on which she'd written some notes about Theo. She got the number of Blandin Builders from Texas directory assistance. After dialing, a woman's voice answered, "Blandin Builders. How may I direct your call?"

"Hello. My name is Jane Lawless. First of all, are you a construction company?"

"Yes ma'am."

"Great. Okay, I'm calling for Mr. Rob Wilson." That had been Theo's alias.

"Just a minute."

Jane was put on hold. She drummed her fingers on the arm of the chair and waited.

After several seconds the woman returned. "I'm sorry, Mr . . . Wilson no longer works here."

"Really? As of when?"

"I can't say."

"Is there anyone there who can say?"

"Just a minute."

She was put on hold again.

Finally, a male voice answered. "This is Fred. Can I help you?"

"I hope so. My name is Jane Lawless. I'm a friend of Rob Wilson's. I was told he no longer works for you."

"That's right."

"Was there some problem?"

"No. "

"Do you know why he quit?"

"I'm sorry. I don't."

"Can I ask what he did at Blandin Builders?"

"Sure. He was an estimator. Went out and gave bids on various jobs."

"How long had he worked there?"

"Sorry, but that's all I can tell you. If you need further information, I suggest you write to our personnel office."

"Thanks," said Jane. She knew this was all she was going to get. "I appreciate your time."

"No problem." He hung up. When Jane had seen the name Blandin Builders on the death certificate, her immediate reaction was that a job in construction was a poor choice for a man with a heart condition. But if he'd been an estimator, major physical exertion probably wasn't part of it. So, it fit. He could have been ill and still employed there. Yet she knew she'd been lied to. What wasn't she being told?

Returning the phone to the foyer, Jane decided it was time to have a chat with Hilda. She walked back to the kitchen. As she came through the door she saw a bowl of radishes sitting on the counter next to a salt shaker. In between wiping plates, Hilda would select one, salt it and pop it into her mouth. So much for local idiosyncrasies.

"Can I help you with anything?" asked Jane, moving to the center island and pouring herself a cup of coffee.

Hilda turned, surveying her visitor. "Nope. I'm almost done." As she returned her attention to the sink, the phone rang. "I'll get it," she said, wiping her hands on a kitchen towel. She picked up the receiver. "Stanwood residence." She leaned against the counter. "No, sorry Mrs. Albern. Orson isn't here right now. Would you like to leave a message?" A pause. "Fine. I'll tell him you called. Goodbye." She dropped it back on the hook. "That woman calls here every day. You'd think she doesn't trust the man."

Jane let that pass. "I don't know if you remember my name. I'm Jane Lawless."

"I know who you are." She began wiping off the large coffee urn that had been used in the dining room. "All you people say you're Diana's friends. Well, if you ask me, you're pretty miserable excuses."

Jane sipped her coffee. "I understand your feelings. You like Diana, don't you?"

An eyebrow raised over an eagle eye. "And why not? She's a fine woman. Has a good heart. And talk about talent? Why she could act circles around any of you."

"I don't doubt it."

"I've been here ever since she came, and let me tell you that woman's in trouble. I've tried to help. I've even hid the booze. Watered it down whenever I could. But nothing works. You people've got to do something. But all you've brought is your own kind of trouble."

"What do you mean?"

"I see what's going on around here."

"Can you be more specific?"

"No." She walked back to the sink.

Jane decided to try another approach. "The night Theo died, did you notice anything unusual?"

"Like what?"

"I don't know. What about the wine he was drinking. Do you know what happened to it?"

She shrugged. "Your friend Cordelia asked me the same question. Maybe Diana took it upstairs with her, although I know she hates sweet wine. She ordered it especially for Mr. Donati."

"You didn't see anyone with the bottle before dinner?"

She shook her head. "That night was a blur. Diana was angry about something. She wouldn't say what. Before dinner, she'd called down for another bottle of vodka. A bad sign. Then, at dinner, your friend Theo had his heart attack." She put a thoughtful finger to her chin. "Come to think of it, I did notice something kind of strange."

"What?"

"Well, as they were leaving in the ambulance, I walked out on the porch. No sooner had they headed up the highway than this car pulled over the rise and proceeded to follow them. Not too close, you understand, but close enough."

"What kind of car?"

"It was a Cadillac. White. I'd seen it a couple of nights before just sitting across the road."

The judge, thought Jane. He was obviously keeping a very close watch on the house. "One more question. Does Diana get the local newspaper?"

"Sure does."

"I suppose you've thrown all the recent ones out."

"No. I save them. Everything that hasn't been burned is in a kindling box next to the fireplace."

"Great," said Jane. "Thanks."

"What do you want them for?"

"Oh, I just thought it might be interesting to read up on the local news."

Hilda gave her an appraising look and then turned back to the sink. "You people kill me, you really do."

33

After searching out the newspapers and confirming what she had already suspected, Jane stepped onto the porch once again for a breath of fresh air. She was close to the truth now. For the first time since coming to Summer Green, she could allow herself a moment to relax. She loved being in the country. Except for the hum of crickets, she couldn't hear a sound. No airplanes or freeway noise interrupted her thoughts. Perhaps someday she'd retire to her parents' cabin on Blackberry Lake. Spend her later years surrounded by a comfortable solitude. But that was a long way off. And even then, she knew another part of her would miss the familiarity of the Twin Cities—the bustle of Uptown, the popcorn stand at Lake Harriet, the Como Park Conservatory, her favorite bookstore and coffee house. So many conflicting feelings were at war inside her. She wondered if it had been like that for Theo. From what she'd found out, he'd been a man of many faces. But only one of them could be real.

At the sound of giggling, Jane turned. Inside Cordelia's car she could see movement—two heads bobbing up and down and laughing. She climbed down off the porch and crossed to the parking lot. Sure enough, Amity and Chickie Johnson were in the front seat. They were having such a good time, they didn't even see her walk up—until it was too late. An open wine bottle sat in the seat between them. Jane recognized it as one of Diana's. She rapped on the window.

Both kids froze.

"Uh . . . Jane," said Amity, rolling down the window. Her smile was something less than confident.

Jane could smell cigarettes. Cordelia would be hysterical. "Good evening."

"Hi." She swallowed hard. "See . . . Chickie and I were just—"

"Can I talk to you for a minute?" asked Jane. She motioned for her to get out.

"Uhm . . . sure." She didn't look particularly thrilled. Slamming the door behind her, she squared her shoulders, bracing herself for the worst. "What can I do for you?"

"First, I think you and Chickie should find someplace else to smoke."

"I don't smoke," said Amity, a bit indignantly. "And, you're right. I'll tell him to beat it."

"Second, where did you get the wine?"

"Well, I, ah . . . borrowed it."

"Borrowed?"

"You're probably not going to believe this, but I don't drink either."

"But Chickie does."

"Right."

"Kind of a mass of bad habits, isn't he?"

"Yeah. Kind of."

"He does drugs too?"

"Well—"

"Do you do drugs?"

"Certainly not."

"Kind of hard not to when your friends do them."

She nodded weakly. "But he quit."

"Really? Why?"

"Well . . . something happened. Something bad."

"Like what?"

She drew Jane further away from the car. "He's trying to go straight. You understand." She gave Jane a knowing nod.

"You make him sound like he's done hard time. Amity, he's only fourteen."

"So?"

Jane realized she was far too removed from teenage life to approach this rationally. It was best to let Amity do the talking. "What happened?"

"Do you promise not to tell?"

Jane sighed. "All right." What could the kid have done? It couldn't be that big of a deal.

"Did you hear about the church fire?" Her eyes flicked furtively to the playhouse.

Jane raised an eyebrow. "I did."

"Well, Chickie and some of his friends accidentally set it."

Jane blinked. "Are you serious?"

"Absolutely."

"Were they doing drugs?"

"Well . . . sort of. It's a long story. See, before the mall was finished, there weren't many places to go at night. And in the winter, if you wanted to keep warm, and you didn't have a car, and you didn't want to stay home—"

"They broke into the church."

"Well, not exactly. Chickie had keys. His father's a deacon. Anyway, they were inside one night . . . and they all fell asleep. Chickie said a velvet pew pad caught fire. But see, they couldn't tell their parents. Chickie's been totally freaked ever since it happened. He's sure someone's going to send him to reform school."

"Reform school."

"Sure. Anyway, he stopped doing the drugs. Now he just

smokes . . . and, well, drinks a little wine every now and then. He's going to stop smoking next week."

"Do tell."

"Look, I know he's kind of a mess, but he's my friend. I don't see that there's any difference between him and Diana. They both got problems, but that doesn't mean we should push them away—refuse to love them."

She had a point. "Let me ask you something. The night Theo died, did you take a bottle of wine off the dining room table?"

She lowered her eyes. "Yeah. I did. For Chickie, though, not for me. He gets super stressed sometimes."

"And you sat in Cordelia's car that night, just like tonight."

"Yup."

"Did he drink it all?"

She nodded.

"Did he feel sick afterwards?"

"Come on, Jane. There was less than a third of the bottle left. That's why I chose it."

"And he never felt sick?"

"Not that I know of. He's sort of the original chronic whiner, if you know what I mean. If he'd started to feel crummy, I would have heard about it."

Jane gave her a serious look. "All right. But you two've got to leave Cordelia's car alone. And the rest in the lot as well."

"No problem. We're history." She ducked back inside the car and yanked Chickie out. "I'll be back in a few minutes."

"All right," said Jane, taking the bottle from Chickie's hand. She watched them as they ran around to the other side of the parsonage. Well, she thought, shaking her head, so no one had tampered with the wine. It was just as she'd suspected. Tomorrow, if everything went as planned, she would be able to put the last pieces in place. And then she'd have to explain everything to Cordelia.

That, in the end, might be the hardest part.

34

The day of the intervention had finally come. Jane headed downstairs, knowing she had less than fifteen minutes before the psychologist arrived. The tension in the house was as thick as a Lake Superior fog. She wondered if Diana could feel it.

As she walked into the foyer, she saw that Annie was in the kitchen, sitting at the center island with a cup of coffee. She was going over some notes. Curt was doing the same, only he was in the parlor with a glass of orange juice. Orson was reading the newspaper in the dining room, and Cordelia was pacing on the front porch, waiting to intercept the doctor. Lastly, Diana was in her room, upstairs, preparing herself for what she thought was the final breakfast before everyone left for home.

As Jane stood alone in the quiet house, she knew one of four people held the answer she'd come all the way from Minneapolis to find. It was now or never. Glancing again in each direction, she walked resolutely into the dining room. Orson looked up as she took a seat next to him.

"Morning," he mumbled.

"Good morning," she said, keeping her voice low.

"We need to talk."

He put down the paper. "About what?"

"Theo."

He gave an exasperated sigh. "Do you realize what's happening this morning?"

"I know the psychologist will be here any minute. I'm willing to wait until after the intervention. But as soon as it's over, we have to talk."

"I have nothing to say to you." He started to rise.

"All right. That's your privilege. But if I don't speak to you, I'm going to speak to the police—and I don't mean the police in Summer Green. I'm talking about the police in Green Bay, Orson. I think they'll be very interested in what I have to tell them."

Slowly, he sat back down. "Why are you doing this?" His expression was a strange mixture of anger and caution.

"You know why. Cordelia asked me here to see if I could shed some light on Theo's death. And that's what I've done."

He ran a shaky hand over his forehead. "How much . . . do you think you know?"

"Enough to make your friend the judge very upset."

"He's not my friend."

"I know."

He tapped his fingers nervously on the table. "What do you want?"

"The entire story."

"You don't know what you're asking."

She looked him square in the eye. "I'm asking for the truth, Orson."

He stared at her a moment and then looked down, laughing bitterly. "I haven't told the truth in so many years, I'm not even sure I'd know where to start."

"Start with the body that was stolen from the cemetery when

you were a college student."

His head snapped up. "What do you know about that?"

"I know it's where this all started. But I don't know why."

He held her eyes. "You think you're pretty smart."

"Yes," she said. "Smart enough."

The sound of voices broke their concentration. Cordelia and the psychologist had just entered the parlor.

Orson rose quickly.

"So," said Jane. "Do I talk to you or do I talk to the police?"

He hesitated. "All right. After this is all done, I'll meet you out on the porch."

"Fine."

Diana appeared in the foyer, all decked out in a cashmere sweater and gray wool slacks. "Who's that?" she asked, seeing the stranger. She turned to Orson for an explanation.

In an instant, Orson was by her side, his arm around her shoulders giving them a protective squeeze. "Diana," he said, his manner sober and yet very gentle, "I'd like you to meet Dr. Bernson."

"*Doctor*?" She scowled.

Orson maneuvered her into the parlor and saw to it that she got a comfortable chair.

"My name is Lynn Bernson," said the doctor. "I'm a family therapist from Minneapolis, and I work with families all over the country. Your friends asked me here today to facilitate a family meeting. They're concerned about you, Diana, and they didn't know how to handle it. That's why I'm here."

Diana froze. "Is it about my—" She looked from face to face, her manner growing tentative. "—drinking? Because if it is, I suppose . . . I owe all of you an apology. I've behaved badly these last couple of days. But it was because of Theo. You all know that. A drink calms me down. It's going to change now, I promise. And besides, I don't always drink this much. It's just . . . the stress."

The room was silent.

"Diana," said Orson, sitting down next to her, "since we've

been here, we've all done a lot of reminiscing. It struck me last night when we were talking to Theo's brother, how many of our stories are colored by your drinking."

"That's not true."

"It is," said Orson, his voice firm. "The first night we were here, Annie brought up that time in college when we all went sledding. Do you remember?"

Hesitantly, she nodded.

"You nearly landed in the river. The day could easily have ended in tragedy."

"But I didn't know how to steer my sled, Orson. That's all. Why are you making such a big deal out of it?"

"It was a big deal, Diana. And it had nothing to do with steering the sled. You'd brought a flask with you. Everyone saw it, but like always, we ignored it. Or maybe we thought it was cool—dangerous. We were young and we took chances. Some of us did it one way—" He paused. "You did it with booze."

"So?" Her body grew rigid.

"You don't get that many chances in life, Diana. And you've just about used yours up."

"We all have stories we want to tell you," said Annie. "Please, if our friendship means anything to you, you've got to listen."

"This is a trap," said Diana indignantly.

As Curt shut the double front doors, Jane could hear Cordelia say, "I suppose, in a way, it is. But we just can't leave you here, knowing that—" Her voice grew very gentle. "You're drowning, dearheart. We've got to try to get you to see that. And also . . . that there's hope."

Jane stuffed both hands deep into the pockets of her jeans and walked out onto the porch. She stood for a moment looking at the marigolds which lined the sidewalk all the way to the house. She'd heard enough about Dr. Bernson's style to know the intervention wouldn't include angry confrontation. This meeting, even though painfully honest, would be full of love. Jane hoped it could work. Yet even if Diana consented to go into treatment, that was only the beginning. Jane felt that, deep down, Diana knew her life was hanging by a thread. She wanted help, she just didn't know how to get it. What her friends were asking of her now was to take a hard road, but one that, in the end, would give her back her life.

Jane turned as Hilda came around the side of the house. She had a shovel over one shoulder and was carrying a basket of freshly dug potatoes. As she stepped up on the porch, Jane nodded a good morning.

"Well," said Hilda, setting down the basket, "you people finally did something. It sure took you long enough."

"It was all planned from the beginning."

"That right." She took off her gardening gloves and shoved them into the back pocket of her overalls. "Well, let's just pray this doctor of yours knows what she's doing. Annie seemed pretty high on her."

"You talked to Annie about the intervention?"

"This morning. Just after dawn. I was making muffins."

Jane nodded.

"Well, anyway, I got to change my clothes. I promised I'd help Amity pack."

"Where's she going?"

"Back to Chicago with Curt and Annie. They're taking care of her until Diana gets on her feet. Then they can all have a powwow about her future. If you ask me, I think the Whittigs would like to keep her permanently."

Jane smiled at the thought.

"Oh," said Hilda, her hand on the screen door. "And one more thing. If you're looking for that oil portrait of Diana, I've got it."

"You what?"

"I took one look at it and decided that artist was just plain mean. It was the last thing Diana needed. She already thinks she's over the hill—a lot of crap, if you ask me."

"How did you do it?"

"I took it Monday morning. When I was setting up the buffet

table. I hid it in the basement. I know that old church like the back of my hand, I even used to run the bells for our pastor. I came back to get it that night—I thought I'd store it in my garage and hope some water dripped on it. That's when I ran into you and Cordelia. Sorry about the light show, but I had to remove the evidence without being caught. I mean, I didn't want to get arrested or anything, I just wanted to keep Diana from being hurt."

"You're a good friend." Jane was touched by the woman's gruff kindness.

"So, if you want it, it's over at my place."

"Thanks."

"Don't mention it. If it was up to me, I'd sell it at a garage sale."

Jane grinned. "I'll pass along your suggestion."

"You do that." She disappeared inside the house, leaving Jane alone with her thoughts.

35

Cordelia was the first to emerge from the parlor a little less than three hours later. She saw Jane sitting on the porch and immediately came outside. "She's agreed to go." Her tone was a mixture of exhaustion and elation.

"Great. What happens next?"

"She has to pack a small suitcase and then Hilda will drive the three of us to the airport in Green Bay. I've decided to accompany Diana and the doctor. Diana asked if I would, and I couldn't say no. Anyway, we'll fly directly to Twin Cities International." She rubbed her hands together. "Mission accomplished, Janey."

"Congratulations."

"Thanks. So, what are your plans?"

"Well, I'm leaving pretty soon too. I've already got your car packed."

"What about—" She glanced back into the house.

"Theo?"

She gave a confidential nod. "You said you'd know the truth about his death before you left."

"I will."

Cordelia gave her a skeptical look. "And?"

"I haven't left yet."

"Very funny." She put a finger to her lips. "Here come the hordes. Act natural."

The door opened and out flowed Curt, Annie and Amity, each carrying a suitcase, and each with a big smile on their face. If not a happy day in the Stanwood household, this was at least a hopeful one. Cordelia gave them all a huge goodbye hug and made them promise to visit her soon. Then she begged off, saying she had to find Diana and help her pack. They had to leave for the plane in less than an hour.

Jane took Amity's suitcase and walked them to their car.

"Well," said Curt, after stuffing the cases into the trunk and shutting it with a thud, "it was good seeing you again, Jane."

Annie was helping Amity get situated in the back seat.

"Thanks. It was good seeing you too."

"Tell me something." He reached into his pocket and drew out his keys. "Do you still think one of us murdered Theo?"

Her eyes moved to the graveyard just over his shoulder. "No. I don't."

"I'm glad. None of us would ever hurt him."

"I know that now."

"Well, I guess we'd better shove off." He took one last look at the parsonage. "This has been quite a visit."

Jane could only guess at the full meaning of his words.

"You know, Theo was trying to tell me something important in the note you found in his belongings. He made a comment about the book, *Beau Geste*. It's really got me stumped. Are you familiar with the story?"

She nodded.

"I'm convinced he took some sort of secret to the grave with him. I've always felt there was something important he wasn't telling me. Truthfully, it's driven me nuts. Now, I may never know what it is."

"He probably had his reasons."

"That's just it. By mentioning that story in his note, he was telling me he had a *good* reason for not taking me into his confidence. Not that it makes it any easier." He looked off in the distance. "But, I guess learning to live with incomplete answers is all part of life."

"You may be right."

"I think I am. For now, it's enough to know that he really cared. I feel like my life has been stuck in the past far too long. I want to get on with it now."

"I envy all of you," said Jane.

"Why?"

"I think your love for each other is remarkable."

"Yeah. We're still friends after all these years, and that's a lot." He walked to the car door and opened it. "Everyone all set?"

"All ready," came Amity's eager voice from the back seat.

Curt gave Jane a wink. "She's going to help me get unstuck."

"You couldn't have picked a better person."

"I know." He grinned. Then, slipping behind the wheel, he started the motor and backed up. Everyone waved excitedly as the car sped out onto the highway and disappeared over the rise.

"Good luck," called Jane, knowing they couldn't hear. She felt a very real sadness, watching them leave.

Half an hour later, after the rest of the group had left, Jane found Orson sitting in the parlor, his body bent forward, his head resting in his hands.

"I think we're finally alone," she said, sitting down opposite him.

He didn't look up.

Jane could see he'd been crying.

"God, for a minute there, I thought Diana was going to

change her mind." He took out a handkerchief and wiped his eyes.

"But she didn't."

"No." He patted his brow. "You'll have to forgive me. This has been an emotional morning."

The phone interrupted them.

"I better get that," he said. "It's probably my wife." He rose and crossed into the foyer, picking up the receiver. "Orson Albern," he said, his voice once again completely controlled. "Yes, hi." He glanced back at Jane. "Sure, no, I'm glad you called. How's everything?" A pause. "Good. Good. What? No, not right now." Another pause. "I'll do that. Let me write it down." He found a note pad and pencil on the phone table. "Okay. Repeat that again." He scribbled quickly. "Fine. Right. I love you too, honey. Bye." He carefully folded the paper and stuffed it into his pocket. Then, returning to the parlor, he sat back down on the couch.

"How is he?" asked Jane.

His hand froze halfway to his face. "What?"

"I said, how is he?"

"How's who?"

"Theo."

"What do you mean?"

"Maybe I should ask, where is he?"

Orson remained motionless.

"I told you I knew the truth. Theo's not dead. That was him on the phone, wasn't it?"

"I—" He ran a hand through his hair.

"It's time for the truth."

"This is preposterous."

"No more than this charade, Orson. I told you, either you talk to me, or I talk to the police. It's your call."

He shot to his feet and crossed to the mantel. Keeping his back to her he asked, "How . . . I mean . . . how did you find out?"

"From the moment I got here, I knew things weren't what

236

they seemed. Someone was lying. It took me a bit longer to figure out it was an act. I just wasn't sure who was doing the acting until yesterday."

"What do you mean? What happened yesterday?"

"Your performance at the grave site, Orson. The tears. They weren't real."

He turned around, a slow smile pulling at the corners of his mouth. "You're accusing me of being a lousy actor?"

She wondered why he would find that so amusing. "I'm accusing you of feeling relieved. You thought you'd pulled it off. You were simply allowing yourself a momentary character break. That is, until the judge showed up."

The smile evaporated.

"I want the whole story, Orson. But first, I want you to say it. Theo's alive, isn't he?"

He stood with his face in profile, considering his options. Finally he said, "What I tell you has to be kept in the strictest confidence. Your life would be in danger if . . . certain people found out what you know."

"I have to tell Cordelia. That's part of the deal."

He rested an arm on the mantel. "All right. But you *must* understand the danger."

"Believe me, I do. And so will Cordelia. Whatever you tell me today will go no farther than the two of us."

He gave a slow nod.

"I know this is hard for you."

"You have no idea." He sat down wearily on the couch and took several deep breaths. Then, very slowly, he began, "Once upon a time, there were two very silly young men. One was named Orson. The other, Theo. Each thought he was the best actor the world had ever seen. To prove who was the greatest talent, a competition was devised. And thereby, Jane . . . hangs the tale."

36

The Blackburn Playhouse in Shoreview was an old log building built shortly after the end of World War II. Orson had purchased it from the Blackburn family in the early eighties, and had turned it into a thriving business. The next play on the theatre's agenda was *The Mousetrap*, by Agatha Christie.

Late the following evening, Jane drove to the deserted parking lot in back of the building and got out. The moon rose low over the wood-shingled roof. Cordelia had handled the rehearsals tonight. She'd gotten a ride out with one of the actors. Jane was supposed to pick her up afterwards and drive her back to Minneapolis.

As she entered the front door, she carefully locked it behind her. What she had to tell Cordelia must be done in absolute privacy. Cordelia had called around noon wanting to be filled in on all the details, but Jane had put her off. What she had to say had to be done in person.

She found Cordelia up on the stage, rearranging some of the props on the mantelpiece. The setting was a cozy English drawing room, complete with antique furnishings and a large, floor-to-ceiling window. On the other side of the glass, the machine that dropped the fluffy plastic snow was still on, giving the set a sense of protected warmth, even in the dead of winter. An electric fire in the fireplace cast shadows against the far wall. Above the hearth was a portrait of Agatha Christie.

Even though none of it was real, Jane was pulled in by the atmosphere. Just as she had been in Summer Green.

"Ah, you're finally here," said Cordelia, throwing herself into one of the two wing chairs on either side of the fireplace. "Just give me a minute and I'll turn everything off. Then we can leave."

"No. Leave the snow on. It's beautiful."

"I forget that you're a winter freak."

Jane smiled. "Are we alone?" She hopped up on the stage and sat down opposite Cordelia.

"That we are. Everyone took off an hour ago. It was a good run through. Orson will be pleased."

Jane made herself a bit more comfortable. "I have some things I need to tell you."

Cordelia seemed to come to life. "I should hope so." She sat up straight.

"Before we start, how's Diana doing?"

"Fine. Dr. Bernson and I got her all checked into the Institute. She'll be staying there for at least a month. On the plane ride back to Minnesota, she was pretty quiet. I started to get worried. But when we left her, she thanked us. I think she really wants to change her life. She's got a lot of work to do, but I feel the motivation is there. I promised to visit sometime next week. Orson will too, once he gets back from Summer Green."

Jane looked up at the fake snow. It was *so* convincing.

"So, give, Janey. Is it time to call the police? What happened to Theo? Did someone . . . god, I can't even say it. Did someone murder him?" Her voice was eager, yet she looked as if she was steeling herself for a blow.

On the drive home from Wisconsin, Jane had thought over what Orson had explained to her. They'd sat and talked in Diana's parlor for almost three hours. It was an incredible story. And just like Orson, she wasn't quite sure where to begin. "No, Cordelia," she said, her tone serious, "none of your friends tried to hurt him."

Cordelia let out a deep sigh. "I'm so glad. Then his death . . . it was natural."

"Well, not exactly."

She gave Jane a blank look. "Was it that judge? I could tell right off he was trouble."

"It wasn't the judge, Cordelia."

"Then who."

Jane reached for her hand. "I'm glad you're sitting down."

"Why?"

"Well, because . . . the truth is, Cordelia, there was no death. Theo's alive."

Cordelia blinked. Then she blinked again. "Repeat that?"

"It's true. He didn't die."

"That's . . . incredible." Her amazement slowly turned to joy.

"It was all an act. He faked the heart attack. The two men you saw come in the ambulance really were volunteer paramedics, but they were also Orson's friends. It was all staged."

"Staged," she repeated, still smiling. Then, "*Staged?*" Her smile gradually became clenched teeth. "This is . . . monstrous. What possible reason could they have for doing something so . . . so cruel? We've been mourning that little turd all week. And now you tell me it was just a bit of theatre. A joke?"

"Calm down, Cordelia. It was no joke. Theo's life was in danger. He didn't think he'd get out of Summer Green alive unless—"

Cordelia ignored the explanation. "All I can say is, if he thought his life was in danger before, wait until I get my hands on him."

"But he's alive. Aren't you glad?"

"What? Of course."

"Then just relax and let me tell you the whole story."

She yanked her sweater into place. "I'm completely calm."

"Good. It all began when you were in college. You remember the day Orson found that sack of bones in the back seat of his car? The remains of a body stolen from Eastwood Cemetery?"

"Of course I remember. It was the same day Theo was arrested for impersonating an IRS agent."

"Right. But, the fact of the matter is, Orson was the grave robber. He'd dug up the grave two nights before and planted the remains in his car. It was all part of a . . . competition of sorts—an acting contest between Orson and Theo. They wanted to prove once and for all who was the greatest actor. Each was to choose a situation within the larger community in which to test his skills. It had to be *real*—for real stakes. And it had to have an element of danger associated with it. If they were caught, there would be repercussions. That would only serve to heighten the tension—make it even more imperative that they give the performance of a lifetime. They were both in love with the idea. Couldn't wait to test their mettle."

"They were idiots."

"Of course they were. But they were young and—"

"Full of testosterone."

"I suppose. And as Orson was quick to point out, terribly arrogant. The rules stated that neither was to know what the other was planning. Orson acted first. And, much to his delight, he got away with it. Not only did he receive a reward for finding Edgar Collingwell's remains, but he ended up marrying his granddaughter and inheriting the man's company. But if the truth had come out early on, he would have gone to jail. And if it had come out years later, not only would he have been ruined personally, but financially."

"The only one who knew was Theo?"

"Exactly. Unfortunately, Theo hadn't made out so well. The

same day Orson turned the remains over to the police, Theo decided to try his luck impersonating an IRS agent. Everything went well at first. He'd done some studying. Thought he knew the best approach. He picked a small company in Bloomington. And he actually succeeded in intimidating the head of the firm into letting him see his books. While he was there, he called in the bookkeeper and made him explain various parts of their most recent tax statements. He was having a ball watching them sweat. He even brought along a small tape recorder which he'd concealed in his briefcase. He wanted Orson to be able to hear how well he was handling the whole affair. But he hadn't counted on one of the secretaries recognizing him. He'd been in far too many theatre productions over at the university to remain totally anonymous. After he left, the police were called. Then the FBI. You know the rest. He was arrested at your apartment that night. He was assigned a lawyer, but the woman's hands were tied because Theo refused to say why he'd done it. He knew if he revealed anything, the authorities would put two and two together and Orson would be arrested as well. He couldn't let that happen. As much as he feared going to jail, he refused to drag Orson along with him. So, in essence, he took the rap for both of them. After all, they'd both known and supposedly accepted the risks. He cared deeply about Orson. They were like brothers. And so, unable to form a credible defense, he went to jail."

"Did he take that money he was accused of stealing?"

"No. He never touched it. Probably someone in the company saw an opportunity to help himself to a nice vacation or a new car."

"Good. That always bothered me. You know, I was there the day he was sentenced. The judge seemed to really have it in for him. No one could understand why he received so much time. After all, it was his first offense."

"I think his very vocal stand on the Vietnam war may have had something to do with it. Orson told me that he found out years later that the judge's son had died in combat only months before Theo's sentencing. He thought guys like Theo were scum. He had the chance to throw the book at him and he took it."

"So, Theo went to jail. Seven years of his life down the drain." She made a sour face.

"And when he got out," continued Jane, "he headed straight for Chicago to see Curt. He knew Curt felt shut out—all of you did. He couldn't talk about why he'd been put in jail, so he just withdrew. Orson was the only one who knew, and therefore the only one he kept in contact with. But he really had loved Curt. He'd always hoped that some day they would have a life together. Still, he refused to ask him to wait until he got out of prison. He thought that kind of request was not only melodramatic, but pointless. By the time he was finally released, Curt and Annie were living together in Winnetka. They hadn't married yet, so Theo made a beeline for Chicago to feel out the situation. See if he still had a chance. In the meantime, a man he'd met in prison had arranged a job for him. Theo knew it might not be totally on the up and up, but he didn't have a dime, and he knew getting a regular job would be difficult. So he took it. He became the chauffeur for a judge."

"Not the one who sentenced him to prison?"

"No, the bald guy in Summer Green. All Theo had to do was drive the guy from Chicago to the Twin Cities two or three times a month. The judge had a girlfriend he kept secret from his wife. He'd installed her in a house in south St. Paul, and Theo would drop him off, drive the car to a specific parking lot in downtown Minneapolis, and spend the rest of the day roaming around. He would stay the night in the hotel of his choice, and then the next day pick up the judge and head back to Chicago. He did this exactly twice before he realized what was really happening."

"Some kind of drug deal."

Jane nodded. "On his third trip to Minneapolis, he waited in the parking lot. Sure enough, two guys appeared and removed several packages from the underside of the car. Before they took off, they deposited a suitcase in the trunk. When Theo got to the judge's girlfriend's house the next morning, he saw that the place was surrounded by cops. He knew there was probably a bust in progress, so he just split. He dumped the car at a grocery store in west St. Paul, but not before checking out the suitcase. Sure enough, it was full of money. Over a million dollars. So, not knowing what else to do, he bought a used Toyota, stuffed the suitcase in the back, and headed south. No one ever caught up with him. But he found out several months later that there was a contract out on his life. Apparently the judge thought Theo had blown the whistle on him. Since the police found no money or evidence of drugs at the house, they just let the judge go. But he was highly connected. Theo was on the run for years. He couldn't contact any of you because he was sure all his friends were being watched. The only good thing to come of it was that he didn't have to worry about money any more. He sent most of it to Orson, and Orson invested it for him. Whenever he needed anything, he'd just send a note. Theo became a very rich man. He also learned how to buy himself different identities as he needed them. Remember the name on his Texas driver's licence? Rob Wilson?"

Cordelia nodded.

"He used that name when he traveled in the South. You never saw the coroner's report, but it said his place of employment was Blandin Builders in Houston. That was only partially true. He didn't work there, he owned it. Another man ran it for him. His involvement was totally anonymous. It was the same all over the country. He owned a number of businesses. Then, about five years ago, he heard through a Chicago contact that the contract on his life had been withdrawn. He still didn't feel safe enough to come out of hiding, but he did take a few more chances. That's why he felt he could go to New York for Jill's funeral."

"But he never dared return to Chicago?"

"No. That was too dangerous. The contract might have been withdrawn, but that judge was still alive and well, and no doubt pissed as hell."

"And he never got to explain to Curt why he disappeared so abruptly."

Jane shook her head. "That was the saddest part. He couldn't expect Curt to drop everything and risk his life to go underground with him. So he didn't do anything. A year later Curt married Annie. For Theo, that was the end of the story. He would never have tried to interfere with that kind of commitment. But I know from talking to Curt that he felt the situation with Theo was never resolved. It drove him nuts. Theo felt the same way, of course, but his hands were tied. And even if he had made contact, what would he say? He couldn't tell the truth. It would just be more non-answers. There were already too many secrets. It was best to simply leave Curt and Annie alone."

"Which he did. Until the intervention."

"That's right. Coming back to the Midwest so openly was taking a real chance. Yet, he felt he had no choice. Diana needed him. He couldn't turn his back on her just because there was some risk involved. He never dreamed she would include his name in that interview she did with the *Chicago Sun Times*. When he got to Summer Green, he was already a sitting duck. That's who you saw the first night. The judge was already there, staking out the house. That same night he met with Theo, and Theo denied any involvement in the drug bust. But he couldn't exactly deny that he'd taken the money and run. The judge wanted it back. Theo promised he'd get it if he could just have a couple of days. He knew the minute he handed it over, he was dead meat. So he and Orson cooked up another little plot."

"Another bit of theatre."

Jane gave a grave nod. "Theo's life depended on pulling it off. Which, for all practical purposes, they did. They were lucky. Orson knew just about everyone in the town since he'd grown up there. The chief of police was an old high-school buddy. So were a lot of other guys on the police force. And so were the paramedics and the coroner. Everyone who was essential to making it work was in his pocket, so to speak. He convinced them all that this was a grand mission. Saving a good man from the clutches of evil. You should have heard him yesterday, Cordelia. He was so persuasive. He could have talked the devil himself into giving heaven another try."

"That's Orson," said Cordelia with more than a hint of pride.

"So they faked the heart attack. Theo was taken to the funeral home where he spent the night. The next day, he was driven to a farm just outside of town. Orson immediately went to work on getting him a new fake passport, credit cards and other necessary papers. Because of Theo's connections, it took less than two days. But Orson couldn't make phone calls from the parsonage. That's why he rented the room at the Sunburst Motel. He hooked up an answering machine so that he could receive messages when he wasn't there. That woman we saw meet him on Tuesday afternoon—she came to see him several times. He tried to make it look like a sexual liaison, just in case the judge was watching. But she was actually the one who messengered the papers. As soon as Orson got everything together—including having his bank in Minneapolis wire cash to the First Bank of Summer Green, Theo was off. He rode a milk truck to Madison where he bought a car and drove to Cleveland. He made a couple of plane connections, and right now I believe he's in London. I think he's planning on settling in Paris. Orson will fill you in on the details later. But remember, Cordelia, this can't go any farther than this room."

Cordelia gave Jane a freezing stare. "You mean, Diana, Curt and Annie are never to know?"

"The fewer people who are privy to this information, the better. You have to promise."

She tapped her fingers impatiently on the arm of the chair.

"Just say you understand."

"Of course I understand. But I think it's awful."

Jane had to agree.

"What about the fight Theo and Orson got into at the Roadhouse? Was that real?"

"No. Also a fake. Remember, Theo's life was in danger. Who knew if the judge was going to wait until Theo handed back the money before he made a move on him. I mean, they had no guarantees of anything. The safest place for him until he could die of that heart attack was jail. So, they staged the fight. Very simple. Theo was whisked away for his own protection."

Cordelia shook her head. "This is too incredible."

"I know"

"If I didn't know better, I'd think those radishes in Summer Green *were* hallucinogenic."

Jane gave a weak smile. "Only if you smoke them."

"So what tipped you off?"

"Several things. The night I arrived, Curt showed me a note he'd received from Theo. Orson had given it to him two nights before, explaining that Theo had written it while he was in the squad car before the police hauled him off to jail. In it, Theo asked Curt if he'd come down to the police station in the morning to talk. They'd apparently had a conversation earlier in the day, and Theo didn't like the way it ended."

"So?" said Cordelia. "Theo wrote him a note. What's strange about that?"

"Well, first of all, the police chief put handcuffs on Theo before taking him outside. Remember, Theo did have a record, and he'd just assaulted Orson. He might be dangerous. It seemed unlikely that the handcuffs would be taken off just so he could write a note."

"Good point."

"But the real tip off was the fact that the note was written on a piece of colored stationary. I don't think small towns stock their police cars with writing paper. That was a major flaw in their plan. Theo had obviously written the note earlier, when he'd had more time and could give it more thought. If that was true, then he knew he was going to be arrested, and that meant the fight had been staged. Orson and Theo were both in on it. And if *that* was a setup, what else was? If the police chief was also in on it— and he had to be, otherwise it might not have gone as planned—then who else in the town was in cahoots with Theo and Orson—and for what reason? It still didn't offer a complete answer, but it did point me in the right direction. What I saw was not necessarily what was real."

"Amazing," said Cordelia. "What else did you see that I missed?"

"Well, I was immediately suspicious when I found out the coroner hadn't ordered an autopsy. His explanation didn't satisfy me at all. Then we found the fake heart pills. I found out from Orson that he'd slipped them into Theo's things after I came. He knew my reputation for—"

"Being a busybody," replied Cordelia, with a small smirk.

"*Sleuthing*," said Jane. "So, he thought he'd better be as thorough as possible. Unfortunately, the druggist in Summer Green *wasn't* an old buddy, so he was forced to make something up on his own. Faking prescriptions is not one of his strong suits."

Cordelia gave another nod. She was totally mesmerized.

"The next thing to catch my eye was something Diana found in Theo's belongings. She was packing them for James when she found a piece of notebook paper. It was another note Theo had written to Curt. I remember her saying she'd started going through his suitcase the day before and hadn't seen it, but she said she'd probably been preoccupied. She simply dismissed it."

"But you didn't."

"No. And fortunately or unfortunately—however you want to look at it—Diana read the whole thing to me. I felt it was completely inappropriate for us to be reading another person's correspondence, but I just sat there."

"How utterly unethical."

Jane resisted rolling her eyes. "In it, Theo mentioned the weather. He'd been in town since Friday. He died Sunday night. With the exception of Monday—after he was dead I should point out—the weather in Summer Green had been perfect. But in the letter, he mentioned something about dark mists—or some such thing. Curt should just enjoy the summer sun and the dark mists. But he hadn't seen any dark mists—there weren't any until after he died. It just seemed odd to include that in what he'd written."

"And he couldn't do that from the grave."

"Exactly. Diana found the note Tuesday night. I asked Orson about it yesterday, and what I'd suspected was accurate. Orson planted it in Theo's things Tuesday afternoon. Theo was heartsick that he hadn't had a chance to talk to Curt privately just one last time. He knew he'd hurt him and was terribly upset that he hadn't made a better attempt to put things right."

"But Theo is never going to let Curt know he's alive."

"No. Never. He feels it's better to let things simply be. It would just cause Curt and Annie more pain if they ever found out the truth. Theo has taken all his secrets to the grave with him, and frankly, I think that's where they belong."

"His love for Curt," said Cordelia. "The truth behind Orson's wonderful good luck."

"All buried in that cemetery in Wisconsin."

"Just like *Beau Geste*. That was his favorite book in college, Janey. He talked about it all the time. In a very real sense, by going to prison, he sacrificed part of his life for a friend. By coming to Summer Green, he made another sacrifice. And by dying, he's made the most important sacrifice of all. He's finally set Curt free."

"Not without pain and not without confusion," said Jane. "But I think, under the circumstances, he made the only decision he could." She stared into the fake fire. "If only he and Orson had never made that bet."

"Crazy idiots," said Cordelia, her eyes welling with tears. She wiped a heavy hand across her face. "But I can't be angry with them."

"I know."

"The Shevlin Underground," she repeated, her voice wistful. "Who would have thought." A small sniff. "Diana, a beautiful and internationally loved actress, in treatment because she couldn't love herself. And Curt, the Jay Gatsby of the bisexual crowd, finally married and settled down with Annie—who has just given birth to a bouncing fourteen-year-old girl. And Orson, a famous Midwest cookie maggot—I mean, magnate. Such talent we all have. "

"And Theo?"

She smirked, placing a finger against her cheek. "How about, *Dead, and living in Paris.*"

Jane laughed out loud. "That's quite an epitaph."

"Yes," said Cordelia, stretching her arms high over her head. She lifted her feet up on the footstool in front of her and gazed up at the oil portrait of Agatha Christie. "Under the circumstances, he could have done a lot worse."

Publications from
Bella Books, Inc.
The best in contemporary lesbian fiction

P.O. Box 10543, Tallahassee, FL 32302
Phone: 800-729-4992
www.bellabooks.com

WALTZING AT MIDNIGHT by Robbi McCoy. First crush, first passion, first love. Everybody else knows Jean Harris has a major crush on Rosie Monroe, except Jean. It's just not something Jean, with two kids in college, thought would ever happen to her. $13.95

NO STRINGS by Gerri Hill. Reese Daniels is only in town for a year's assignment. MZ Morgan doesn't need a relationship. Their "no strings" arrangement seemed like a really good plan. $13.95

THE COLOR OF DUST by Claire Rooney. Who wouldn't want to inherit a mysterious mansion full of history under the layers of dust? Carrie Bowden is thrilled, especially when the local antique dealer seems equally interested in her. But sometimes secrets don't want to be disturbed. $13.95

THE DAWNING by Karin Kallmaker. Would you give up your future to right the past? Romantic, science fiction story that will linger long after the last page. $13.95

OCTOBER'S PROMISE by Marianne Garver. You'll never forget Turtle Cove, the people who live there, and the mysterious cupid determined to make true love happen for Libby and Quinn. $13.95

SIDE ORDER OF LOVE by Tracey Richardson. Television foodie star Grace Wellwood is not going to be golf phenom Torrie Cannon's side order of romance for the summer tour. No, she's not. Absolutely not. $13.95

WORTH EVERY STEP by KG MacGregor. Climbing Africa's highest peak isn't nearly so hard as coming back down to earth. Join two women who risk their futures and hearts on the journey of their lives. $13.95

WHACKED by Josie Gordon. Death by family values. Lonnie Squires knows that if they'd warned her about this possibility in seminary, she'd remember. $13.95

BECKA'S SONG by Frankie J. Jones. Mysterious, beautiful women with secrets are to be avoided. Leanne Dresher knows it with her head, but her heart has other plans. Becka James is simply unavoidable. $13.95

PARTNERS by Gerri Hill. Detective Casey O'Connor has had difficult cases, but what she needs most from fellow detective Tori Hunter is help understanding her new partner, Leslie Tucker. $13.95

AS FAR AS FAR ENOUGH by Claire Rooney. Two very different women from two very different worlds meet by accident—literally. Collier and Meri find their love threatened on all sides. There's only one way to survive: together. $13.95

NIGHT VISION by Karin Kallmaker. Julia Madison is having nightmares. So are all the lesbians she knows. What secret in the desert could be responsible? $13.95

AFTERSHOCK: Book two of the Shaken series by KG MacGregor. Anna and Lily have survived earthquake and dating, but new challenges may prove their undoing. $13.95

BEAUTIFUL JOURNEY by Kenna White. Determined to do her part during the Battle for Britain, aviatrix Kit Anderson has no time for Emily Mills, who certainly has no time for her, either, not when their hearts are in the line of fire. $13.95

MIDNIGHT MELODIES by Megan Carter. Family disputes and small town tensions come between Erica Boyd and her best chance at romance in years. $13.95

WHITE OFFERINGS by Ann Roberts. Realtor-turned-sleuth Ari Adams helps a friend find a stalker, only to begin receiving white offerings of her own. Book 2 in series. $13.95

HER SISTER'S KEEPER by Diana Rivers. A restless young Hadra is caught up in a daring raid on the Gray Place, but is captured and must stand trail for her crimes against the state. Book 6 in series. $13.95

LOSERS WEEPERS by Jessica Thomas. Alex Peres must sort out a possible kidnapping hoax and the death of a friend, and finds that the two cases have a surprising number of mutual suspects. Book 4 in series. $13.95

COMPULSION by Terri Breneman. Toni Barston's lucky break in a case turns into a nightmare when she becomes the target of a compulsive murderess. Book "C" in series. $13.95

THE KISS THAT COUNTED by Karin Kallmaker. CJ Roshe is used to hiding from her past, but meeting Karita Hanssen leaves her longing to finally tell someone her real name. $13.95

SECRETS SO DEEP by KG MacGregor. Glynn Wright's son holds a secret that is destroying him, but confronting it could mean the end of their family. Charlotte Blue is determined to save them both. $13.95

ROOMMATES by Jackie Calhoun. Two freshmen co-eds from two different worlds discover what it takes to choose love. $13.95

WHEN IT'S ALL RELATIVE by Therese Szymanski. Brett Higgins must confront her worst enemies: her family. Book 8 in series. $13.95

THE RAINBOW CEDAR by Gerri Hill. Jaye Burns' relationship is falling apart inspite of her efforts to keep it together. When Drew Montgomery offers the possibility of a new start, Jaye is torn between past and future. $13.95

TRAINING DAYS by Jane Frances. A passionate tryst on a long-distance train might be the undoing of Morgan's career—and her heart. $13.95

CHRISTABEL by Karin Kallmaker. Dina Rowland must accept her magical heritage to save supermodel Christabel from the demon of their past who has found them in the present. $13.95

VESTAVIA HILLS
LIBRARY IN THE FOREST
1221 MONTGOMERY HWY.
VESTAVIA HILLS, AL 35216
205-978-0155